THE
LIGHT AFTER
THE WAR

THE
LIGHT AFTER
THE WAR

— A Novel —

ANITA ABRIEL

ATRIA BOOKS

New York   London   Toronto   Sydney   New Delhi

ATRIA
BOOKS

An Imprint of Simon & Schuster, Inc.
1230 Avenue of the Americas
New York, NY 10020

First Atria Books hardcover edition February 2020

ATRIA BOOKS and colophon are trademarks of Simon & Schuster, Inc.

For information about special discounts for bulk purchases, please contact Simon & Schuster Special Sales at 1-866-506-1949 or business@simonandschuster.com.

The Simon & Schuster Speakers Bureau can bring authors to your live event. For more information or to book an event, contact the Simon & Schuster Speakers Bureau at 1-866-248-3049 or visit our website at www.simonspeakers.com.

Interior design by Jill Putorti

Manufactured in the United States of America

1 3 5 7 9 10 8 6 4 2

Library of Congress Cataloging-in-Publication Data
Names: Abriel, Anita, author.
Title: The light after the war / Anita Abriel.
Description: First Atria Books hardcover edition. | New York : Atria Books, 2019. | ATRIA fiction original hardcover—Verso title page.
Identifiers: LCCN 2019016972 (print) | LCCN 2019018018 (ebook) | ISBN 9781982122997 (eBook) | ISBN 9781982122973 (hardcover) | ISBN 9781982122980 (pbk.)
Subjects: LCSH: Jewish women—Fiction. | Jewish refugees—Fiction. | Refugees—Venezuela—Fiction. | Jewish fiction.
Classification: LCC PS3601.B84 (ebook) | LCC PS3601.B84 L55 2019 (print) | DDC 813/.6—dc23
LC record available at https://lccn.loc.gov/2019016972

ISBN 978-1-9821-2297-3
ISBN 978-1-9821-2299-7 (ebook)

To my mother

CHAPTER ONE

Spring 1946

Vera Frankel had never seen the sun so bright or streets teeming with so many people. Lovers held hands, teenagers zoomed by on Vespas, and old women carried shopping bags laden with fruits and vegetables. Vera smelled sweat and cigarettes and gasoline.

The experience of arriving in Naples from Hungary made Vera remember the early spring days in Budapest when she was eight years old and recovering from diphtheria. The curtains in her room had been drawn back and she was allowed to sit outside and eat a bowl of plain soup. Nothing had ever tasted so good, and the scent of flowers in the garden was more intoxicating than her mother's perfume.

All around her, people felt the same way now. The outdoor cafés overflowed with customers enjoying an espresso without fear of bombs exploding. They nodded at neighbors they had been too afraid to stop and talk to, and kissed boys returning from the front until their cheeks were raw. Eleven months ago the Allies had defeated the Nazis and the war in Europe was over.

"I didn't know pizza like this existed," her best friend Edith said as she bit into a slice of pizza. For the last year and a half they had been hiding in the small village of Hallstatt in Austria, where all they had to eat was soup and potatoes. "The tomatoes are sweet as honey."

Vera consulted the clock in the middle of the piazza. They sat at an outdoor table with two slices of pizza in front of them.

"My appointment is at two p.m.," Vera announced. "I won't get the job if I'm late."

"We've been in Naples for forty-eight hours," Edith protested, tying her blond hair into a knot. "We haven't seen the palace or the gardens or the docks. Couldn't you schedule your interview for to-morrow?"

"If I don't get the job, we won't be in Naples tomorrow," Vera replied grimly. She thought of the pile of lire that was carefully folded under the pillow in their room at Signora Rosa's pensione. It was barely enough to cover a week's accommodation for her and Edith. "You need to find a job, too."

"When was the last time you saw women who weren't wearing gold stars, men not in uniform, people eating and drinking and laughing." Edith scanned the piazza. "Can't we have one day to relax and enjoy ourselves?"

"You eat my slice." Vera pushed her plate toward Edith. "I'll meet you at Signora Rosa's in the evening."

"I promise I'll look for a job after the noon *riposo*." Edith's blue eyes sparkled. "We are in Italy now, we must behave like Italians."

Vera walked briskly through the winding alleys, consulting the map Signora Rosa had drawn her with directions for the American em-bassy. Signora Rosa owned the boardinghouse where they were staying, and in two days, she had already taken Vera and Edith under her wing. The American embassy was in the eleventh quarter, which had once been one of the most elegant parts of Naples. But the war had left gaping holes in the streets, obstructing her route. Daisies grew where buildings once stood, and sides of houses were missing, leaving their abandoned interiors exposed. Vera thought of her home in Budapest, the shattered windows of her parents' apartment building, the women and children huddled together in the dark. Hungarian soldiers, young men who in another time would have asked her to dinner, had herded families toward the trains.

She thought of her father, Lawrence, who had been sent to a forced labor camp in 1941 and hadn't been heard from since. And of her mother, Alice, who had continued to set the table for him every night, as if one evening he would appear in his dark overcoat and scarf and sit down to her schnitzel.

And she thought of Edith, who was more like her sister than her best friend. They were both almost nineteen years old, born three days apart at the same hospital. They lived across the hall from each other their whole lives, and the doors to their apartments were always kept open.

Edith had always been the wild one: at fifteen she had borrowed one of her mother's dresses and convinced Vera to crash a New Year's Eve gala at the Grand Hotel when Vera would have rather sat at home with a book. Edith hadn't wanted to flirt with boys; she wanted only to see the fashions worn by the most glamorous women in Budapest.

But Edith had changed when her childhood sweetheart, Stefan, didn't return from the labor camps. She was like a racehorse whose spirit had been broken and could barely trot around the course. It was Vera who propelled them forward after the war: acquiring the train tickets to Naples and finding Signora Rosa's pensione. It was Vera who encouraged Edith to get dressed in the morning and do her hair. It was only when Edith was all dressed up and socializing at one of the piazzas that she seemed like her old self. Edith never let anyone see her without a belt cinched around her waist and her hair perfectly brushed.

Vera put the map away and turned off her mind. She could worry about Edith later; right now she had to focus on finding the embassy.

"Excuse me." Vera approached an old man selling dried chestnuts. "I am looking for the American embassy."

"The Americans," the old man scoffed. "They bombed our city and now they eat our pasta and steal our women. A pretty girl like you should marry an Italian boy!"

"I'm not looking for a husband." Vera smoothed her black hair, suppressing the fact that she was Hungarian, not Italian. "I'm trying to get a job."

"Behind those gates," the man said, pointing across the street. "Tell them we can rebuild our own city. We've been doing it for centuries."

Vera walked quickly to the villa. It had a rounded entry and marble columns. Ivy climbed the walls and the shutters were painted green. She straightened her skirt and wished she had splurged on a pair of stockings. But the money had to last until she and Edith were both working, and it didn't stretch for makeup or hosiery. Vera wet her lips and climbed the stairs to the front door.

"Can I help you?" A man wearing a khaki uniform answered the door. He was tall and blond, and his face was freshly shaven.

"I'm looking for Captain Wight," Vera said, trying to keep her voice from trembling.

The man slipped his hands in his pockets. He stood in the doorway, but Vera could see the circular entry behind him.

"I'm Captain Wight. But I'm sorry, we're not making donations today. You could try back on Friday." He tried to shut the door, but Vera put her hand out and stopped him.

"Please, wait. I'm here for the secretary job." She gave him a sheet of paper. "Captain Bingham sent me."

Captain Wight glanced at the paper. He looked as if he was about to say something, but then shrugged.

"Come in. It's too hot to stand outside."

Vera followed him through rooms decorated with marble floors and intricate frescoed ceilings. Sheets half covered brocade furniture, and velvet drapes hung from the windows.

"It's like a palace," Vera breathed.

"It was a palace," he said, leading her to a room lined with tall bookshelves. There was a large wooden desk in the center and an Oriental rug covering the floor. "The Palazzo Mezzi was built in the eighteenth century. We commissioned it in 1943 from the Count and Countess Mezzi. The Mezzis fled to Switzerland, but we have not been able to contact them. We are lucky it escaped the bombs; some of the frescoes are priceless."

"The old man on the corner who sells chestnuts thinks the Americans are taking everything that isn't theirs," Vera said lightly.

Captain Wight's eyes grew serious. He sat in a leather chair and motioned Vera to sit opposite him. "I want to leave Naples the way it was before Hitler got his hands on it."

"I'm sorry." Vera sat down and twisted her hands in her lap. "If the Americans hadn't won the war, a German would be sitting in that chair. And he wouldn't be offering me a job."

At least, she hoped Captain Wight would give her the job.

"I'm not offering you a job either." Captain Wight frowned, the letter sitting unread on his desk. "Captain Bingham promised me an experienced secretary who was fluent in four languages."

"Five," Vera gulped. "I'm fluent in five languages: Italian, French, Hungarian, Spanish, and English. I can type and take shorthand, and I know how to brew American coffee."

Captain Wight gazed at Vera for so long she turned away, blushing. His hair was short and slicked to one side; his eyes were a pale blue. He had a dimple on his chin and a small scar on his left hand.

"How old are you?"

"Eighteen and three quarters," Vera replied. "I can press your shirts and make a bed," she added in desperation.

"I'm not looking for a maid. Gina comes to clean every day. And I'd much rather drink Italian espresso than American coffee." He tapped his fingers on the desk. "It is a difficult position, not suitable for a young girl."

"Please," Vera pleaded. She felt the breath leave her lungs. Captain Wight was the only lead she had. If she didn't get the job, she'd have to find work in a restaurant or bar, and she wasn't well-suited for that. Her secretarial skills were much stronger. "Read Captain Bingham's letter."

Vera glanced at the desk while he read the letter. A collection of gold fountain pens and an ashtray full of cigarette butts sat off to the side. Papers were strewn everywhere; a crystal paperweight was covered in dust.

She grabbed the ashtray and emptied its contents into the garbage. She collected and fastened the papers with a paper clip. Then she screwed the tops on the fountain pens and dusted the paperweight with the hem of her skirt. When Captain Wight looked up, his desk was in perfect order.

"I'm very organized." She smiled, sitting back in the chair.

"Is all this true about what happened to your parents?" Captain Wight waved the paper in the air.

Vera flashed on the picture of her mother and father taken before the war that she kept in her purse. Her mother wore a mink coat and evening shoes with satin bows. Her father had a bowler hat and carried a briefcase.

"Yes." She nodded, blinking away tears.

"The pay is twenty lire a week," Captain Wight said as he fiddled with a fountain pen. "Dictation can be very boring. You'll get cramps in your hands and a bad back from sitting so long."

"I'm a hard worker," Vera said simply.

"My last secretary ran off with a sailor." Captain Wight stood up and strode to the fireplace. "I was hoping for someone with more experience."

"I could never marry a sailor." Vera smiled. "I'm afraid of the sea."

"In that case"—he held out his hand, and there was a twinkle in his eye—"the job is yours."

Captain Wight showed her the morning room where he drank his coffee and read the newspapers. He led her into the kitchen, which had thick plaster walls and worn oak floors. The gray stone counters were covered with dirty plates, cups, and silverware.

"I thought you had a maid," Vera reminded him, instinctively collecting knives and spoons and loading them into the sink.

"Gina's husband was killed in Africa and she has five children at home." Captain Wight picked up a red apple and polished it on his sleeve. "Sometimes she has to leave early or come in late."

"I could help," Vera offered, noticing the pot of congealed oatmeal, the half-eaten pieces of fruit.

"I'm happy with dry toast in the morning and an omelet at lunch," Captain Wight answered. "But you're welcome to help yourself. Louis, the gardener, grows excellent fruits and vegetables."

Vera followed him through halls hung with crystal chandeliers. The walls were lined with paintings in gilt frames and doors opened onto salons and ballrooms. She imagined men in silk tuxedos, women in glittering evening gowns, the tinkling of glasses, the sounds of a ten-piece orchestra.

They returned to the library, and Captain Wight took his seat at his desk.

Vera tried to concentrate on Captain Wight's words, but her eyes started to close. She had barely slept, sharing the narrow bed at the pensione with Edith. That morning she woke early so she could bathe and iron her cotton dress.

"Vera," Captain Wight repeated.

"I'm ready." Vera started, shifting in the chair on the other side of the desk from him. She grabbed a pen and notepad. "Please begin."

"I have a better idea." Captain Wight looked at her. "Go to Marco's trattoria on Via del Tribunali. Tell Marco to feed you his best linguine with prawns and prosciutto and put it on my tab. We'll start in the morning."

"I can't take your charity," Vera protested, her stomach growling with hunger.

"In America we call it an advance." Captain Wight stood up and moved to her side of the desk. He took her arm and gently led her toward the entry. "Don't worry, you'll earn it."

Vera skipped through the streets of Naples like a schoolgirl freed for the summer. She felt lighter than she had since they arrived. She had a job! Now she could pay for their cramped room at Signora Rosa's; she could buy lipstick and stockings for her and Edith.

Vera passed the Piazza Leone and saw Edith sitting at a table. Edith was eating a gelato and whispering to a man with slick black hair. Their chairs were pressed close together; the man had his hand draped across Edith's shoulder.

"You're back so soon!" Edith exclaimed. "This is Franco. He bought me a gelato."

"We don't accept presents from strangers," Vera announced as she approached the table. The sun was bright and Edith's pale cheeks were flushed.

"A present is jewelry or stockings," Edith protested. "A gelato is something to share. Franco has a motorcycle; he's going to drive me around the Bay of Naples."

"Tell Franco another time," Vera instructed, ignoring the young man with brown eyes and long, thick lashes.

Edith leaned in and whispered something to Franco. He laughed and tucked a stray blond hair behind Edith's ear.

Vera started walking, waiting for Edith to catch up with her. She passed trattorias with pasta hanging from the windows and bakeries with cannelloni and chocolate tortes displayed on silver trays.

"Franco was lovely," Edith said as she strode beside her. "He called me *bella*."

"Italian men call all women under the age of ninety 'bella.' " Vera scanned the shops for Marco's trattoria. She found it on the corner, a narrow restaurant with red awnings and tables covered in checkered tablecloths.

Vera entered, a bell sounding over the door. A woman swept the floor and a man counted money at the cash register.

"Signor Marco?" Vera inquired.

"We are closed," said the woman. "We will open again for dinner."

Vera smelled olive oil and garlic and onions. Her stomach rose to her throat and suddenly she felt dizzy. Her knees buckled and she sank to the floor.

"Drink this," a voice said.

Vera blinked at the man who stood over her. He pressed a glass to her lips and shouted commands in Italian. The woman brought two plates of spaghetti to the table. There was a loaf of bread and a pot of olive oil.

"Captain Wight sent me. I'm his secretary," Vera explained, eyeing the spaghetti. "He said to put it on his tab."

Marco handed them each a fork. "Start eating, but not too fast, your stomach will not allow it. Then my wife will bring dessert."

Vera and Edith waited until Marco disappeared to the back room. Vera twirled the spaghetti around her fork, inhaling the fresh oregano. The tomato sauce was rich and oily and dripped onto the plate.

"Why is your boss buying our dinner?" Edith dipped a chunk of bread in olive oil. "Did you sleep with him?"

"Don't talk like that," Vera snapped. "He is only kind."

"He's probably old and wants to get his hands up your skirt." Edith chewed the bread.

"Not old at all," Vera mused. "He looks like an American cowboy."

"And you wouldn't let me ride on the back of Franco's Vespa," Edith grumbled.

"I'm working for Captain Wight, not dating him." Vera soaked the tomato sauce up with bread. "You have to be careful with Italian men; they only want one thing."

"Franco has the most beautiful eyes," Edith sighed. "I want to wrap my arms around his waist and hold on forever."

Vera looked sharply at Edith. When she wasn't lying in bed all day with the curtains drawn, this was the way Edith had behaved ever since the camps were liberated and Stefan wasn't accounted for. She spent her days mooning over photos of actors in movie magazines and flirting with any male that crossed their path: the engaged American soldier on the train to Naples, the boy who helped Signora Rosa with chores and smelled like fish. It was only at night, when Vera curled her arm around her, that Edith whispered Stefan's name and let the tears roll down her cheeks.

Vera started to reply, but she didn't have the strength. She concentrated on scraping every strand of spaghetti from the plate. Only after Marco had given them thick slices of chocolate cake and cups of black coffee did Vera turn to Edith.

"You can't throw yourself at a man because he reminds you of Stefan."

"You think I should save myself for him." Edith's brown eyes flashed. "You think I should sit in our room and wait for Stefan to appear at the door."

"He could be alive." Vera avoided Edith's eyes. "You have no proof he's dead."

Edith's voice rose. "I don't need them to identify a body. I know here." She touched her chest.

"The war has only been over eleven months," Vera pleaded. "They're finding survivors every day."

"Even if Stefan were lying wounded in a hospital, he would find a way to get word to me. Stefan and I loved each other. He wouldn't let a few gunshot wounds keep us apart. Nothing you say can convince me that he's not dead." Edith's cheeks flamed and she pushed her chair back. "We're in a new country with men who are alive. Men who can buy us flowers and chocolates and recite poetry."

Edith flung open the door and ran down the street. Vera thanked Marco and hurried outside. She ran after Edith and wrapped her arms around her. Edith sobbed onto Vera's shoulder, her breath coming in short gasps and a low, guttural sound emerging from her throat.

Vera pictured Edith and Stefan strolling along the Danube. They used to swim in the baths, splashing and playing like young seals. She remembered Stefan's large brown eyes, his hands holding Edith's face to say good-bye. Stefan vowed he would return, and Edith promised to wait for him. But Vera and Edith hadn't returned to Budapest after the war. She was certain her parents and Stefan hadn't made it back. The war had been over for almost a year. Someone would have alerted them by now. Without the people they loved, there was nothing for them in Hungary.

"You're right." Vera stroked Edith's hair. "We're in a new country, and everything is before us."

CHAPTER TWO

Spring 1946

Vera walked briskly to the American embassy. She had left Edith in bed with a pillow over her face to block out the morning light. She hated leaving Edith alone, but Edith promised she wouldn't talk to strange men and that she would ask the neighborhood seamstress for work.

Vera opened the front door of the embassy and checked her reflection in the hall mirror. Her black hair was brushed and curled under her chin. She had rubbed blackberry juice on her lips to give them color.

"I'm in here," Captain Wight called from the morning room.

Vera took a deep breath and followed the sound of his voice. The curtains were open and the room was flooded with sunlight. A record player played classical music and a silver tray held porcelain cups and a plate of dry toast.

"I didn't mean to interrupt your breakfast." Vera blushed, hovering at the door.

"Do you like Mozart?" Captain Wight set aside his paper. "He is my favorite composer."

"The Nazis wouldn't let anyone wearing a gold star attend the opera," Vera replied. "They took away our gramophone and all our records."

"I'm sorry." Captain Wight noticed her anguished expression and turned off the record player immediately. "Music helps me remember the world wasn't always full of barbarians."

"I can wait in the library." Vera turned toward the door.

"No, it's time to get to work." He led the way down the hall. He stopped in front of the library and waited while Vera entered. Vera took her seat on one side of the oak desk and Captain Wight sat in his chair.

"This is a hard job for anyone," Captain Wight counseled, flipping through the stack of papers in front of him. "Mostly we write letters of condolence, we extinguish hope, and we bring home reality. Perhaps you should think twice about this job."

"I don't want another job." Vera picked up the steno pad and unscrewed the fountain pen. "Because of this job, yesterday I ate the best chocolate cake I ever tasted. You have given me hope. I am ready whenever you would like to begin."

Captain Wight fired off letters, pacing the room and tapping an unlit cigarette against his palm. He stopped only when Vera's pad was full and she had to retrieve another from his desk. By lunchtime, Vera's fingers were stiff and there were ink stains on her dress.

"The greatest crime in Naples is to work during lunch." Captain Wight placed his pack of cigarettes on the desk. "When the clock chimes noon, everything stops."

"I brought my lunch," Vera announced, holding up a paper bag. "If you don't mind, I'll eat in the garden."

"I told Gina to prepare lunch for two for your first day of work," Captain Wight said kindly, slipping his hands in his pockets. "She was so excited, she cleaned the kitchen all morning."

"I couldn't intrude." Vera shook her head.

"You're doing me a favor." Captain Wight smiled. "If you don't join me, I'll have to eat Gina's pasta all by myself."

Vera followed Captain Wight to the kitchen. It looked completely different from the day before. The floor was scrubbed, the counters sparkled, and the table was set with white china and sterling silverware.

"Oh," Vera murmured, noticing a bowl of lettuce, red peppers, and cucumber. There were plates of linguine and platters of sliced melon and oranges. A vase of sunflowers was arranged on the sideboard and the French doors were open to the garden.

Gina was a small woman with coarse dark hair. She wore an apron tied around her waist and heavy black shoes.

She turned Vera around as if she were inspecting a beautiful doll. "It is wonderful to have another woman in the house. Captain Wight thinks a sandwich eaten at his desk is lunch, but in Italy the noon *riposo* is meant to feed the soul as well as the stomach." She waved at the table. "Sit down; I will bring soup and bread."

"I thought people in Naples were starving." Vera tasted her soup. "But everywhere there is fruit and pasta and cake."

"For years they were starving; sixteen-year-old boys looked like they were twelve." Captain Wight agreed, pouring a glass of orange juice. "But since the war ended, supplies have improved. The Neapolitans treat every day like a celebration."

"I've never seen such a vibrant city," Vera agreed. "In Budapest the buildings are dark brick, and a thick fog lies over the streets.

Naples is like a girl in a bathing suit, half-naked and craving sunshine."

"I'm glad you like it." Captain Wight lit a cigarette. He blew out the match and looked at Vera curiously. "Tell me, how do you speak so many languages?"

"My father loved languages. He studied them at university." Vera felt momentarily shy under his gaze. "He thought Latin was the most romantic language in the world. He taught me in the evenings when he came home from his law practice. My mother would serve us slices of almond torte and we'd sit at the kitchen table together."

Captain Wight exhaled a puff of smoke. "I studied Latin at school, but I never became proficient. My Latin professor at Yale mangled every line of the *Aeneid*."

"My mother studied dance in Paris when she was young," Vera continued, her words faltering. "She taught me French."

Vera's eyes clouded over as if she had seen a ghost.

"I couldn't eat another bite," she declared and pushed back her chair. "We must get back to work."

They worked until the sun moved behind the hills. Captain Wight dictated letters to local authorities. He wrote short, pained letters to families in America, informing them that their sons were no longer missing in action, they were dead. Vera copied his words down, silently admiring the way he phrased the sentences to show that he really cared. She found herself blinking back tears that she didn't want Captain Wight to see. Every now and then, when she thought she couldn't transcribe another paragraph about a son lost on the battlefield, he would fire off a letter to General Ashe in Rome about trees he wanted to plant in a park or a school he was going to rebuild. The passion in his voice when he dictated those notes was infectious, and she found herself scribbling even faster.

"I told you it was a difficult job," Captain Wight said when the stack of papers on his desk had been cleared. "I understand if you don't want to come back tomorrow."

"I'll be here at eight a.m.," Vera said with confidence. She was about to leave when there was a knock at the door. Gina poked her head in and waved an envelope.

"Telegram, Signor Wight."

He ripped open the envelope and Vera gulped. She had seen enough movies before the war to know that a telegram was almost always bad news. Captain Wight's expression changed, and she waited anxiously for him to speak.

"Is everything all right?" Vera inquired.

"My mother used to send me letters telling me my father needs me at home." Captain Wight grimaced, stuffing the paper in his pocket. "That didn't work, so now she sends telegrams. I wouldn't be surprised if one day she shows up with a ticket for my passage to New York."

"If the army wants you in Rome and your mother wants you in New York, why are you still in Naples?" Vera asked. The thought of Captain Wight leaving the embassy upset her.

"I can only answer by showing you." Captain Wight grabbed his cap from the side table. "Follow me."

They walked down the steps, passing villas with small gardens enclosed by iron gates. They turned onto a street where there were no houses, only rubble. Gaping holes formed where shops once stood, and there were abandoned cars with crushed hoods. Vera's stomach dropped and she wondered what could be buried under the piles of stones. Perhaps a beloved dog that didn't have time to escape or a favorite doll left behind by a little girl. Captain Wight walked beside her and she could see her own revulsion reflected in his eyes. His shoulders were hunched, and he stuck his hands in his pockets.

"Did you know that Naples was bombed two hundred times, with over twenty thousand civilian casualties?" Captain Wight asked, looking at her apologetically. "The Allies freed Naples from Axis rule, but this is what we left behind."

"It's not the Allies' fault. In a war there are casualties," Vera murmured.

"We gutted the city!" Captain Wight's eyes flashed. "When I arrived, the people were like cats in the Colosseum. If you turned your back for a minute, your pockets would be empty and there'd be a knife in your chest."

"The Americans set Naples free," Vera insisted.

"My father owns hotels in New York and Boston," Captain Wight continued. "It inspired me to study art and architecture in college. I can't leave the city like this. We have to give Neapolitans back their buildings and their pride."

"Everyone's war has to end sometime." Vera hugged her chest. It was almost evening, and a cool wind blew in from the bay.

"I didn't mean to drag you out here for so long." Captain Wight touched her hand. "I'll walk you home."

Vera shook her head. "I'm meeting a friend in the piazza."

"It's almost evening. It's not safe for a girl to walk by herself at dusk." Captain Wight drew a pack of cigarettes from his pocket.

"I won't walk, I'll skip." Vera smiled. "I'll see you in the morning."

She set off before he could stop her. She turned at the end of the street and saw him standing on the sidewalk, puffing his cigarette as if it were a contest.

Vera searched the piazza for Edith, but no one had seen her. A young man zoomed by on a motorcycle, a blond girl's arms wrapped around his waist.

Vera hurried to the pensione, feeling suddenly uneasy because she couldn't find Edith and everything seemed so foreign. The piazza was almost empty, and it reminded her of the time when her mother sent her to the bakery to buy rugelach for dessert. The street was so quiet when she walked home, she could hear her footsteps echoing on the pavement. When she turned the corner she saw her mother, Edith, and all their neighbors standing in a circle. Vera thought they were holding some kind of meeting, and then she saw the Hungarian officers in their dark coats.

It was spring of 1944 when Vera learned of the ghettos: small houses in the countryside where Jews from all over Hungary were being sent. They were told it was for their own good. They would be closer to synagogues and away from civilians who were angry with the Jews. But as neighbors left their apartments wearing layers of clothing and carrying all their belongings in suitcases, Vera sensed this wasn't true. As soon as they were gone, the Nazis raided their apartments. They even took up residence in some of the more elegant ones: sipping cognac that was left on a silver tray and listening to the records that sat on the phonograph.

"Are we leaving?" Vera asked her mother, following her back into the warmth of the apartment. It was the end of April and the night air was frigid.

"Of course we're not leaving." Her mother busied herself in the kitchen, as if she had merely stepped outside to borrow a cup of sugar.

"But I passed the Weinbergs and they were leaving Budapest." Vera handed her mother a coffee cup. "The officer said it isn't safe here any longer, someone could shoot us in the street or break our windows."

"Of course the Hungarian soldiers will say that," her mother spat. "Then they'll let themselves into our flats and sleep in our beds. I saw a Hungarian soldier walking down the street carrying Golda Feinstein's sheets! They were a wedding present from her in-laws and now they're going to be slept on by filthy Nazi lovers."

Vera flinched. Her mother never talked like that. She believed in turning the other cheek. When other girls at school mocked Vera for wearing a gold star, her mother told her to be proud. Hadn't they longed for gold stars on their schoolwork as children?

"I had a better idea," her mother continued. "I told the captain in charge that I will cook just for him. Every day at five thirty he can come and there will be stuffed cabbage and potato nokedli and a whole rugelach. His mouth watered so much, he needed to wipe it with his handkerchief," she laughed. "No one is sending us to the ghetto yet."

They didn't have to move, and as long as Edith was across the hall, everything was all right. Then Vera heard a commotion outside; there was the sound of orders being barked in Hungarian and people screaming and sobbing. She avoided looking out the window and wondered how long their reprieve would last. When would she have to pack all her books into a suitcase? What if one day Edith and her mother were gone?

Vera opened the door of the pensione and tried to get the memories out of her mind. People didn't disappear anymore. The war was over and Edith was perfectly safe.

Signora Rosa was in the kitchen peeling potatoes. She was a tall woman with pendulous breasts. Today she wore a flowered dress and her brown hair was tucked in its usual bun.

"Have you seen Edith?" Vera asked. "I'm late from work."

"She went to the piazza an hour ago," Signora Rosa said with a frown. "You girls are too pretty to wander around Naples alone."

Vera was sure Edith would be home any moment, repeating this to herself to make her heart slow. She went up to their room and stood at the window. She leaned outside, listening for Edith's voice. Two cats fought in the alley below her. Vera set down her purse and thought she'd go down to the garden and pick some plums for Gina. Gina had been so kind, serving her soup and bread. It would be nice to bring her something in return.

The door opened and Edith entered, wearing a white dress of the thinnest cotton. Her long blond hair was tied with a ribbon. Her shoulders were shaking and her cheeks were wet with tears. There was a small cut on her cheek and dried blood on her mouth.

"Who did this?" Vera gasped, grabbing a handkerchief and dabbing Edith's mouth.

"Signora Stella gave me work," Edith sobbed. "She gave me this dress as payment. I felt so pretty, I wanted to go out."

"It's a beautiful dress." Vera ran her hands over the fabric.

"I met Franco in the piazza," Edith began. "He said I looked like an angel. He wanted to take me up to the hills and show me the view of the Bay of Naples."

"Oh," Vera whispered.

"He packed a delicious picnic," Edith continued. "We ate bread and prosciutto and figs. There was red wine and strawberries for dessert. He kissed me softly." Edith flinched as Vera dabbed her cheek. "Then he put his hand up my skirt. I tried to get away, but he laughed and said I wanted it."

"What did you do?" Vera asked.

"I grabbed the knife and said I'd rip a hole in his chest," Edith replied, touching her mouth. "We fought like tigers. Then he called me a whore and drove me home."

Vera held her in her arms. "It's all right. You are safe now."

They sat at the edge of Edith's bed.

"I want our apartment in Budapest and our house in the country," Edith cried. "I want our mothers. I want to eat stuffed cabbage and kugel."

Vera waited till Edith's sobs subsided. She stroked her hair and ran her finger down her cheek. "I can't bring them back, but I promise we can get coffee and whipped cream." Vera stuffed some lire in her pocket. "Come, we will show Naples not to mess with two Hungarian girls." She took Edith's hand, just as she had been doing since they were little girls playing on the playground while their mothers watched from a bench. Vera didn't let go until they were outside and the sun setting over the Bay of Naples glittered before them, warming the cold place in Edith's heart.

* * *

They sat in the piazza, watching the tables fill with people. Men smoked cigarettes and moved figures around a chessboard. Children played near the fountain, squealing with joy when the water sprayed their faces.

"Italian men are so beautiful." Edith sipped her coffee. She was already over the incident with Franco. "They look like Michelangelo's *David*."

"We're going to be in Naples for a while." Vera gazed at the men walking by. They wore leather jackets and nodded in their direction. "You could try making friends with them first."

"Like your Captain Wight?" Edith laughed. "I want to hear everything about him."

"He's from New York," Vera mused. "He's very serious and sad, as if he is responsible for the whole war."

"Perhaps he just wants your sympathy," Edith suggested. "So he can lay his head on your shoulder and you can comfort him."

"He's my boss," Vera retorted. "Nothing is going to happen."

"Wouldn't it be wonderful if you fell in love and he took us both to New York?" Edith sighed. "I'd become a famous fashion designer and you'd be a great playwright. He'd squire us around and I'd meet fabulous men."

"I'm happy transcribing his letters so we can pay Signora Rosa and buy stockings," Vera murmured.

"You've wanted to be a writer since we were ten years old," Edith reminded her.

Vera had scribbled whole plays in her schoolbooks since she was a little girl; she and Edith used to perform them for their mothers. Alice and Lily would become so wrapped up in the performances, their husbands would come home and dinner wouldn't be on the table.

They spent hours digging through their mothers' closets, choosing their costumes. Vera remembered a play where she dressed in her mother's pearls and heels. Edith wore a velvet robe and clutched a pearl cigarette holder in one hand and a brandy snifter in the other. Edith's father came home and thought they were drinking real brandy and made Edith wash her mouth out with soap.

Edith's mother snapped that she would never let the girls near his precious brandy, then went to her bedroom and slammed the door. It was only later, when Edith's father ran off with his secretary, that Vera learned the true reason Edith's mother was upset. It wasn't because he punished Edith or scolded her. It was the scent of perfume on his coat and the receipt from a hotel bar in his pocket.

"Edith," Vera said now, touching her hand. "This isn't the time to think about following our dreams. We have to earn enough money to survive."

"Why do we always have to think about money?" Edith said stubbornly. "We're young; we're supposed to have fun. I'm going to get a gelato." She jumped up and ran across the stones to the café on the corner.

Vera gazed at the young people chattering. She longed for the tearooms in Budapest, the rich milky coffee and powdered cakes. She longed to see a schoolmate or one of her mother's friends dressed in boots and a fur coat.

Edith returned, dragging a dark-haired boy to the table.

"Meet Marcus," she announced. The man wore a leather jacket and had a red bandana knotted around his neck. "Marcus is a photographer. He wants to take our picture."

"We don't talk to strangers," Vera replied.

"Marcus is from Ravello." Edith sat down, ignoring her. "He's going to submit the photos to the newspaper and make us famous."

"Two beautiful Hungarian refugees," Marcus said with a bow. "It will be a wonderful story."

"Excuse us." Vera stood. It was dinnertime, and they had to go back to the pensione. "We have to work in the morning."

"I will be here tomorrow," Marcus said hopefully. "Same time."

Vera waited till they left the piazza before she turned to Edith. "Didn't you learn your lesson?"

"He's only nineteen; he's harmless," Edith said with a shrug. "He has eyes like a puppy."

"One day you're going to get in trouble and I won't be around to help you," Vera retorted.

Edith stopped walking, her dress blowing around her legs. "I have to have love, otherwise I'd rather be dead."

Vera put her arm around Edith and led her to the pensione. "We don't know what it's like to be dead."

CHAPTER THREE

Spring 1946

Vera buttoned her dress and brushed her hair. Edith still lay in bed, the sheet pulled up around her cheeks.

"I'll be back by noon," Vera said. "You promise you won't go out by yourself?"

"I'm going to lie here all day." Edith yawned. "No one works on Saturday. Your captain is a slave driver."

Vera was in her third week working for Captain Wight, and she found it more satisfying than she had imagined. It felt good to know that the letters sent to the embassy in Rome would make a difference in rebuilding Naples. She even took some solace in the blue airmail envelopes waiting to be mailed to America. Surely it was better for the families to know the worst so they could grieve and begin to heal, rather than to live with the uncertainty of wondering whether or not their loved ones were alive. Vera knew something about that.

"He has to go to Rome on Monday." Vera studied her reflection in the mirror. "We need to finish some letters."

Edith smirked. "Maybe he can't stand a day without his secretary."

"He doesn't even look at me," Vera insisted.

"That's what you think, but he's a man," Edith rejoined. "How can he not notice a pretty girl who sits across from him all day?"

Edith was wrong. Sometimes while they worked, she stole a glance at Captain Wight, but he was always sifting through papers. It momentarily made her feel sad, but then she would brush the thought away. She was at the embassy to work, not to receive the attentions of a man.

Vera skipped onto the street, the sunshine warm on her back. She was beginning to recognize the faces in the neighborhood. The women smiled toothless grins and the men offered her free oranges and figs.

"I brought a present," Vera announced, finding Captain Wight in the morning room. He wore navy slacks and a tan polo shirt. His blond hair was brushed to the side and his cheeks were freshly shaved.

"I have a present for you, too. As a thank-you for working on the weekend." Captain Wight closed his newspaper and handed her a small stack of books. "These are some of my favorite American authors, but the stories are set in Europe." He pointed to the covers. "I thought you might enjoy reading books in English."

Vera read the names of the authors: Ernest Hemingway and F. Scott Fitzgerald. There was also a book of poetry by T. S. Eliot.

"Thank you. I'll start reading them tonight," she said awkwardly.

Did Captain Wight think her English needed improving or was he being thoughtful? She tucked them under her arm and handed him a bag of plums.

"Signora Rosa grows these in her garden. She said Gina could make a pie."

"I'm sure she would love to when she returns. She took the day off." Captain Wight walked toward the kitchen. "Gina's youngest son is turning four. They are going to ride bicycles in the park."

"Where did they get bicycles?" Vera asked curiously. Gina couldn't afford bicycles for her children.

"I bought them at the outdoor market," Captain Wight said easily. "All children should learn how to ride a bicycle."

Vera entered the kitchen. A vase was filled with sunflowers, and ceramic plates were stacked on the counter.

"Something smells delicious," she announced. Pancakes warmed on a skillet and there was a jug of syrup and a bowl of berries.

"Pancakes are my specialty," Captain Wight said, putting the plums in a bowl. "When I was a boy my mother spent every Saturday with her friends. Our cook, Elsie, let me help with breakfast. Would you like some?"

"In Hungary, we fill pancakes with fruit and eat them for dessert," Vera replied.

Captain Wight smiled. His teeth were white and his hair was golden in the sunlight that streamed through the window.

"Americans like their sweets in the morning." Captain Wight put two golden pancakes on a plate. "My brother would eat the first batch before anyone else filled their plates."

"Is your brother an officer, too?" Vera asked, taking a bite of the pancake.

"Brad was hit by a taxi on Fifth Avenue in 1942. He was only twenty-four. He was on leave from his desk job in Washington." Captain Wight's eyes went dark. "It seems silly to get run over when the whole world is at war, but Brad was always in a hurry. He was running to say good-bye to a girl."

"I didn't mean to pry," Vera said uncomfortably. She was embarrassed for asking about his private life.

"My sister's husband died in Japan and my youngest brother is a freshman at Princeton." Captain Wight picked up his fork. "That's why my father wants me to come home and manage the hotels, but there's still so much here that needs to be done."

Captain Wight's brow furrowed, and sadness clouded his face.

"It must have been lovely growing up in a large family." Vera noticed his expression and tried to lighten the mood. "I always wanted brothers and sisters. My best friend Edith was born three days before me in the same hospital. Once we had a birthday party at our country house in Szentendre and our parents rented a pony. We were so disappointed that we didn't get to keep him."

"That sounds like my sister's parties," Captain Wight laughed. The brooding look vanished and he was more like himself. "Only the pony was in Central Park, followed by lunch at Tavern on the Green."

Without his uniform on, Captain Wight seemed younger. He spoke freely and the lines around his eyes relaxed.

"What is Tavern on the Green?" Vera asked.

"A fancy restaurant that shouldn't be full of ten-year-old girls with marzipan on their fingers." Captain Wight grinned. "My father loved spoiling Carol. She was his angel."

"All fathers spoil their daughters," Vera agreed, picturing her father in a camel-colored coat and holding a jewelry box on her fourteenth birthday. He presented her with a gold chain and said that when she was older, she'd only wear diamonds.

"I'm sorry." Captain Wight frowned, noticing her mouth wobbling. "I didn't mean to make you think about your father . . ."

"I should be taking dictation instead of eating your delicious pancakes," Vera said. "If Signora Rosa and Gina fatten me up, soon I won't fit into my dress."

Captain Wight opened his mouth to say something but changed his mind. He put the plates in the sink and glanced at the clock.

"If we hurry, you'll be home by lunchtime." He stood in the doorway. "I don't want to ruin your afternoon."

Vera closed her stenography pad and screwed the top on the fountain pen. They had worked past the noon bells but neither of them wanted to stop.

"I'll be back on Saturday." Captain Wight handed her a wad of lire. "Perhaps you could check the mail every day."

"You mean collect your mother's telegrams," Vera laughed, stuffing the money in her purse. "You might send her a reply."

"I'll reply when I can give her the answer she wants to hear," Captain Wight responded. "Will you help me with an errand? I need a woman's opinion."

Vera walked with him toward the piazza, wondering if he was buying a present for a girlfriend in New York. She imagined a tall blonde with long legs and an impossibly small waist.

Captain Wight stopped in front of a small boutique. The window held trays of silk scarves and leather wallets. Earrings and charm bracelets and gold necklaces rested in cases within.

Captain Wight ushered her inside. He walked around the shop, tapping his fingers on the display cases.

"Do you like the red or blue scarf?" He pointed to two gossamer scarves with gold specks.

"The blue is pretty." Vera nodded.

"I'll take the blue," Captain Wight said to the shopkeeper.

They waited while the girl wrapped the purchase in tissue paper and tied it with a silver bow. Captain Wight clutched the box and walked into the sunlight. Vera turned to say good-bye, but he put his hand on her arm.

"I would be grateful if you could deliver this for me."

Vera nodded. "Of course." She had been wrong. He had a local girlfriend, a young Italian with wild black hair and high, full breasts.

"Her name is Edith, and she is staying at Signora Rosa's pensione."

"You know Edith?" Vera's eyes widened.

"You talk about her all the time," Captain Wight explained. "You've worked for me for three weeks and you wear the same dress every day. I figure the money must be going somewhere. If I buy Edith a present, perhaps you'll spend some money on yourself."

She glanced down at her dress, embarrassed that he had noticed.

"Edith lost the boy she was going to marry." Vera's cheeks turned red. "Pretty things keep her happy. But I don't need anything." She handed him the box. "I can't accept your present."

"That's why I'm giving it to Edith." Captain Wight grinned. "Summer is coming; buy yourself a gift."

Vera stroked the silver ribbon, imagining Edith's face when she saw the delicate scarf. "Thank you, that's very kind," Vera said finally. "It's Edith's birthday on Wednesday. She will jump with joy."

Vera said good-bye and hurried toward the pensione. She was about to cross the street when she saw an older woman standing in a butcher shop. She wore a navy dress and her black hair was styled in a pageboy.

Vera stood, mesmerized. The woman accepted her package from the butcher and opened the door. Suddenly Vera ran across the street.

"Mama, Mama," she cried in Hungarian. "*Kerlek besszelj hozzam. Sajnalom. Nem akartam hogy ez megtortenjen.* Please talk to me. I'm sorry. I didn't mean for it to happen."

The woman stared at her and backed away.

"I'm not your mother," she answered in Italian.

"I'm sorry, I didn't mean to intrude," Vera replied in Italian, the tears streaming down her cheeks. "You look so much like my mother."

The woman hurried off and Vera felt a hand on her shoulder. She looked up to find Captain Wight beside her. Her dress was stained with tears and she let out a moan.

"It's all right," Captain Wight soothed her.

"I was sure it was my mother," Vera cried. "Her dress, her hair. I thought she didn't answer because she hasn't forgiven me."

"Why don't we sit down and get something to drink?" Captain Wight replied softly. He took her arm and steered her across the street.

"It's my fault she isn't here." Vera gasped. "She died because of me."

Captain Wight guided her to an outside table at a nearby café and ordered two glasses of sherry. He sat quietly until Vera stopped trembling.

"The things Captain Bingham wrote in the letter, about your mother and escaping from the train to Auschwitz," Captain Wight asked, rubbing the rim of his glass. "Are they true?"

"Yes," Vera whispered.

"Perhaps it would help to talk about them," Captain Wight suggested.

"You are busy." Vera shook her head. "You must pack for Rome."

"I have nowhere to go," Captain Wight encouraged her. "I want to hear your story."

Vera took a deep breath. She needed to tell her story. She gazed at Captain Wight's pale blue eyes, the lines on his forehead and the dimple on his chin, and began to speak.

Vera stood in the back of the train and tried to breathe. Edith dozed in front of her, Stefan's scarf wrapped around her neck even though the air was as stale as old bread. Edith's mother, Lily, crooned a melody. Only Vera's mother seemed alert. Her brow was furrowed as if she was trying to decipher a difficult recipe or rectify the month's household accounts.

Two weeks before, in May of 1944, they had finally been moved to the ghetto. Vera's mother pretended things were normal, making Vera do her schoolwork and set the table at night. But their food supplies had dwindled, and for the last few days, Alice pushed her own tiny portion of bread toward Vera and claimed she wasn't hungry.

Edith remained happy and calm until Stefan was put on a train to a labor camp called Strasshof in Austria. Stefan said it was actually good news. The rumor was that the Jews in Strasshof were needed to work on the farms. The inmates weren't starved and he might get to work outdoors instead of in a factory.

The train lurched and Vera fell back. It wasn't really a train: trains were the luxurious silver cars Vera had seen at the station in Budapest. Where porters carried steamer trunks and first-class passengers sat on plush velvet seats, admiring the scenery on the way to Vienna.

Vera and the rest of the ghetto had been herded into cattle cars that were sealed as tightly as cans of sardines. There was no food or water, and the smell was worse than the garbage in the streets of the ghetto.

"Vera," her mother whispered. "Come here."

Vera's heart raced. Her mother had whispered on the way to the train that she was going to think of an escape plan.

"What is it?" Vera asked, and glanced around. Everyone on the train was so intent on their own pain, they didn't pay attention to each other.

"At the next stop, a guard will come on board to make sure no one is causing trouble. Edith will say it is her birthday and insist he share a bottle of schnapps. When he finishes the bottle, he will fall asleep. We'll wait until he does and then I will steal his key and open the door. You and Edith will slip out and Lily and I will follow."

"Where did you get the schnapps?" Vera worried. It was against orders to carry alcohol. And the guards were instructed to shoot troublemakers on the spot. "And how do you know he'll fall asleep?"

"The guards are practically children; they've never had a shot of schnapps in their lives." Alice tapped the lining of her coat. "This is extra strong. It could put a cow to sleep. He'll be out within fifteen minutes."

"Are you sure?" Vera whispered. "Perhaps where we are going is not that bad."

Her mother's face clouded over and Vera noticed tears in her eyes.

"Tell Edith our plan," her mother instructed. "We must be ready when the guard arrives."

The train stopped and a guard in the brown Nazi uniform leaped into the car. A prominent Adam's apple protruded from his neck. Her mother was right, he couldn't have been more than sixteen.

"Adolf," Edith whispered to him in German. "Today is my birthday."

The guard glared at her.

"Why did you call me Adolf?" he asked warily.

Edith had taken off Stefan's scarf and unbuttoned the top of her blouse. She had pinched her lips to give them color. She reached up and touched the guard's cheek.

"All handsome Germans are named Adolf," she murmured. "I'm eighteen today, you have to help me celebrate."

"Happy birthday," the guard wished stiffly.

"That's not enough; you must drink this." She pushed the flask into his hands. "It's a special day."

The guard refused. Edith moved closer.

"Please," she begged. "I might not have another birthday."

The guard swallowed the schnapps and handed the flask back to Edith. Edith pretended to drink and urged him again.

"One more sip," she whispered. "Then perhaps a kiss."

Vera glanced around nervously. Ten minutes passed, and she tried to pretend everything was normal. She hummed a little tune to herself and fidgeted with the buttons on her dress. When she finally looked back, the guard was slumped against the wall. Her mother slipped the key out of his pocket and motioned Vera and Edith toward the door. It barely budged; Vera wondered if it was wide enough for them to jump.

Alice nudged it open further and Vera inhaled the night air. She inched closer and heard a groan.

Vera turned to see the guard clutching his leg. His face contorted as he moaned again.

"What's happening?" Vera asked her mother.

"He has a cramp," Alice answered.

The guard's eyes flickered open, and then everything happened quickly. Alice moved Edith in her place and blocked the guard so he couldn't see the two girls. The other passengers were crammed too tightly together and consumed by their own fears to notice what was going on.

"Jump now," she ordered. "We will follow."

Vera stared at the thin line of darkness outside the train. If she and Edith jumped, there might not be time for her mother and Lily to follow. But if they didn't, the guard might fully wake up and notice something was wrong.

Before she could decide, her mother pushed her through the opening. Vera grabbed Edith's hand, and together they tumbled off the train.

The ground was hard and she landed awkwardly. Pain shot through her ankle and she was afraid it was broken. She lay perfectly still until the train disappeared. Then she sat up, hoping to make out her mother's navy coat or Lily's favorite red dress despite the darkness.

"What happened?" Edith sat beside her. She had blacked out for a minute. Brambles were caught in her hair and there was a rip in her dress.

"My mother pushed us off the train," Vera replied. "She and your mother must have jumped off a moment later. We'll wait here and they'll find us."

They huddled together and waited for their mothers to appear. The sky was black and there weren't any stars to light the field.

"I don't see them, and I'm so cold," Edith whispered, her teeth beginning to chatter.

"They'll be here any minute." Vera stared straight ahead like a hypnotist she had seen at a birthday party. He could bend a spoon just by concentrating on it.

"We must get back on the train!" Edith exclaimed, clutching her neck. "I left Stefan's scarf. I promised I'd keep it always."

There was the sound of a cow mooing, and then quiet. If her mother and Lily had escaped, they would have found them by now.

"That's not all we left on the train," Vera said, and her heart was a dam that was about to break.

"The train carried my mother and Lily to Auschwitz. They died in the gas chamber." Vera looked at Captain Wight. The glasses of sherry were long gone, and the waiter had brought two more. "Do you mind if we finish the story another time? I'm sorry; I can't go on right now."

"Of course." Captain Wight nodded. "But you mustn't blame yourself; five hundred and fifty thousand Hungarian Jews were killed at concentration camps."

Vera had heard the figure before, but she ignored it anyway. She wasn't responsible for the death of all the other Hungarians, but she could have saved her own mother. If only they had jumped off the train together.

"You don't understand, my mother would have done anything for me. When I was eight years old I had diphtheria and the doctor thought I was going to die. My mother sat at my bedside for two weeks, willing me to live," Vera responded. "She should have jumped off the train with us, instead she stayed behind so we could live. She was afraid the guard would become alert and see us trying to escape.

The train would have been stopped and we could have been shot. It's my fault that she's dead."

Captain Wight signaled the waiter for the check.

"Your mother may have been determined, but she was no match for the Nazis," he assured her. "Every day she woke up knowing you were safe. That's the greatest gift of all."

Vera sat silently, her body trembling. She pictured her mother being led to the gas chamber, her hair shorn, her arm inked with a tattoo.

"You'll fall in love, get married, have children," Captain Wight continued. "You'll look at their faces and see your mother's eyes and you'll tell them how brave their grandmother was."

"All I want is to see her again." Vera wiped her eyes.

"I'm taking you home," Captain Wight soothed her. He stood up and pulled back her chair. "Tomorrow everything will be brighter."

"I didn't mean to tell you so much," Vera apologized as they approached the pensione. "I ruined your Saturday."

"Give Edith her present." Captain Wight handed her the box. He looked at her and there was tenderness in his eyes. "Then go out and buy yourself a spring dress. It would make your mother happy."

Vera reached up and kissed him briefly on the cheek. His skin was smooth and smelled of shaving lotion.

"I'll see you next Saturday." He smiled and turned back to the piazza.

CHAPTER FOUR

Spring 1946

Vera and Edith entered the pensione's small parlor. Yellow daisies sat in a ceramic vase atop a lace tablecloth.

"You shouldn't have gone to all this trouble," Vera said as she observed the basket of fresh bread, the bowl of fruit, the jars of jam and honey.

"It's Edith's birthday and you are my favorite guests," Signora Rosa insisted. "I'm going to fatten you up so you find good husbands."

"Vera won't let me talk to men," Edith grumbled, biting into a plum. She wore a print dress and white sandals. Her cheeks were powdered and her blond hair was tied in a knot. "She thinks I'm going to get into trouble."

"You can talk to men," Vera responded. "You shouldn't drive off on their Vespas."

There was a knock at the door and Signora Rosa peered through the window. A dark-haired young man stood outside, clutching a bouquet of lilies.

"Can I help you?" Signora Rosa opened the door.

"Marcus Sorrento." The man bowed. "These flowers are for your lovely home. I came to wish Edith a happy birthday."

"What beautiful lilies!" Edith jumped up and dragged Marcus inside. "They would look gorgeous on the sideboard."

Marcus smiled and handed Edith a flat package. "A small token for your birthday."

Edith opened the parcel. Inside was a photo in a silver frame. At first Vera didn't recognize the two girls sharing an iced coffee. Their eyes sparkled and their cheeks glowed in the camera's flash.

"I took it the night we met in the piazza." Marcus beamed.

"It's wonderful," Edith gushed. "We'll put it on our nightstand."

"A friend of mine owns a restaurant on the bay," Marcus said. "He makes the finest pizza marinara in Naples. I would be honored if you and Vera joined me for your birthday dinner."

Edith was about to answer but Vera interrupted. "If you'll excuse us, we'll be right back." She dragged Edith upstairs to their room, shutting the door behind them.

"What are you doing?" Vera demanded.

"Having a lovely birthday," Edith replied innocently. "Isn't it sweet that Marcus stopped by?"

"Have you been seeing him behind my back?" Vera demanded.

Edith shrugged. "He walked me home a few times. He has four older sisters; he's very polite."

"Today he'll bring flowers, tomorrow he'll put his hands up your skirt!" Vera declared, waving her hand. "All men are after one thing."

"You're wrong. Some men want to gaze at the clouds and talk about life," Edith said dreamily. "Some men want to ride bicycles and splash in swimming holes and stuff their faces with cake."

Vera remembered when they were children and spent every summer in the countryside. Their fathers stayed in Budapest to work, but Alice and Lily and Edith and Vera shared a house in the country near Szentendre. There was a lane, and fields with cows, and a lake perfect for swimming.

At first, Edith and Stefan were just friends. Stefan's family lived in Budapest and they went to the country every year at the same time. Vera and Edith and Stefan spent lazy days making daisy chains and eating stuffed crepes that seemed to multiply in the kitchen.

But when they became teenagers, everything changed. Vera noticed the way Stefan looked at Edith: as if she were a sculpture to be admired behind a velvet rope at the museum. He appeared at the door in a clean shirt and brought flowers or a piece of fruit picked from an orchard.

The girls giggled about it, until one afternoon Vera had a headache and left the swimming hole early. Edith came home that evening with flushed cheeks and a new womanliness: her hips swayed when she walked, and her breasts pushed against her bathing suit.

"Vera," Edith whispered, climbing into bed beside her. It was only seven p.m., but Vera's head throbbed. She had been sleeping fitfully for hours.

"What is it?" Vera roused herself awake. Edith felt hot, like she might be coming down with a fever.

"Stefan kissed me," Edith revealed. Her breath was sweet, like the coffee cake they had taken on their picnic. "We were sitting under a tree and watching the ducks in the lake. He touched my hair and said it reminded him of a princess in a fairy tale."

"What was the kiss like?" Vera sat up immediately. They were fifteen, and the only kissing they had done was practicing in front of the mirror.

"At first our noses bumped, and Stefan was so embarrassed." Edith hugged her knees. "But I urged him to try again and it was warm and soft," she sighed. "I can't wait to kiss him again."

"By next summer you'll have kissed a dozen boys and I'll still be practicing on a pillow," Vera complained.

Edith's eyebrows arched in surprise. "I'm never going to kiss another boy. Stefan and I will be together forever."

"It was different for you and Stefan. You had known each other since you were children," Vera said gently, pushing away the images of Edith and Stefan. "You just met Marcus; you don't know anything about him."

"I'll never meet a man if I stay locked up like Rapunzel!" Edith protested. "I'm nineteen. I want to dance and laugh and flirt."

"All right," Vera relented. "We'll go to dinner with him."

Edith grinned. "It's going to be so much fun!" She embraced Vera.

"You have to promise we won't keep secrets from each other," Vera warned, returning her hug.

"I promise. I must wash my hair." Edith walked to the staircase to tell Marcus they would go to dinner. "Maybe Signora Rosa will lend me her perfume."

Marcus picked them up promptly at seven. Edith wore a red dress with a flared skirt, her waist cinched by a thick belt.

Marcus stood at the door. His hair was damp and his camera was slung over his shoulder. He took in Edith's dress and whistled. "They say Italian women are beautiful. But they are no match for such perfection."

They stepped into the cool evening air. The street was full of young people laughing and smoking cigarettes. Marcus talked easily, pointing out the places he wanted to photograph.

"There were only a few men left in our village of Ravello, and my mother insisted I stay home after the war," Marcus explained. "All I ever wanted to do was take pictures. So I ran away. I'm going to become a rich and famous photographer and buy my mother a villa big enough for her and all my sisters."

They entered a café overlooking the Bay of Naples. Wooden tables were crammed near the window and a piano stood against the wall. The ceiling was hung with garlic, and Vera could smell tomato sauce and onions.

"Two beautiful dates?" A young man thumped Marcus on the back. "I should be a photographer instead of spending my days chopping oregano."

"This is Paolo." Marcus introduced them. "He is the best chef in Naples."

"A year ago I was a busboy, now I own a restaurant." Paolo led them to a round table. "There is much opportunity after the war."

"Paolo sold cigarettes on the black market," Marcus whispered. "Now he is rich and can do what he loves."

"I want to design evening gowns," Edith declared. "Gorgeous dresses that women wear to the opera and the symphony."

Marcus held out his hand. Vera sat opposite them at the table, and Paolo filled their wineglasses.

"You must come to Rome with me," Marcus suggested. "We will live in an apartment above the Spanish Steps and throw parties that last all night."

"Vera is going to write scripts," Edith continued, sipping a glass of red wine. "Her name is going to be in big letters on a theater marquee."

"A toast." Marcus raised his glass and gazed at Edith. "To new beginnings and great fortunes."

Edith's face lit up. She was like a flower blooming after a long winter. Her eyes were wide and blue; her skin was the finest porcelain. For once, Edith didn't seem to be watching a sad film that only she could see. Could their dreams come true? Did Vera even want to be a playwright anymore? She thought of leaving her job at the embassy to write plays, and there was a lump in her throat. Every day she looked forward to going to work and seeing Captain Wight drinking his coffee in the morning room.

"We must eat." Marcus opened his napkin. "Paolo will be disappointed if we don't clean our plates."

Vera surveyed the plates of spaghetti and clams, the loaves of garlic bread, the platters of vegetables. She suddenly thought of Captain Wight in Rome. He would be sitting at a café near the Trevi Fountain, sipping espresso and reading a newspaper.

"Every Sunday we would have lunch that lasted three hours," Marcus interrupted Vera's thoughts. He heaped Edith's plate with spaghetti. "My sister's boyfriend, Donato, would compliment my mother's cooking while putting his hand on my sister's thigh. My mother kept a ruler at the table. The minute Donato started praising the meal, she'd rap him across the knuckles."

"She sounds frightening," Edith laughed.

"She taught me to respect women and keep my hands to myself." Marcus gazed at Edith. "Women are goddesses; men are their servants."

Vera ate a bite of bread and listened to what Marcus was saying. Did women want men to be their servants, or did they simply want loving husbands? Wasn't it better to find someone to share things with: someone who looked at the world in a similar way and had the same goals?

After dinner, Paolo played the piano and Marcus and Edith danced between the tables. Vera watched Edith twirl and dip, remembering dances with boys in stiff shirts and narrow ties. She wondered if any of those boys made it back, if Budapest would ever know the sound of youthful laughter. Her heart tightened and she missed Hungary with a physical ache. All those young men with hopes and dreams were now piles of bones in the yards at Auschwitz and Bergen-Belsen. And Hungarian girls like Vera and Edith who dreamed of getting married and having houses full of children had to find new meaning and reinvent their futures.

"Marcus knows a nightclub," Edith said breathlessly. Her cheeks were flushed and tendrils of hair stuck to her forehead. "He wants to take us dancing."

Vera shook her head. "I don't want to go to a club."

"You see how sweet Marcus is," Edith tried again. "He hasn't laid a hand on me."

"Marcus is sweet," Vera agreed, watching Marcus point his camera in their direction. "But you don't need to rush. Let's go home; you can see him again tomorrow."

"I am tired, and it has been a lovely birthday," Edith relented. "But you must promise on Saturday we'll go dancing. You can't forget your birthday; it's in three days."

Marcus paid for dinner and they strolled onto the docks. The wind had picked up and he put a tentative arm around Edith's shoulder.

Vera walked behind them, the cold air nipping her ankles. Edith and Marcus whispered together, and Vera suddenly felt very alone.

She remembered when she was a girl, dreaming about her future. She would have a loving husband, a lawyer or an engineer, and four beautiful children. They would own an apartment in Budapest and a house in the country. The children would ride horses and play tennis and swim in the lake. At night they would curl up in front of a fire, and she would read Tolstoy and Chekhov.

"I forgot how much I love to dance!" Edith exclaimed, after they said good night to Marcus and crept up to their room.

"I have a present for you." Vera handed her the box wrapped in tissue paper.

"We weren't going to buy each other presents," Edith reminded her. She unwrapped the delicate scarf and gasped. "It's beautiful! But it must have cost a fortune."

"It's a gift from Captain Wight." Vera watched Edith wrap the scarf around her neck.

"Why would he give me a present?" Edith asked. "I've never met him."

Vera shrugged. "He likes to help others."

"I thought we weren't supposed to accept presents from men." Edith looked at Vera curiously.

Vera pictured Captain Wight in his khaki uniform. She remembered reaching up and kissing him on the cheek. "Perhaps we can accept a small present now and then."

CHAPTER FIVE

Spring 1946

Vera folded the letter and slipped it in her pocket. She glanced in the mirror and adjusted the collar of her dress.

"He can't make you work on your birthday!" Edith protested, sitting up in bed. It was already the afternoon, but Edith had spent the morning lounging around the room. "You promised we'd go dancing. Marcus is going to pick us up at eight."

"Captain Wight doesn't know it's my birthday." Vera smoothed her hair. "I'll be home by six; I'll have plenty of time to get ready."

"Marcus invited his friend, Pico. Pico has the profile of a Roman god," Edith said dreamily.

"I'm not interested in men," Vera insisted. "I'm only going to the nightclub to keep you company."

"You're going to keep an eye on me and Marcus," Edith laughed. She pulled the covers over her and went back to sleep.

Vera skipped down the steps and onto the street. She took the letter out of her pocket and read it again.

Vera,

I arrived back in Naples this morning and have some correspondence that must be finished before Monday. Would it be possible for you to come to the embassy for a few hours this afternoon?

Yours,

Anton

In the month Vera had been working for Captain Wight, she had never seen his signature. She hadn't even known his first name. Captain Bingham had only referred to him as Captain Wight, and that's how he had introduced himself. And she always transcribed the letters and left them on his desk for him to sign. Then Gina took them to the post office, so she had never had occasion to see his full signature.

"Captain Anton Wight," Vera said aloud, laughing at herself. He probably signed his first name by accident, hastily giving the letter to Gina to deliver to the pensione.

"Thank you for coming." Captain Wight opened the front door. He wore a black tuxedo with a white silk shirt. His hair was combed and his cheeks were closely shaven.

"You're going out!" Vera blushed, suddenly flustered.

"I'm hosting a dinner party this evening." Captain Wight ushered her inside. "You must think I'm an ogre to make you come to the embassy on another weekend."

"I don't want to keep you," Vera murmured. "I could come back in the morning."

"I'm not such a beast to make you work on Sunday!" Captain Wight exclaimed.

Captain Wight dictated letters for an hour, but Vera was distracted. He looked out of place in his starched collar and gold cuff links. She imagined him seated at a sumptuous banquet, sipping champagne and discussing politics.

"When I was in Rome, General Ashe kept insisting I close the Naples embassy and join him there," Captain Wight said finally, leaning back in his chair.

"I hope you don't leave us soon." Vera clutched her fountain pen tightly, realizing she could lose her job as quickly as she found it.

"I don't want to think about moving to Rome right now. I haven't had a proper meal all day and I'm always grumpy when I'm hungry. I was on the train for hours and the sandwiches tasted like wax paper." Captain Wight stood up and stretched his legs. "Let's raid Gina's kitchen."

Captain Wight made plates of bread and mascarpone cheese. They sat at the oak table overlooking the garden, and Vera mentioned how much Edith had enjoyed her birthday present.

"You haven't bought yourself anything new," Captain Wight said, pointing to the green dress she wore every day.

"I might today," Vera mumbled self-consciously. "Edith and I are going dancing."

"Then I shouldn't keep you, you must have dates waiting." Captain Wight got up abruptly and loaded dishes in the sink.

"And your guests will be arriving shortly." Vera wrapped up the cheese and put it in the fridge.

"Could you bring me my mother's telegrams before you go? I didn't see them on my desk," he said.

"I left them on the table in the morning room," Vera replied, glad for an excuse to leave the kitchen. "I'll run and get them."

The curtains in the morning room were closed and Mozart played softly on the phonograph. Vera rustled around looking for the pile of telegrams, but they were missing. She glanced up five minutes later and Captain Wight stood at the door, holding a square box.

"Gina must have moved them," Vera explained.

"No, I took them earlier," Captain Wight admitted. He walked toward Vera and handed her the box. "I didn't want you to leave until I gave you this."

Vera opened the box and took out an emerald-green evening gown. It had a heart-shaped bodice and capped sleeves. Buried in the tissue paper were delicate heels with gold straps.

Vera held up the shoes and her eyes sparkled.

"I can't accept this," she breathed, touching the sheer silk of the dress.

"Wear it dancing tonight." Captain Wight slipped his hands in his pockets. "Your date will love it."

"I don't have a date." Vera shook her head. "I don't need to wear such a pretty dress. I'm only going to keep Edith company."

"In that case," Captain Wight said, shifting his feet. "Perhaps you'd join me for dinner."

"But you're having a dinner party," Vera objected.

Captain Wight reached down and touched her cheek. "You are my only guest."

Vera broke away and sat down on the sofa. She clutched the box, her hands trembling.

"I'm sorry if I upset you," Captain Wight implored, striding across the room. "I wanted to give you a wonderful dinner with champagne and dessert and then tell you my feelings."

"Feelings?" Vera choked. Captain Wight had always been so polite and serious, could he really have developed feelings for her? And how did she feel about him? She recalled the way he popped into her thoughts when she crossed the piazza after work or when Marcus called on Edith and there was a fluttering in her chest.

"When I was in Rome I couldn't stop thinking of you," Captain Wight admitted. "I couldn't sleep, I couldn't eat. I just wanted to come home and be with you."

"You hardly know me," Vera replied, her heart hammering.

"You're beautiful and courageous and I'd like . . ." Captain Wight stopped, as if he couldn't decide what he wanted. "I'd like to invite you to dinner."

Vera had promised Edith she would go dancing with her. She couldn't abandon her best friend.

"Perhaps another night. I have to go," Vera said reluctantly. She stood up and walked to the door. "Edith is waiting for me."

"I have a confession to make." Captain Wight stopped her. "I asked Edith's permission to have dinner with you tonight. She gave us her blessing."

"Edith knows?" Vera remembered Edith saying Captain Wight was a slave driver to make her work on Saturdays.

"I swore her to secrecy. I didn't want to pressure you."

Vera studied his serious pale blue eyes, the fine lines around his mouth. She admired the elegant fabric of the dress, feeling young and pretty. "I accept."

"Thank God," Captain Wight exhaled, smiling. "Gina will take you upstairs to change. Dinner will be in the Red Salon."

Vera knew there was a whole floor of bedrooms furnished with four-poster beds. She suddenly wondered if Captain Wight just wanted to get her into bed. He would ply her with drinks and take her to one of the suites.

"We could dine at a restaurant if you prefer," Captain Wight suggested as if he could read her thoughts. "I just thought the rooms in the villa are so beautiful and no one uses them. It seems a waste."

He walked into the hall and called for Gina. She appeared swiftly from the kitchen.

"Vera is concerned about the propriety of dining alone with me," Captain Wight explained. His eyes were serious, but a smile played across his mouth. "Could I ask you to be our chaperone this evening?"

"*Si*, signor," Gina agreed, glancing from Captain Wight to Vera.

"You promise not to leave us until we have finished dessert and I have escorted Vera home?" he asked.

"My pleasure, signor." Gina nodded and smiled at Vera. "You have my word."

Captain Wight turned to Vera, as innocent and hopeful as a young boy.

"What do you think?"

Vera's chest swelled. She picked up the evening gown and turned to Gina. "Where do I change?"

Vera followed Gina up the marble staircase to the second floor. They passed sitting rooms with brocade furniture and frescoed ceilings. Rich tapestries and damask curtains covered the bedroom walls.

Gina opened a door at the end of the hall. Vera stepped through the entrance and gasped. A canopied bed occupied most of the room, across from shelves of leather-bound books and a fire crackling in the fireplace.

"The bathroom is through here." Gina showed her the bathroom's black-and-white marble floor and gold fixtures. "And the dressing room is in here." Gina led her to the area with velvet walls and a dressing table covered with pots and jars.

"Signor Wight said you may use anything you desire." Gina pointed to the rows of lipsticks and bottles of perfume.

"I've hardly worn makeup since the war." Vera hesitated, picking up a bottle of perfume.

Gina smiled. "I have two daughters. Every night I brush their hair one hundred strokes. I will turn you into a princess."

Gina opened a jar of powder and dusted Vera's cheeks. She applied a coat of eye shadow and thick strokes of mascara. She found a gold clip and pinned it in Vera's hair.

Vera stepped into the evening gown and let Gina close the pearl buttons. She gazed in the mirror, feeling like a countess in a Russian novel. Her hair was glossy, her lips were painted red, and her wrists were sprayed with a floral perfume.

"It needs something to draw attention to the bodice," Gina said as she studied the dress critically.

"I don't want to draw attention to my breasts!" Vera was shocked.

"Not your breasts, your neck. Why does a woman dab her neck with perfume? Because it is the most sensuous spot on the body." Gina opened a drawer and took out a gold locket. "You're too young for jewels. A locket has mystery; anything could be inside it."

Vera fingered the locket and remembered finding her mother in her dressing room in 1943, her jewels scattered across the table, as if she were conducting some kind of treasure hunt.

"What are you doing?" Vera asked. Alice sat on the red velvet stool, ruby earrings and gold necklaces and brooches made of ivory in front of her.

"I'm taking them to Stein's jewelry store." Alice inspected a pearl brooch.

"Why would you sell your jewelry?" Vera asked in alarm.

"It can't buy veal and potatoes sitting in a heap," Alice said, waving at the small tower of gold. Vera's father had disappeared to a labor camp two years before. "Abram Stein will probably rob me blind. He has the morals of a street cat, but that's why he's still in business. Do you know how many Jews have closed their stores? They can't stay open if no one will buy from them."

"The war could end any time and father will be released. We have no reason to believe he's not still alive," Vera replied. "What will he say if you've gotten rid of everything he bought you?"

"Or the war could go on for years," Alice countered. "Do you think the Germans would be living in our apartments and eating in our cafés if they expected to leave anytime soon? Moshe Goldberg sells bratwurst made with pork and German sauerkraut at his delicatessen. His mother is turning over in her grave, but the Germans are his only customers. If he doesn't stock pork, they'll shop somewhere else. There isn't even any difference between Hungarian and German sauerkraut. He only writes German sauerkraut on the label to attract the German soldiers," she spat. "They are too stupid to realize that."

"You've collected jewelry for years," Vera tried again. "Every piece has a special meaning."

Alice picked up a gold locket and showed it to Vera. "This is the first piece your father gave me. It was in Paris when we met. Your father was a law student on holiday and I was at dancing school. I was only nineteen, but I lied about my age because you had to be twenty to live in the boardinghouse," she laughed. "Your father thought he was dating an older woman, so he bought this to impress me. I told him to return it and use the money for his studies. But he fastened the locket around my neck and said it was going to be the best investment he ever made."

"Keep it, then," Vera urged. "It can't be worth much."

Alice turned it over in her palm and her shoulders heaved. Then she resolutely dropped it on top of the pile.

"If it buys a carton of eggs it will do more good than gathering dust." She leaned forward and kissed Vera. "Don't worry about your father. All he would want is for us to be warm and fed."

Vera glanced in the mirror in the bedroom of the Palazzo Mezzi and wondered what had happened to the locket. Had her mother sold it or kept it hidden with the small bundle of jewels she set aside to bribe German officers? In any case, it was gone now.

"Thank you, it's perfect." Vera turned to Gina and her eyes sparkled. "I'm ready."

"A great beauty doesn't descend the stairs in haste." Gina motioned Vera to sit. "You must keep Captain Wight waiting."

"But that's impolite." Vera frowned.

Gina smiled. "That's part of being a woman."

Vera waited for ten minutes until the grandfather clock chimed. Captain Wight paced the entry holding an unlit cigarette. He looked up and stared as she made her way toward him.

"You are breathtaking," he gasped.

"Anyone would look beautiful in this dress," Vera murmured.

"I have only two requests this evening." Captain Wight offered her his arm and they walked toward the dining room. "That you accept my compliments and call me Anton."

"Anton," Vera repeated, and burst out laughing. His grip was firm, and she glided along the polished floor beside him.

"Why is that funny?" Anton asked. He turned to look at her and his expression was warm and curious.

"It just sounds funny with your American accent. I thought all American men were named something like Dick or Bud," Vera explained.

"I got a lot of grief in school," Anton admitted. "The other children put on French accents and asked whether I was going to be a painter and live in a garret."

"I'm sorry, it's a lovely name." Vera suppressed her giggles.

"When my mother was pregnant, she became infatuated with Flaubert and Stendhal." Anton guided Vera to the Red Salon. "She bought a poodle and named her Fifi."

"We haven't yet had dinner and I've embarrassed you," Vera replied. She had been insensitive and now she'd made Anton feel bad.

"On the contrary"—Anton stopped walking and touched her cheek—"you're even more beautiful when you laugh."

They entered the grandiose salon and Vera gazed around her. The table was set with gold china, gleaming silverware, and flickering candles. There was a phonograph and music played softly.

"I've never seen such ceilings," Vera gasped, studying the naked cherubs drinking from silver goblets.

"The first Countess Mezzi was Venetian," Anton explained. He walked to the sideboard and poured two glasses of sherry. "She thought Naples was full of peasants, so her husband built her a palace. The ballroom can fit five hundred people."

"I can't imagine owning a home with a ballroom! Our apartment in Budapest was small, but we had a house in the country to accommodate my mother's family." Vera sipped her sherry. "My mother had four siblings and they often visited with their children. My mother would cook a feast. I'd lie on my bed afterward unable to move."

"Are your relatives still in Hungary?" Anton inquired.

"One uncle died of tuberculosis," Vera said stiffly. "My other uncle was sent to a labor camp, and my aunts and cousins were sent to Auschwitz."

"They may have survived," Anton countered. "I can try to contact them on your behalf."

Vera gripped the sherry glass. Suddenly she wasn't a glamorous young woman dining with an American captain. She was a refugee, without anyone in the world except Edith.

Vera shook her head. "I'd rather they think I'm dead."

"Why?" Anton asked, alarmed.

Vera put down the glass and waved her hand around the dining room.

"I don't deserve any of this," she gulped.

"You have to stop blaming yourself." Anton put his hand on Vera's shoulder. "You deserve beauty, love, and happiness," he whispered.

He led her to the table. As they ate, he talked about showing her New York City one day, ice-skating in Rockefeller Center and carriage rides in Central Park.

"I was never good at dinner parties," he mused after they had eaten veal parmigiana and stuffed eggplant. "I wanted to study the architecture instead of making polite conversation with the guests."

"I bet you were popular with girls," Vera said with a small smile.

"I attended my share of cotillions," Anton conceded. "My mother was anxious to marry me off to a Roosevelt or a Jewett, the old established families in New York. We're still considered new money; her lifelong ambition is to see her name in the pages of the *Social Register* for New York society: Mr. and Mrs. Harry and Margaret Wight of Park Avenue."

"What about your brother?" Vera asked.

"My mother knew Brad was more likely to get a girl pregnant than put a ring on her finger," Anton replied.

"I see." Vera put her fork on her plate. She was no longer hungry. She imagined a sleek blonde waiting for Anton at the dock in New York. She saw them stepping into a black motorcar and driving to their town house near Central Park.

"What about you?" Anton asked. "Did you have many suitors?"

"I was busy with school, and on the weekends I wrote. I wanted to be a playwright." Vera remembered the manuscripts hidden under her bed. She wondered if the Germans found them. She imagined them laughing at the scribblings of a young girl. "I always thought boys would come later, when I was at university."

"I'm glad you waited." He stood up and offered her his hand to dance. Vera rose and he pulled her toward him.

He kissed her slowly, tasting of sherry. Then he kissed her harder, crushing the green silk against his chest. Vera stood on tiptoes and felt like she would faint. She was delighted and shaken at the same time. The ornate frescoes, the glittering chandeliers, the candles faded away and all that remained were his lips on hers.

"It's getting late." Vera pulled away. "If I'm not home when Edith arrives, I'm afraid she'll invite Marcus upstairs."

"You can't leave yet." Anton fixed his bow tie. "Gina has been working all afternoon on dessert."

Vera reluctantly sat down and waited while Gina cleared plates and silverware. She had forgotten about Gina. Where had she been during dinner when she was supposed to be their chaperone? But Vera was too happy and excited to think about it.

Anton dimmed the lights and Gina appeared carrying a beautiful chocolate cake. It was shaped like a heart and illuminated by nineteen flickering candles.

"I bribed the chef at the Grand Hotel in Rome to make the cake." Anton smiled. "I wanted him to top it with pink flowers, but he said Americans had terrible taste. A cake isn't a garden."

"It's beautiful." Vera noticed her name scrawled in pink icing.

"How did you know it was my birthday?" She turned to Anton, pushing away her memories of birthday parties in the country with her parents and aunts and uncles.

"You said that Edith was born three days before you," Anton replied.

"And you remembered?"

Anton cut two slices of cake and placed them on Wedgwood plates. He handed Vera a dessert fork and a white linen napkin.

"I remember everything about you."

They ate thick slices of chocolate cake and shared a bottle of Tia Maria that Anton had brought from Rome. Vera remembered Anton's lips on hers and wondered if he would kiss her again. Then she shook herself and listened to him talk about plans for new schools and parks.

"I'm boring you." Anton put his napkin on his plate.

"Liqueur makes me sleepy," Vera admitted. "I should go home."

"I'll walk with you." Anton pushed back his chair.

Vera shook her head and stood up.

"You have work to catch up on," Vera she reminded him. "I'll be fine; I just need some air."

"I promised I'd walk you home." Anton took her arm and walked to the entry. "An officer always keeps his word."

They walked quietly through the piazza, Anton's tuxedo brushing her arm. Vera suddenly felt out of place. Anton was used to women who wore diamond earrings and silver-fox coats. Vera's wardrobe consisted of two cotton dresses and a new pair of stockings.

They reached Signora Rosa's and Vera stood on the first step.

"Last Saturday you let me tell my story and I was too tired to go on," Vera said nervously. "I would like to tell you more."

"You don't have to," Anton said. "We can just stand here and enjoy the balmy evening."

She waved at the ball gown. "It isn't right for you to see me all dressed up and drinking wine without knowing who I was before. It would make me feel better."

"If you're sure . . ." Anton took off his jacket and draped it over the step.

"Perfectly sure." She nodded and sat down. Stars twinkled against the black sky and she was transported to the night she and Edith jumped off the train and there were no stars to guide them.

Vera held her arms to her chest to keep from shivering as she and Edith walked in the dark. Edith had begged Vera to let them stop and rest. But if they lay down on the hard ground they would freeze, and if they waited until morning, someone might find them.

"We don't even know where we're going," Edith moaned, trudging beside Vera. For the last hour they had hummed the Maurice Chevalier and Josephine Baker records their parents had played on the phonograph.

"There must be a farmhouse somewhere." Vera squinted into the dark. She assumed there would be, and yet she didn't even know what country they were in.

"And do you really think we can knock on a door and be invited inside?"

Vera had been worrying about that since they jumped off the train. With her blond hair, Edith might pass as Aryan, but Vera's dark hair and slightly longer nose marked her as Jewish.

They turned at the sound of an engine. Edith stepped onto the gravel path and waved her arms.

"What are you doing?" Vera asked in alarm. It sounded like a car.

"Hoping someone might see us." Edith waved her arms wider.

"Are you mad?" Vera gasped. "What if it's a German soldier?"

"I'd rather sit in a car with a gun to my head than freeze to death in this field," Edith retorted.

Edith was right. If they stayed there any longer, they would get sick from the cold. And Edith was a wonderful actress. She had been so convincing with the guard on the train. Maybe it would be wiser to take their chances with the driver of the car than spend the night in an open field. Besides, what would a German soldier be doing out here in the middle of the night? It was probably a farmer returning home from visiting a neighbor.

Before Vera could protest, a truck emerged from the fog. She squinted in the dark and made out a man sitting in the driver's seat.

"What are you girls doing out here?" the man asked in German, jumping out of the truck. He was a few years older than Vera and Edith and wore a thick vest.

"We were at a party and got lost." Edith stepped forward. Edith might have been a good actress, but she was a terrible liar.

"A party out here?" The man glanced around the empty fields.

"It was a very small party." Edith smiled provocatively. "Our dates were expecting it to be more exciting and we disappointed them." She rubbed her hands. "They left us here and we're going to freeze to death."

The man noticed Vera and he turned toward his vehicle.

"I'm sorry, I can't help you. I hope your dates return soon," the man said brusquely. His jaw was set in a firm line and he shifted his feet.

"Please." Edith touched his arm. "It's so cold and I'm afraid of the dark."

The truck light illuminated Edith's blond hair and blue eyes. The man coughed and opened the passenger door. "My name is Lukas. There is a farmhouse not far from here I can take you to."

The girls squeezed in beside him and he started the engine. Vera kept glancing at Lukas, terrified he'd pull out a gun.

After ten minutes, the truck stopped in front of an overgrown lane.

"It's down there." Lukas pointed into the darkness. "The Dunkels lost their only son at the battle of Kursk. Ottie Dunkel is a kind woman and she has a soft spot for young people." He opened the car door. "Next time make up a better story. There are no young men left to party with; they're on the front lines. Be careful."

Vera knocked on the farmhouse door and waited for someone to appear. They heard footsteps before the door opened no wider than a needle.

"What do you want?" a woman's voice called.

"We are lost." Vera leaned closer. "We haven't eaten all day and we're very cold. Can we come in?"

"I'm sorry, you must leave," the woman said coldly.

"Please, we'll freeze out here," Vera tried again. "Lukas said you would help."

Vera tried to stop the panic rising inside her. The latch opened and the woman peered outside.

"Lukas?" the woman repeated. "Come inside, quickly."

A candle flickered on the mantel and a single log sat in the fireplace. There was a rocking chair and a side table with framed photographs.

"My husband is asleep." The woman pointed to a ladder that led to a loft. "Come into the kitchen."

They followed her. The small space held a table and two chairs next to a stove; the window was covered with heavy drapes.

She motioned the girls to sit down. "I'm Ottie Dunkel. First you will eat, then we can talk."

Ottie took a pan that smelled of potatoes and beef and garlic off the stove. She placed two plates in front of them. Vera thought she might have dreamed it.

"It's Eintopf stew." Ottie handed them spoons. "The farmers are supposed to make it once a month and bring it to the German soldiers living in the village. I make extra and keep it for us. There's hardly any beef in it, but it's better than eating plain carrots and onions."

"It's the best thing I've ever tasted," Vera said, momentarily forgetting the chestnut purees of her childhood.

"We are fortunate." Ottie hovered over them. "We keep cows

and chickens. There is enough milk and eggs and sometimes por-ridge."

"Do you have coffee?" Edith asked, looking up from the stew.

Ottie shook her head. "Occasionally we trade a chicken for spoon-fuls of coffee. But if we did it too often, we wouldn't have a way to get eggs."

"Coffee is my favorite drink," Edith sighed. "I love it made with cream and lots of sugar."

"It's very kind of you to let us in and feed us stew. We lost our way," Vera said between mouthfuls. She was starving and couldn't eat the Eintopf fast enough. "Where are we? Germany?"

"Austria, though the Germans would like to believe Austria doesn't exist." She let out a slow sigh. "Just because Hitler was born in Braunau am Inn in Austria, he thought he could march in and take the whole country. For six years we've lived under German officers who believe they're superior because their boots are shiny."

They were in Austria! And where were their mothers? How many days until the train arrived in Auschwitz and they were led into the concentration camp?

"You girls are not from around here," Ottie commented. "Farm-ers don't own pretty dresses or wear fancy shoes."

Vera hesitated. Ottie had to suspect they were hiding from some-thing. If she told the truth, Ottie might make them leave. Or worse, turn them in. But she had no other story.

"We are from Budapest," Vera admitted. "We were on a train to Auschwitz."

Ottie walked back to the living room and Vera's heart raced. What if she woke her husband, or worse, there was a German truck waiting outside? But Ottie returned and handed them a photograph.

"This is my son, Emil. Emil and Lukas were best friends. Emil lied about his age and enlisted in the German army in 1941. He died in 1943 at the battle of Kursk on the Eastern Front. He'd never been to Russia; he'd never been past our village. I like to think he saw something before he died: the orthodox churches in Moscow or the inside of a Russian home, where someone offered him borscht with sour cream."

Vera and Edith stared at the photo and Vera knew what Edith was thinking. Emil resembled Stefan, with the same blond hair and strong jaw.

"He was very handsome," Vera commented.

"He was sixteen," Ottie said shortly. "He'll never make love to a woman or hold his son in his arms." She stuffed the photo in her apron. "Come, we can't sit here or my husband might hear us and come downstairs. I have some blankets you can take to sleep in the barn. But you have to be gone by morning."

"Oh, thank you!" Vera breathed.

"You must be quiet as mice." She took the blankets from a closet and opened the back door, walking them to the barn. "My husband is not so open-minded. I understand his thinking." Her mouth wobbled as she spoke. "He has to believe that Emil died for a worthy cause, otherwise there is no point living."

Vera and Edith climbed up to the loft in the barn and Ottie handed them the blankets.

"We will be grateful forever," Vera said, as Ottie turned to leave the barn.

"Emil didn't know what he was doing when he joined the army. He was just like you girls: young people full of hopes and dreams, eagerly waiting to see what the world would bring them."

*　　*　　*

Vera stopped talking and looked at Anton.

"There's more," she said. "But I'd like to stop for now."

They stood outside the pensione. Anton was so close, Vera could smell his cologne. He touched her arm and she realized the evening was coming to an end.

"I wanted to wait until after dinner to tell you my feelings," Anton said slowly, putting on his dinner jacket. "Then I blew it by kissing you, but I still haven't told you how I feel. The last thing I wanted was to get involved with a woman in Naples. Rebuilding a city is a grueling task and I shouldn't let anything get in the way." He paused. "But I can't help it. I loved you from the first moment I saw you."

Vera studied Anton in his dinner jacket and bow tie and wondered how she could be so lucky. Anton was in love with her and she was falling in love with him.

She opened her mouth to answer when she heard the window in Rosa's pensione open upstairs.

"There you are!" Edith called. "Marcus bought a bottle of Chianti and we had to drink the whole thing ourselves."

Vera glanced up to see Edith waving a silk handkerchief out the window. Her cheeks were flushed and she leaned dangerously over the ledge.

"I'd better go." Vera turned and smiled at Anton. She lifted her skirt and ran up the stairs. "Thank you for a wonderful evening."

In their room, Edith lay on the bed. She wore the red dress she had worn on her birthday. Her eyes were closed and her chest rose and fell in a steady rhythm, but she wasn't asleep.

Vera slipped off her evening gown and stuffed it in the wardrobe dresser. She stood at the small sink and wiped the powder from her cheeks.

"Marcus and I danced for hours and then we walked along the dock," Edith opened her eyes and said drowsily. "We ate warm chestnuts and he didn't even try to kiss me." Edith sighed, clutching the sheet against her chest. "I think I'm falling in love."

Edith yawned again and moved over in the narrow bed. "You haven't told me about your dinner with Anton."

"Go back to sleep." Vera lay down beside Edith. "I'll tell you in the morning."

She wanted to tell Edith about Anton but it was late and Edith was practically asleep. She pictured Anton's pale blue eyes and square chin. She remembered the way he touched her cheek, and for the first time, she understood how Edith felt.

CHAPTER SIX

Vera stood in Signora Rosa's narrow kitchen, eating an orange.

Over the last two weeks she and Anton had spent every spare moment exploring Naples and falling in love. No matter how much time they spent together, they wanted more. She cherished every moment: picnics of figs and grapes and ricotta cheese with crusty bread in the Parco Virgiliano; the massive paintings by Titian and Raphael and Caravaggio at the Museo di Capodimonte; the spot on the Triumphal Arch of the Castel Nuovo where they had scratched their names.

Vera felt guilty about leaving Edith alone, but Signora Stella kept Edith busy with more work than she could handle. During the day Edith sewed until her fingers bled, and at night she and Marcus zoomed around Naples taking photos. She promised that Marcus behaved like a gentleman. Edith's guarded expression had been replaced by an open smile.

Anton seemed content holding hands at the cinema and kissing on Vera's doorstep. Sometimes she imagined his mouth on her breast or his hands massaging her thighs. But she pictured all the women he must have known during the war and knew it wouldn't stop there.

She didn't want to become a young unwed mother abandoned by her American lover, as other women in Naples had become.

Vera grew nervous when Anton read his mother's telegrams. He knew hardly any Jews in New York; he was raised Episcopalian. Perhaps Anton would give in to his mother and return, his wartime romances forgotten. His mother would hold endless cocktail parties until he met a girl with a suitable pedigree. They'd have a large church wedding followed by a reception at The Plaza. Vera pictured sheaths of pink and yellow roses, and a six-tier raspberry fondant cake.

"You'll never guess what happened," Edith announced, racing into the kitchen at the pensione, clutching a copy of *LIFE* magazine.

"Tell me." Vera poured sugar into a cup of coffee.

"Marcus got a photograph published in *LIFE*!" Edith opened the magazine and flung it on the counter.

Vera studied the photo of children playing in the fountain. She read the caption and found Marcus's name in small print.

"That's wonderful!" Vera beamed. "He must be so happy."

"They asked him to take a series of photos of street life in Naples," Edith gushed. "But that's only the first thing. Last night we had dinner at Paolo's, and the owner of a boutique in Amalfi asked where I bought my dress." Edith grabbed a green apple. "I told her I made it myself and she wants to sell it in her store."

"Well, she has wonderful taste!" Vera clapped her hands.

"I still haven't told you the best part," Edith said as she danced around the kitchen. "I saw Marcus in the piazza whispering with Leo Grimaldi—you know, the one who owns a jewelry store on Via Port'Alba." She stopped and turned to Vera. "I think Marcus is going to ask me to marry him."

Vera frowned.

"But you've only known Marcus a few weeks," she protested. "You haven't even kissed."

"Kissing is for children," Edith said dismissively. "What we have is deeper. I can feel it here." She touched her chest and giggled. "Of course, Marcus is so handsome, when we kiss it will be like the fireworks over the Danube on New Year's Eve." Her face grew serious. "I know he will propose. All he talks about is moving to Rome together and becoming rich and famous. And he says the nicest things; he makes me feel like a princess."

It was wonderful to see Edith happy, but Vera felt a niggling doubt, like when a ladybug flew onto her arm and she brushed it away. Edith and Marcus had only just met. Could she really consider marrying him? That was the thing about Edith: she believed falling in love was the answer to everything, even escaping the war.

"Signora Rosa will make your wedding breakfast," Vera said finally and hugged her. "Omelets and melon slices and a meringue cake topped with strawberries."

Vera skipped through the piazza to the embassy. It was midmorning and by noon the pavement would be burning hot. The greengrocer and the butcher would close for the siesta and only a few old men would remain outdoors smoking cigarettes and playing chess. She thought about Edith's wonderful news and remembered the time when Edith had all but secured her and Stefan's future. If Edith and Stefan had succeeded, where would they be now? Would Vera have come to Naples and met Anton?

*　　*　　*

It was early spring of 1944 and life was growing harsh in Budapest. There wasn't any money, and even when her mother sent her to the delicatessen, all Vera could find was roux to make soup, and dry gnocchi. She couldn't remember the last time she had eaten meat or seen her mother add milk to her coffee.

Vera and Edith started sharing a bed at night. It was more comforting to curl up together. They kept each other warm and, more important, they knew the other wouldn't disappear before morning.

"Vera, wake up," Edith whispered, climbing into Vera's bed in Budapest one morning. "I have news."

"Can it wait?" Vera turned over. She was in the middle of a dream in which she and Edith were eating corn on the cob and Dobos torte with chocolate buttercream filling for dessert.

"This is important." Edith nudged her. "Stefan and I are leaving Budapest. We want you to join us."

"That's nice," she replied sleepily. Her eyes fluttered closed, wanting to go back to her dream. "We'll live in a mansion in Hollywood and become friends with Errol Flynn and Ginger Rogers."

"Not Hollywood, Switzerland," Edith said. "Stefan knows a guy who forges papers. We're leaving next Thursday."

"You're not serious?" Vera opened her eyes, fully awake now.

"We're going to be Mr. and Mrs. Christian and Heidi Mueller, newlyweds traveling to the Swiss Alps on our honeymoon. You will be my sister, Agnes, with sickly lungs, joining us for the fresh mountain air."

Vera could scarcely understand Edith's words.

"It would take days to get to Switzerland; you have to pass through Austria and Germany," Vera responded. "It's impossible; it's the fastest way to end up before a firing squad."

"Stefan's guy is excellent. He gives a money-back guarantee," Edith insisted. "Stefan sold his gold coin collection to afford it."

"Anyone who fails probably can't return to get their money back," Vera said grimly. "It's out of the question."

"Any day we could get sent to the ghetto and then the camps." Edith shivered. "Jews are safe in Switzerland. When we arrive, Stefan and I will get married and you'll be my maid of honor."

"You're only seventeen. You want to be a fashion designer."

"So? Stefan doesn't mind if I work," Edith declared. "He's going to be a modern husband."

"The trip is too dangerous," Vera insisted. "And besides, we can't leave our families."

"You and Stefan are my family. We'll send for our mothers when we're settled," Edith said firmly. "We'll get an apartment in Geneva, and I'll open a dress salon. In the summers we'll go to Montreux and listen to jazz under the stars."

"That's a lovely fairy tale." Vera lay down and closed her eyes. "I'll stick to my dream of buttered corn on the cob."

A week later, Vera was sitting in her room. Edith and Stefan had decided to go through with their plan and Edith had sworn Vera to secrecy. Every night Edith debated whether to pack her party dress and necklaces as if she and Stefan were really going on holiday. Vera escaped by rereading her favorite Rudyard Kipling jungle stories, and for a moment she forgot her hunger pains and the Nazi officers strolling up and down the street.

Footsteps pounded down the hall and soon Edith rushed into the room. Her eyes were red and her cheeks were stained with tears.

"What happened?" Vera gasped.

Edith threw herself onto the bed. "The guy who was going to

forge our papers was caught. He was shot this morning." She began to cry.

Vera sat on the bed beside her. "I'm sorry."

"We can't go to Switzerland. We don't have the papers, and Stefan thinks it's too dangerous." Edith sniffled. "We won't get married after all."

"We'll have a double wedding after the war," Vera consoled, stroking her hair. "You'll marry Stefan and I'll marry some handsome law student at the Grand Hotel. It will be the most elegant wedding of the year."

"It would be nice to have a hotel wedding," Edith sighed. "With a band and flowers and a chocolate cake."

"You can sew our dresses, with long trains like the one Empress Sisi wore," Vera said, recalling the history lessons about Hungary's greatest empress.

"How long until the war is over? What if none of us live long enough to get married?" Edith's eyes darkened.

Vera blotted the memory from her mind and climbed the steps to the embassy. Perhaps she should stop worrying about Edith. After all, Marcus brought her flowers and took her dancing, and when she was with him, Edith seemed like her old self.

She opened the front door and wondered what Anton had in store for today. She loved Saturday afternoons after they completed the endless permit applications and official correspondence. Perhaps they would explore the ruins of Pompeii and Herculaneum or visit the Royal Palace.

The downstairs rooms were quiet, and a leather suitcase stood in the entry. Perhaps Anton had to go to Rome and forgot to tell her.

"You're early!" Anton walked down the staircase. "I wanted to surprise you. Gina is packing you an overnight bag. I'm taking you to Capri."

Vera looked down at the black-and-white marble floor and tears sprang to her eyes. Now she would have to pay for the elegant dinners, the pretty dresses, the nights at the cinema. Anton would expect her to put on a silk negligee and climb into his bed, and in the morning she would wake up ashamed at what she'd done.

"I booked us two rooms at the Hotel Quisisana," Anton said as if he could read her thoughts. "On different floors, at opposite ends of the hotel. Your room has one key, which will be safely in your possession. I have to show you Capri. It's my favorite place on earth."

Vera sat next to Anton on the ferry. Edith hadn't been home when she went to Signora Rosa's to pack, so she left a note saying she had gone to Capri with Anton and would be back tomorrow. Now the Island of Capri glimmered in the distance. Bright flowers dotted the cliffs, and boats bobbed in the harbor.

Capri seemed to be completely untouched by the war. There were no bombed-out buildings, no closed shop fronts, no children with frightened eyes and thin limbs playing under a fountain. The air smelled of oranges and lemons.

They took the funicular to the Piazzetta and left their luggage with the concierge. Anton grabbed her hand and they hiked to the top of the island. Far below them were the green grottoes and Rocks of Faraglioni. Vesuvius loomed in the distance, and the white clouds looked like cotton balls.

"During the Roman Empire, Tiberius built twelve villas in Anacapri," Anton said as he leaned against a stone railing. "He ruled the most important empire on earth from this spot. After the Roman Empire fell, civilization went dark. For centuries the world revolved around war and disease and death." Anton paused. "But now we have the Sistine Chapel and the Louvre. We have Shakespeare and Dante and Proust. Symphonies perform Mozart and Beethoven, and museums display Rembrandt and Monet. Europe will recover from Hitler's atrocities, and a new crop of artists and philosophers will emerge." Anton clasped Vera's hands. "No one man can wipe out truth and beauty. Human beings were born to create great things, and they will do so again."

After his speech, they walked down the steep path in silence. The yellow-and-white awnings of the Quisisana greeted them as they reached the Piazzetta. Vera was about to enter the hotel when Anton took her hand. He kissed her gently and her heart lifted.

"I'm the luckiest man," he whispered. "We're going to drink the finest champagne and swim and explore the island. I want you to have the most wonderful time and create new memories."

Vera looked up at Anton and couldn't remember being so happy. "I want to create new memories too."

Vera moved around the hotel room, touching crystal vases and gold lamps. She was supposed to be resting before dinner, but she was too excited to lie down. Everything about her suite was beautiful. From the moment they entered the lobby, with its marble floors and pink damask walls, she felt like a film star. French windows opened onto lush gardens and chandeliers dangled from the ceiling.

Now she stood in her slip and bare feet in front of the wardrobe dresser. Gina had packed a pair of black heels and an evening gown with a satin bodice and flared skirt. She held it against her chest and noticed how the red fabric warmed her skin.

Edith would be shocked when she read Vera's note and found out that she had gone away with Anton. But Vera would make her understand that when they were together, she felt like she had known Anton all her life.

There was a knock at the door and she froze. What if it was Anton? She had never done more than kiss a man before and had no idea what to expect. Maybe he assumed they would have a romantic interlude before dinner.

She pulled a robe around her waist and answered the door. A bellboy in a gold uniform held a small box from the hotel gift shop.

"With compliments from Captain Wight." The bellboy handed her the box. "He requests your presence in the hotel bar at six p.m. for cocktails. What should I tell him?"

Vera gave the boy a silver coin and nodded. "Please tell him six p.m. is perfect."

Inside the black velvet box was a diamond solitaire necklace. Vera turned it over, admiring the way the single diamond captured the light. There was a card with the note:

My dearest Vera,

I hope you like the necklace. Even without it, you are so beautiful you would outshine every woman at dinner.

Warmest regards,

Anton

Vera stroked the diamond and it took her back to the nights when her parents went out to dine. Her father would help her mother pick out her jewelry. Her mother would try on a topaz bracelet or ruby earrings and her father would tell her she was the most beautiful woman in Budapest. Now Vera put the diamond necklace back in the box and a sob caught in her throat.

Vera sat across from Anton, sipping a glass of champagne. When she had entered the restaurant with its flickering candles and gilt mirrors, she felt out of place. Less than two years ago, she had been on her way to a concentration camp, and now she was surrounded by luxury. Anton took her hand and led her to a table on the balcony. He had ordered appetizers and a bottle of champagne. By the time the waiter replaced the appetizers with plates of seafood ravioli, she had finally relaxed.

"Where do these people come from?" Vera waved at women in couture dresses and narrow heels. The men wore evening jackets and bow ties. "One would think the war never happened."

"Many Italians made money on the black market," Anton conceded. "Capri has always attracted a wealthy clientele. I came with my parents the summer before the war."

"My mother always wanted to take me to Paris," Vera mused, buttering a warm bread roll. "When she was nineteen, she danced in the corps de ballet of *La Sylphide* at the Opéra National de Paris."

"I was in Paris this spring." Anton smiled. "The masterpieces have been returned to the Louvre and the elevators are functioning in the Eiffel Tower. The Champs-Élysées was bursting with tulips and daffodils. It's still the most romantic city in the world."

Vera studied her plate, wondering if Anton would ask her to go to Paris. Then she blushed, thinking she was being foolish.

Anton's face suddenly turned grim.

"I have to tell you," he said slowly. "I received a telegram from General Ashe. They are closing the embassy in Naples."

Vera felt her chest seize.

"So you're going to Rome?" she inquired.

"Being at the embassy in Rome would be nothing like working with you in Naples." He looked at her and there was a warmth mixed with desperation in his expression. "Rome is full of bureaucrats and red tape. I'd be assigned a desk, and nothing would get done. It's time I went home."

"Of course." She touched the diamond necklace and felt like she couldn't breathe.

"I want to ask you a question, but before you give me your answer you have to listen to everything I have to say." He took her hand. "When I said I was falling in love with you, I was telling the truth. You are the bravest, most beautiful woman I've ever met. I can't imagine not having you by my side."

Vera looked up and Anton's eyes glistened. She sucked in her breath and tried to stop her hands from shaking.

"I love you too," she whispered. "I didn't think it was right, falling in love with my employer. But I couldn't help myself; it just happened."

"Vera, I want nothing more than to ask you to be my wife. But there is something I should have told you." He released her hand and looked embarrassed. "When I was eight I had the mumps. I'm sterile."

"Sterile?" she repeated. "What do you mean?"

"It can't be the only word in English you don't understand," he said gently. His eyes were filled with sadness and he touched her cheek. "I can't have children."

"I see," she whispered, and looked at Anton awkwardly. "And you've seen doctors . . . there is no way to fix it?"

He nodded. "The best doctors in Boston and New York. Unfortunately, it's a very straightforward case. There is no remedy."

Vera's mind spun at Anton's words and her heart hammered. When she and Edith were girls, they had spent full nights describing their future families. Edith wanted a little girl she could dress in colorful dresses. Vera wanted two boys and two girls, so the rooms were always full of laughter. They would live in adjoining apartments in Budapest, where the front doors stayed open. On Sunday nights they would cook paprika chicken and stuffed cabbage.

How could she leave Edith and move to New York? Or envision a future that didn't include baby booties and children's birthday parties?

Anton was kind and handsome and wanted to right every wrong. And when he kissed her, her whole body trembled. She looked up and he was staring at her intently.

"I was wrong to ask the question," Anton said stiffly. "You are young and beautiful and have your whole life ahead of you. You'll find someone who can give you children."

"Yes," she said.

"Yes, what?" he asked.

"Yes, I want to spend the rest of my life with you." She was suddenly giddy. "Yes, I want to marry you."

He leaned forward and grabbed her hand. "Are you sure?"

"Completely sure," she breathed.

He fumbled in his pocket and pulled out a black velvet box. Inside was a square diamond surrounded by sapphires. "I cabled my father. This was his grandmother's ring. We can have it sized if it doesn't fit." He slid it on her finger and it fit perfectly. "We agreed it would be best to wait and tell my mother in person. She'll love you when she meets you."

Vera suddenly thought of Anton's mother. Margaret Wight had her heart set on Anton marrying a member of New York society. She would never welcome a Jewish Hungarian refugee. Could she have a mother-in-law who expected her son and his wife to give cocktail parties at the country club and who hosted elaborate Christmas dinners with ham and stuffing and presents under a giant Christmas tree?

Vera thought about how she would fit in with Anton's friends. They probably had all known each other since nursery school and used nicknames like Buffy and Skip. How would she feel when they excluded her because of her slightly long nose and European accent? And what if they stopped inviting Anton to their gatherings because he was married to her?

"Let's dance," Anton said, interrupting her thoughts. He took her hand and led her onto the dance floor.

Vera rested her head on his shoulder. She wasn't going to let Margaret Wight frighten her. She had jumped off a train to escape the Nazis and spent a year hiding in a barn. She could learn to play croquet and give dinner parties. Anton twirled her around the dance floor and the champagne seemed to lift her off her toes.

Vera stood on the balcony of her room, gazing at the lights of the piazza. It was after midnight and the noise had died down. Guests entered the lobby to smoke cigars and listen to the grand piano. Young couples disappeared into the alley to embrace. Vera glanced at her engagement ring and her thoughts spun like a carousel at the World's Fair.

It was always assumed she would marry a Jew. She had only known Jewish boys at dancing school and art class. But what if she returned to Budapest and there were no Jewish boys left?

New York sounded like a place in a storybook: the Empire State Building, Central Park, and Times Square. Fifth Avenue teeming with well-dressed men and women and long black cars and steel skyscrapers that touched the clouds.

It wasn't the strangeness of New York that was holding her back, or even the fact that Anton wasn't a Jew. So much had changed that she had learned to lock up the past and look ahead. But when she saw a life without children, her heart sank.

But how could she live without him? She had never known before what it was like to be in love. The simplest things made her happy: sharing one of Gina's omelets, arranging his newspapers, taking an evening stroll through the Piazza del Plebiscito.

And he didn't know her whole story yet. She had to tell him how she met Captain Bingham and what he learned when he went to Budapest. It was Captain Bingham who had encouraged her to go to Naples. If it weren't for him, she wouldn't be sitting in a hotel room in Capri with Anton's engagement ring on her finger.

She gazed at her reflection in the mirror. Her lipstick was smudged, and her hair had escaped its clip. There was a tiny run in her stocking and a loose thread on her dress.

Suddenly she knew what she had to do. She grabbed her room key and stepped into the hallway. She hurried to the staircase and climbed the stairs to Anton's floor.

"What are you doing here?" Anton asked when he opened the door.

"I need to speak to you." Vera strode into the room.

Anton's dinner jacket lay across a chair and a book was open on the coffee table. A glass ashtray was full of cigarette butts and a shot glass stood next to a bottle of cognac.

"I couldn't sleep," Anton admitted. "I was afraid I'd wake up and you'd have been a dream."

Vera walked across the room and touched his shirt. She reached up and kissed him.

"You shouldn't be here." Anton's voice was low. "It's late and we've both had too much champagne."

"I shouldn't have said yes before you heard my whole story." She looked at him. "You might change your mind about marrying me."

"It's not your fault that you and Edith jumped off the train and your mother and Lily were left behind," Anton reminded her. "You have to forgive yourself."

"It's not about that. It's about our time on the Dunkels' farm," Vera replied. "The next morning, before we left, Ottie's husband, Peter, fell off a ladder and broke his back. Peter couldn't move and was stuck in bed for months. Ottie couldn't run the farm by herself, and there were no young people left in the village to help. She offered to hide us if we did his work on the farm." She looked at Anton and there was pain in her eyes. "While our mothers were starving at Auschwitz, we were fed breakfasts of eggs and toast. On the farm there were no German officers waiting to escort us to the gas chamber if we broke a rule. Instead, we sat in Ottie Dunkel's cozy kitchen and ate stew and homemade pies," she gulped.

"You were only doing what you needed to survive. How would that make me change how I feel about you?" he asked, puzzled.

"Ottie's son had been in the German army. He was responsible for killing Jews! And Ottie's husband made it clear where his loyalties lay." Her voice grew anguished. "We could have left and tried to make it on our own. But we were there for more than a year. When I met Captain Bingham, Edith and I were still staying in the Dunkels' barn."

Vera stood behind the counter of the bakery and watched children play in the village square. It was September 1945 and the scene was like a postcard: wooden chalets and thick forests of fir trees, and in the distance a shimmering lake. A light dusting of snow clung to the mountains, and the fields were dotted with chrysanthemums.

Everything was different since the war had ended. Vera and Edith ate meals with Ottie and even went to the market together on Saturdays. Ottie's husband still treated them coldly, but he acknowledged the farm wouldn't have survived without them.

All summer and winter they hid in the barn and helped Ottie run the farm. Then in May the war was over, and they waited for news of their parents and Stefan. There was no record of Alice and Lily's fate at Auschwitz, and Stefan's name wasn't on the list of Jews released from Strasshof.

They debated returning to Budapest, but what would they do there if their parents didn't return? Vera wrote a letter to a neighbor in Budapest asking if they had come back to the apartment, but she hadn't received a reply. In the meantime it was easier to stay where they were. Edith assisted the village seamstress and Vera worked at the bakery. Food supplies were still low, but there was a trickle of visitors who passed through on their way to hiking in the mountains.

There was another reason they wanted to stay. Vera didn't want to run into her mother's siblings if they had survived. It was Vera's fault that her mother had gone to Auschwitz, and she couldn't face them until she knew whether or not Alice was alive. And what about Edith? It would be difficult for Edith to be in Budapest where everything reminded her of Stefan. It was better for them to stay in Hallstatt until they heard some news.

"A loaf of pumpernickel, please," a man said in English. He wore a khaki uniform with a smart leather visor.

Vera took the bread out of the case and set it on the glass.

"Is that an American accent?" she asked, thinking it reminded her of the American movies her parents took her to see before the war.

"I hope it is," he chuckled. He was in his midtwenties with reddish hair. He slipped his hand in his pocket and leaned against the counter. "I've been over here so long I might have lost it."

She wrapped the loaf in paper and handed it to him.

"I wouldn't know, I've never been to America." She shrugged and turned to the cash register.

"You speak very good English," he said approvingly. "Are you from around here?"

"Budapest," she answered, embarrassed for starting the conversation. "My friend and I have been here for more than a year."

The officer looked at her and she noticed a quick flash of sympathy.

"I'm on my way to Budapest." He shuffled his feet. "I've been at Bergen-Belsen and Auschwitz."

"Auschwitz?" Her eyes opened wider.

"The Russians liberated it in January, but we were sent to inspect it." His face drained of color. "The army tries to prepare you, but they have no idea."

The man paid for the bread and walked out into the square. Vera untied her apron and ran after him.

"Please, wait!" she called.

"Did I forget something?" he asked, checking his package.

"My mother was at Auschwitz," she said urgently. "I wrote a letter to a neighbor in Budapest to see if she returned, but I haven't received a response. I have to know if she survived. I wonder if you could help me?"

The man moved closer and removed his cap. "Captain Allan Bingham," he said, and held out his hand. "Why don't we sit down and I'll buy you a cup of coffee. I have to return to Auschwitz on army business soon, but I will see what I can learn."

They walked through the square and sat at an outdoor café. Captain Bingham ordered two coffees and Vera told him the story of how she and Edith had escaped. She gave him their mothers' names and asked him to make inquiries.

Six months later, Vera was arranging a plate of Sachertorte. Ever since Captain Bingham left, she hadn't been able to concentrate. All winter, she gave the wrong change to customers at the bakery and at night she tossed and turned so much, Edith said she'd rather sleep on a bale of hay.

The shop door opened and Vera turned around. Captain Bingham stood behind the counter.

"You're back. It's been six months. I thought you had forgotten!" she breathed in relief. "Please tell me, what did you find?"

"Why don't you ask if you can take a break," he said gently. "I'll wait for you in the square."

Vera spoke to the owner and joined Captain Bingham outside. They sat at the same café where they'd met the first time, and he placed his officer's cap on the table.

"There was nothing at Auschwitz," he said after a waiter brought two coffees.

"Nothing?" she said, disappointment washing over her.

"I combed through every name," he continued. "So I went to Budapest."

"Budapest?" Vera repeated.

"I was on my way there anyway. I visited your neighborhood."

"How did you know where it was?" she asked, startled.

"There aren't many Jewish neighborhoods left in Budapest," he answered apologetically. "I figured I'd ask around until I met someone who knew Alice Frankel."

"Did you?" Vera was almost too anxious to breathe.

He nodded. "A woman named Miriam Gold. She attended the same synagogue. She'd been at Auschwitz, too."

Vera remembered a dark-haired woman with two young girls. They sat near them at temple, and the girls passed the time by braiding each other's hair.

"What did she say about my mother?" Vera asked anxiously.

"Alice and Lily weren't sent to the gas chamber when they arrived; they were made to work in the kitchen. Miriam sat with them at mealtimes. Every night your mother prayed out loud in Hungarian over her portion of bread." He looked at Vera. He took a notebook out of his pocket and read from the first page. "*Kedves istenem, keriek, hagy a dragam Vera esžik egy nagyobb darabotd.* Dear God, please let my darling Vera be eating a bigger piece of bread."

Captain Bingham stopped talking and Vera met his eyes.

"Go on," she said quietly.

"One of the other women asked what happened to her daughter, and Alice confided how you and Edith jumped off the train," he went on. "The woman must have turned her in. At the next meal time, Alice and Lily were gone."

"Gone?" Vera stammered.

"To the gas chamber, I assume. There was nowhere else to go."

"I see." Vera put her cup on the table.

"Miriam wanted to tell you how sorry she is," he finished lamely. "Her daughters died at Auschwitz."

"Thank you. You've been very kind."

"I asked about your father, too," Captain Bingham said.

"My father?" Vera repeated, and hope swelled in her chest. Her father had survived the work camp and was waiting for her at the apartment in Budapest. They would grieve her mother together and somehow create a new life.

"I went to the temple and located the rabbi." Captain Bingham sipped his coffee. "I thought your father might go there if he returned. Rabbi Letzig hadn't heard from him. He said to offer his condolences. Lawrence was a good friend."

Rabbi Letzig and her father used to sit in the living room and discuss religion and philosophy. Vera would ask her mother if she could serve the coffee cake so she could listen to their conversations. Who would she learn about these things from now? And how had her father felt when the god he conferred with every Saturday deserted him?

"Thank you. You didn't have to do that, but I'm grateful," Vera said, and noticed her hands were shaking.

"Here, this is for you." Captain Bingham gave her an envelope.

Vera opened it and inside was a ten-schilling note and a letter.

"What's this?" She looked up in surprise.

"It's train fare to Naples, Italy, and a letter of recommendation. The embassy there is looking for a secretary who speaks English." For the first time since he sat down, he smiled. "You have my highest recommendation."

She handed it back. "I can't take your money or your letter. You hardly know me."

"For the last fourteen months I've been at concentration camps, and all I've seen is death," he began. "You can't imagine how a place can hold so much death; it's in the walls and the floors and outside the windows. Then I pass through a village in Austria and all of a sudden there are fresh cheeses and flowers and mountain air." He fiddled with his cap. "I meet a girl who asks me to do her a favor. But instead of bringing her good news, I deliver more death. So every time she stands at that counter she'll remember sitting with me at this café." He glanced around the square. "The least I can do is help you get out of here. Go with your friend to Italy."

The sun gleamed on the church steeple, and all around them people drank coffee and nibbled on cake.

"All right." She nodded and took back the envelope. "I promised Ottie we would stay through the spring; her husband had a relapse and needed help on the farm. But you're right, there is nothing keeping us here any longer."

"You see," Vera looked at Anton. The chandelier in the hotel room made patterns on the rug and Vera could smell the Mediterranean. "While we were eating Ottie's food and sleeping under her blankets, our mothers were hungry and shivering on iron cots. And after the war, when we were alive and healthy and breathing in mountain air in Hallstatt, they were bones heaped in an open grave. How can I live with myself knowing everything that happened?"

Anton stroked her cheek. "None of this was your fault."

"I may as well have escorted her to her death," Vera continued. Her cheeks flamed and the familiar feeling of despair welled up inside her. "If it weren't for me, she would have been one of those women you saw on the movie reels staggering out of the camps."

He drew her close. "You have to stop blaming yourself. The war is over. Nothing can change the past. I love you and I want to marry you."

Vera closed her eyes and listened to his heart beating in his chest. Suddenly she slipped off his bow tie and undid the buttons on his shirt.

"I want you," she whispered.

He shook his head. "In a couple of months we'll be married. Our wedding night will be at the St. Regis."

"Please," Vera breathed, inhaling the scent of aftershave and cigarettes.

"You should go." Anton put his hands on her shoulders and gently propelled her to the door.

Vera turned around and kissed him. His mouth was warm and his arms circled her waist.

"You are so beautiful," he whispered, kissing her hair.

"I want you more than anything," she implored. "If we're going to get married, you have to treat me like a woman instead of a girl."

Anton picked up her up and carried her to the bed. He slipped off her dress and unsnapped her bra.

Vera lay on the satin sheets and studied his smooth chest. His mouth moved down to her stomach and stopped at her thighs. He looked up and his eyes were filled with wonder.

"Are you quite sure?" he asked. "We can stop and go to sleep."

Vera was suddenly filled with a terrible sense of loss. Edith waiting for Stefan to come home and knowing he never would. Her mother and father going to their bedroom after a night at the opera, her mother's gown rustling and her father in a cashmere overcoat.

"I've never been more sure," she said, nodding and drawing him back on top of her. Her legs opened and something hard pushed inside her. She bit her lip, ignoring the sharp pain and tearing flesh.

Her eyes closed and she tried to match Anton's rhythm. He moved faster as if he were running a race. Suddenly he stopped and let out a moan. Then he pushed with such strength, she was afraid she'd be crushed.

Vera lay in the dark, listening to Anton's breathing. They were joined now, and she would never doubt their future again.

CHAPTER SEVEN

Summer 1946

Two weeks after the trip to Capri, Vera stood at the counter while the butcher wrapped a piece of meat. She selected a jar of olives and a thick sausage. She liked to bring Signora Rosa little treats to thank her for her kindness. This afternoon Anton would purchase their tickets, and in a week they would sail for New York.

Vera had been afraid to tell Edith about the engagement. But Edith hugged her and said it was the best news. She was certain Marcus would propose and they would find a small apartment. His photographs were receiving praise, and Maria, the boutique owner, had ordered four more dresses.

Vera studied her reflection in the mirror above the counter. They never repeated their night in Capri, but she knew she looked different. She wanted to tell Edith, but she couldn't find the words. She hid her secret by discussing plans for the wedding and the honeymoon on the coast of Maine.

Vera left the butcher and stepped into the piazza. She passed the jeweler and noticed Marcus standing at the counter. He reached into his pocket and took out a wad of lire. She ducked out of view before he saw her and ran down the cobblestones.

"Guess who I saw at Grimaldi Jewelers," Vera announced, running up the stairs to their room.

Edith sat at the vanity, brushing her hair. She wore a red cotton dress and a silver necklace. Her cheeks were smudged as if she'd been crying.

"Marcus was standing at the counter with a wad of lire." Vera dropped her shopping bag on the bed. "I think he bought your engagement ring!"

"Leo loaned Marcus money and he's paying him back," Edith said, turning to Vera. "He's not going to propose. He isn't in love with me."

"Of course he is!" Vera protested. "He bought lilies for your birthday; he takes you dancing every night."

"He's in love with someone else," Edith replied. Her eyes had lost their sparkle and her mouth turned down at the corners.

Vera shook her head. "I've never seen him with another girl."

Edith threw herself onto the bed. "He's in love with Leo."

Vera thought Edith was being ridiculous. Marcus waited for Edith every evening. He bought her pastries and little trinkets. On Sundays they borrowed Paolo's car and explored Amalfi and Sorrento.

"He first fell in love with a boy when he was seventeen," Edith began. "Luca was a migrant worker and got a job in Marcus's family's orchard. One night his mother discovered them in the chicken coop. She threw Marcus's bags onto the street."

"But his promises of getting an apartment together," Vera protested. "All the talk about your future."

"He wanted to fall in love with me. He said I was his angel and that we'd show his mother he was a real man," Edith sighed. "I didn't understand what he meant until last night. I passed the jewelry store and noticed Marcus standing behind the counter. It was late and the store was dark. I thought he was picking out my ring, so I watched. Leo emerged from the back room and they kissed. Have you seen two men kiss?" Edith's eyes were wide.

"Then you must come to New York." Vera said softly, walking over to the bed. She reached down and stroked Edith's hair. "You'll meet a sweet college boy and open your own dress shop."

"Marcus and I are moving to Rome," Edith announced. "He's going to take photos of models wearing my designs and get them in *Vogue*. I won't have time for men."

"You can have both," Vera whispered.

"I had Stefan," Edith said sadly. "Now I have nothing."

Vera strolled along the sidewalk to the embassy. She had been reluctant to leave Edith alone. Edith pretended to be happy about moving to Rome with Marcus, but what if her heart was still breaking?

She remembered when Captain Bingham gave her the money to buy train tickets to Naples. She had been nervous to show the money to Edith. If Stefan survived, Vera argued, they should return to Budapest so he could find them. But Edith was certain that Stefan was dead, and nothing Vera said would change her mind.

Later on the morning that Captain Bingham returned to Hallstatt in March 1946, Vera climbed the alley to the seamstress's cottage where Edith worked. The Austrian village looked so pretty on a spring day. The chalets were stacked like matchbooks and there were window boxes filled with daffodils. It was impossible to believe that in another part of Europe the buildings of Auschwitz had been some mythical beast, roaring fire and swallowing every soul that came into its path.

She poked her head in the door and found Edith hunched over a table. She had a thimble between her teeth, and a dress with pink and yellow embroidery fanned out on a table.

"Vera, what are you doing here?" Edith took out the thimble. Vera's shift usually ended at six.

"I have something to tell you and it can't wait." Vera entered the workshop.

"I'm almost done," Edith said. "My back aches, but Greta said she'll give me fabric scraps so I can sew my own dresses."

"What if we don't stay in the village?" Vera began. "What if we go to Italy?"

Edith stopped what she was doing and looked up in surprise.

"We don't know anything about Italy," Edith said. "Except they eat spaghetti instead of potato nokedli."

"Captain Bingham didn't find anything at Auschwitz, but he went to Budapest and looked up Miriam Gold."

Edith thought for a minute. "I remember Miriam. She wore beautiful fur stoles during the winter and her daughters always had matching coats."

"Miriam said our mothers weren't sent to the gas chamber right away. Later a woman turned them in because my mother prayed for me over her piece of bread . . ." Vera's voice trailed off. "It's my fault that our mothers are dead."

Edith jumped up and hugged her. "It's the war's fault. But what has that to do with Italy?"

"The embassy in Naples is looking for a secretary who speaks English and Italian. Captain Bingham recommended me and gave us enough money to cover two train tickets and a week's lodging."

"Train tickets to Naples!" Edith gasped.

"We don't have to go," Vera said quickly. "We can wait a few months."

"We've already been here for almost two years, why would we wait?" Edith asked.

"It might be harder for Stefan to find us in Italy. We should stay here or go back to Budapest."

"Stefan is dead, and I don't want to go to Budapest," Edith's voice was sharp.

"The war has only been over several months," Vera replied. "Stefan could be lying in a hospital or recovering in a village not far from here."

"Strasshof was liberated in May, and he wasn't on the list of survivors." Edith pointed to her chest. "If he were alive, my heart would beat as fast as butterfly wings, waiting for him to arrive. Instead it's so slow, sometimes I think it will stop."

"Think about it," Vera urged. "We can take a few days to decide."

Edith waved outside at the sun shining on the cobblestones and the fields dotted with flowers.

"Visitors think this is some kind of Shangri-la with its clean air and wonderful perfumes, but the mountains are a prison," she said darkly. "At least in Naples, there won't be boys with fair hair like Stefan to remind me that he's gone forever."

*   *   *

It was late the next morning and Vera was stirring a pot of porridge. The back door opened and Edith entered the Dunkels' kitchen. Her hair was tied in a knot and she wore a crocheted dress.

"You were so deeply asleep, I didn't want to wake you." Vera turned off the stove. "I made porridge and coffee."

"I had a terrible dream about Stefan," Edith admitted, pouring a cup of coffee.

"Stefan?" Vera repeated.

"We were hiking in the Swiss Alps." Edith took her cup and sat at the table. "Stefan brought a picnic of Edam cheese and rye bread. He wanted to hike further, so we left the picnic and climbed the side of the mountain." Her eyes widened. "He waved at the forests and waterfalls and said, 'You see, we made it to Switzerland.' Then he reached for my hand, but his foot slipped and he lost his balance. I tried to grab him, but he fell."

Vera frowned and put an arm around Edith.

"It was just a nightmare," Vera consoled her. "You drank coffee too late last night, or Ottie's potato soup was too heavy."

"I wanted to throw myself off the mountain after him, but his voice came to me in the dream," Edith continued. "He said his mother and sisters died in the camps. If I died too, there would be no one to remember him. I had to stay alive or it would be as if he never existed."

"Let's walk into the village for ice cream. It's a beautiful day and we can sit outside and breathe the mountain air," Vera suggested gently. "You'll forget about the dream."

"I can't forget the dream." Edith shook her head. "Stefan takes up all my thoughts."

"Then you'll dream something else tonight." Vera tried to coax a smile out of her. "A memory of you and Stefan swimming or eating Dobos torte."

"You don't understand. If I stay here I may as well be lying in a coffin beside him." She looked at Vera. "Why shouldn't we go to Naples? I want to stroll beside a bay filled with boats and sit in a piazza where the music is so loud, I can't think. And I don't want to see another mountain in my life."

"Are you sure?" Vera asked.

"Completely sure." Edith drank the coffee. "And Italian coffee must be better than the coffee in Austria. I love Ottie, but her coffee tastes like dirty water."

Vera passed a piazza where children played in a fountain and realized Edith had been right. Life was easier in Naples. Perhaps she worried too much and Edith would be happy in Rome. Edith would take the money she received from Maria and buy the finest fabric. She was going to dress Anna Magnani and Greta Garbo and one day become as famous as Coco Chanel.

Anton was taking Vera to dinner at Marco's trattoria to celebrate purchasing their ocean liner tickets. She smiled, remembering the night they had dinner at Palazzo Mezzi, how he had asked her to use his first name after chiding her for using his title. She couldn't help it, when she closed her eyes she pictured him in his khaki uniform and officer's cap. But since then, all that had changed; they were engaged and they had become lovers.

The curtains were drawn in the morning room and the sounds of Mozart drifted down the hall. Vera entered the study and found papers scattered across the desk. Anton had been working twelve-hour days, pushing through building applications and construction permits before the embassy's closure.

She straightened the papers and emptied the ashtrays into the garbage. She was going to miss working together: transcribing his notes, putting the official seal on envelopes. She would miss stopping for a delicious lunch of Gina's linguini marinara and stuffed artichokes.

Anton was going to help his father run the hotels in New York and Boston. Vera was expected to furnish their new home and sit on the board of the Library Foundation and Ladies Garden Auxiliary. Vera imagined elegant women with fox stoles and American accents and wondered if they would accept her.

Gina stood in the doorway, clutching an envelope.

"This is for you," Gina said, nervously handing it to her.

Every day Vera was afraid Margaret Wight had learned of their engagement. One of her telegrams would arrive saying: STOP THIS FOOLISHNESS IMMEDIATELY. HAVE FOUND YOU A SUITABLE WIFE. COME HOME.

Vera took the envelope and recognized Anton's handwriting.

"Where did you get this?" she asked.

"It was on the counter in the kitchen," Gina replied.

Vera opened the envelope and extracted three thin sheets of paper.

My beloved Vera,

Even as I write the words on the page, I already miss your bright smile and those luminous green eyes. It seems I am not a war hero; in truth, I am the greatest coward. I should have told you I couldn't give you a family on the first night we danced. I was afraid you'd turn away from me, and the closer we became the more I fell in love with you and couldn't let you go. These past weeks have been the happiest of my life.

I saw your discomfort when I told you my condition. What kind of

98

man proposes marriage and announces he can never have a family at the same time? I couldn't keep seeing you without declaring my intentions, and I couldn't let you accept without knowing the truth.

I have spent most nights imagining our future and have come to a decision. You will grow to hate me when your friends are wheeling baby carriages and shopping for pink or blue blankets. I can't tie you to me when there are dozens of men who will give you the family you rightfully desire. I love you more than life itself, and I would never forgive myself for causing your unhappiness.

Please don't try to find me. I am going to travel until I feel fit enough to be of value to my father. I have already spoken to General Ashe; he can find you a position in Rome. I would have left you money, but I know you wouldn't accept it. Sell the engagement ring and get yourself a nest egg.

You have shown me how wonderful love can be. I will never forgive myself for my moment of weakness in Capri. Please try not to hate me; it was the happiest night of my life. The memory of your perfume will last me for eternity.

Yours always,

Anton

Vera crumpled the paper and turned to Gina. Her eyes were wide and there was a lump in her throat.

"What did Anton say when he left?" she breathed.

Gina shook her head. "He wasn't here when I arrived this morning."

"He's gone," Vera whispered. "He's not coming back."

Gina held out her arms and Vera collapsed against her chest.

"It will be all right," Gina soothed. "Captain Wight is a good man."

Vera thought about Anton's promise not to cause her unhappiness.

"He doesn't understand; he's all I want," she said, almost to herself. She broke away from Gina's embrace and raced out the door. She ran past Grimaldi Jewelers with its rows of diamond engagement rings; she ran past Marco's trattoria with its trays of chocolate marzipan. She stumbled up the steps of the pensione to her room and threw herself on the bed.

CHAPTER EIGHT

Summer 1946

It was late afternoon and the sound of children laughing drifted through the window of Vera's room. It had been three weeks since Anton had left, but she still listened for his footsteps. Sometimes she saw an officer lounging in the piazza and her heart beat faster until he took off his cap and revealed a shock of dark hair.

She spent the first few days in bed, eating nothing except Signora Rosa's chicken soup. At night she lay awake and pictured Anton sitting on a train. Then her mind drifted to her mother praying for her at Auschwitz and she wondered if she was being punished for her mother's death.

She even tried praying herself, but what was the use? Her mother had prayed, and God hadn't listened. But maybe he had. Maybe her mother had prayed only for Vera and not for herself.

In 1935, Vera was eight years old and had been confined to bed with diphtheria. The doctor suggested that her mother hire a nurse. Any contact with Vera could make her sick. Her mother politely declined.

Finally, after nearly a month, the feeling that she was being strangled went away and she got out of bed. She went to read her favorite German children's book, *Der Struwwelpeter*, which was in the library, and as she passed the open door to her parents' bedroom, she saw her mother kneeling, her hands clasped.

"Vera!" her mother exclaimed. "What are you doing out of bed?"

"I was going to get *Der Struwwelpeter*," Vera said, entering the bedroom. "What are you doing?"

"I was having a conversation with God."

"A conversation?" Vera repeated.

"It's God's job to listen," her mother responded. "Like it's your father's job to assist his clients in legal matters, and mine to iron the clothes and make the goulash."

At the synagogue, the rabbi instructed Vera to pray, but he never mentioned God might answer.

"What if God isn't there to listen?" Vera worried. "Like when father had a cold and couldn't go to the office."

"That's what is different about God. He's been listening for thousands of years." She pointed to Vera's flowered dressing gown. "A few days ago you couldn't sit up, today you buttoned your dressing gown and walked down the hall."

"You were talking about me?" Vera wondered.

"What else would I talk about?" her mother asked.

"If I talked to God, I would ask if Edith's dog is going to have puppies or if she's just fat, and if our history teacher will be nicer when she gets married," Vera pondered. "Last week, her fiancé forgot to send her flowers and she was more terrifying than the scariest villain in *Der Struwwelpeter*."

Her mother pulled her close and hugged her. When she released her, Vera saw that she was crying and laughing at the same time.

"God would understand why a mother only talks about her children." She took Vera's hand and walked to the library. "Because he is the father of us all."

If only she had found a way to help her mother, and if only Anton believed that she loved him enough not to have children. The answers wouldn't come to her and so she stayed awake for hours, staring at the ceiling of her room in the pensione.

After a few days of letting Vera wallow in self-pity, Edith insisted that Vera accompany her downstairs. Vera reluctantly put on a dress and combed her hair and joined Edith for Rosa's spaghetti Bolognese.

With the embassy closed, Vera had to find work again, and so she accepted a job at Leo's jewelry store. From morning to night she showed eager young men diamonds and rubies. They handed her wads of black market lire and left with velvet boxes and huge grins.

Now Vera sat at the dressing table in her room at Signora Rosa's and brushed her hair. She heard footsteps, and Edith stood at the door.

"You're not dressed." Edith entered the room. "Everyone is waiting at Paolo's."

"I'm too tired to go out." Vera shrugged. She put down the brush and moved to the bed.

"How many nights did you insist I have iced coffee or gelato when I wanted to lie with a pillow over my head?" Edith demanded.

"That was different," Vera replied.

"Because Stefan was dead? Anton isn't coming back either," Edith reminded her. "Paolo is making seafood risotto and Marcus got the latest copy of American *Vogue*. We can drool over the new designs by Mainbocher and Norman Norell."

Since Marcus had admitted his feelings for Leo, Edith and Marcus were closer than ever. They spent Saturday afternoons at the cinema watching American movies with Italian subtitles. They searched the outdoor markets for the perfect blouse for Edith, and spent hours flipping through fashion magazines.

"I'll come," Vera relented. "But if I eat any more of Paolo's chocolate cake, I won't fit into my dresses."

"The two most beautiful women in Naples." Paolo kissed them on both cheeks when they entered the restaurant. "I made ziti Bolognese with basil and oregano."

"Anthony Guido returned the engagement ring you sold him." Leo turned to Vera. "He said he broke up with his fiancée because he's in love with you."

"That's ridiculous. I hardly spoke to him!" Vera protested. "He doesn't even know my name."

"In truth, I think his fiancée turned him down," Leo admitted. "But if you go out with him, maybe he'll keep the ring."

"You already pay Vera too little." Paolo thumped Leo on the shoulder. "She's not going to go on dates just so you can keep your customers."

They sat at a round table and ate. Paolo poured a bottle of red wine and Marcus displayed his copy of American *Vogue*.

Vera flipped through the pages, admiring women in silk sheaths and empire-waist dresses. She stopped at a full-page ad for a hotel near Central Park. A uniformed doorman stood in front of a gold revolving door and the caption read:

WIGHT HOTELS.

Your home away from home in New York and Boston.

Five-star service starts at the door.

"It's Anton's hotel," Vera exclaimed. She jumped up and paced around the restaurant. She would go to New York and ask Anton's father to help her find him. Harry Wight must know where his son was. Anton wouldn't cut himself off from his family.

"I'm going to New York to see Anton's father," she turned to Edith and announced. Her eyes danced and excitement surged through her body. "I don't know why I didn't think of it before."

Edith waved her hand. "You can't just go to America. How will you afford the fare?"

"I've saved one hundred lire," Vera answered. "I'll go to the Cunard office and see how much a ticket costs."

"Refugees aren't allowed to enter the United States without a sponsor," Paolo interjected. "My cousin fell in love with an American nurse and they were going to get married. He arrived at Ellis Island, but she never showed up. The authorities sent him back on the first ship."

Vera listened to Paolo, and for a moment her hopes deflated. Harry Wight had never written to Anton in Naples. What if he knew nothing about Vera? But then she remembered Anton cabling his father before he proposed, to ask for his grandmother's ring. And she couldn't go to Anton's mother for help. Margaret Wight would be glad that Anton discarded his Hungarian refugee. Anton's father was her only chance.

"I don't have a choice." She sat down and suddenly her throat was parched. She gulped her wine and set the glass on the table. "I have to try."

Three weeks later, Vera stood polishing the glass counter at the jewelry store. Paolo had tried to use his connections to find her a sponsor, but failed. She set aside the money she earned every day. But she was still no closer to getting to New York.

"Look!" Edith burst into the store, waving a copy of the *New York Times*. She had a magazine tucked under her arm.

"Since when do you read English newspapers?" Vera asked.

"Page six, column three." Edith handed it to her.

There was a photograph of an old man with gray hair and thick eyebrows. Underneath was a blurry picture of two young women. It was the photo Marcus had taken of her and Edith when they had first arrived in Naples.

"What is this?" Vera asked.

"Read it out loud," Edith insisted.

"'Millionaire philanthropist Samuel Rothschild to sponsor Hungarian beauties—'" Vera stopped reading and gasped.

"Read the whole article," Edith urged.

"'Samuel Rothschild learned of the plight of two beautiful Hungarian refugees in the pages of *LIFE* magazine. Vera Frankel and Edith Ban escaped from the train that carried their mothers to Auschwitz. For a year they hid in the barn of an Austrian couple, hoping to be reunited with their parents. But their mothers died at Auschwitz and neither father returned to their apartments in Budapest.

" 'The two nineteen-year-old beauties found their way to Naples, where Vera works at a jewelry store and Edith is a seamstress. They spend their weekends at the cinema, dreaming of coming to America. Their wish is to go to New York, where Edith wants to become a fashion designer and Vera aspires to be a playwright.

" ' "When I saw the photos of these two young women, I knew I had to help them," Mr. Rothschild said in an interview with the *Times*. "To witness such tragedy at a young age and still have aspirations is terribly brave. Fifty years ago I arrived at Ellis Island, having lost my parents in the pogroms. Who would have thought a scrawny twelve-year-old boy could go on to own banks and department stores? This country was built on refugees with big dreams, and Gilda and I want to help these girls achieve their goals. They will sail on the *Queen Eliz-abeth*, and my wife and I will be waiting on the docks in New York." '

"I don't understand. I never saw an article about us in *LIFE* magazine." Vera put down the newspaper. "Who told them we want to go to New York?"

"Marcus called his friend at *LIFE* and asked him to write the article," Edith said, handing her the magazine under her arm. "It came out a month ago, but his friend sent it to Marcus by boat mail. It just arrived."

Vera pored over the photos, and for a moment she forgot about Samuel Rothschild's offer. There was the first photo Marcus took of Vera and Edith when they arrived in Naples. They were sharing a gelato and they looked as young and carefree as schoolgirls. She flipped the page and saw a photo of them sipping coffee the day after she returned from Capri. Vera noticed a new womanliness in the way she sat, and a half smile played across her face as if she was keeping a wonderful secret.

"I didn't know Marcus took all these photos," Vera said in disbelief. "We look like film stars and Naples is some incredible movie set."

"I told you Marcus was talented. It was his idea to send the article in *LIFE* magazine to a reporter at the *New York Times*. He hoped some influential person would read it. Americans love to help European refugees. It makes them feel less guilty that we were being shot by the Germans while they ate gefilte fish in penthouses on Fifth Avenue."

Edith had changed over the last few weeks. She wore formfitting dresses and red lipstick. The fear in her eyes had been replaced by a new confidence. It was almost as if Edith had blossomed while Vera had shrunk.

Vera folded the *LIFE* magazine and returned to the *New York Times*.

"We can't accept help from a stranger," Vera protested, rereading the article. "What if he expects something in return?"

"He's sixty-two years old; he's hardly looking for concubines," Edith laughed. "He sent two first-class tickets on the *Queen Elizabeth*. Marcus told me everything. Sam Rothschild mailed the tickets to *LIFE* magazine and asked them to contact the photographer in Naples and find us! We're going to sit at the captain's table and eat filet mignon and strawberry shortcake."

"But what about the dresses you're designing for Maria, and your apartment with Marcus in Rome?"

"You don't think New York has socialites and actresses?" Edith waved her hand. "I read Katharine Hepburn is doing a show on Broadway. Maybe we'll meet Rosalind Russell and Joan Crawford."

"You're making a name for yourself here," Vera protested. "New York must have hundreds of seamstresses."

"Do you remember when we jumped off the train? I was so exhausted I wanted to lie in the bushes. You made me get up and walk six miles to the Dunkels' farm. You wouldn't let go of my hand until we were safely in their barn," Edith began. "What if you get to New York and can't speak to Anton's father? I'm going to stay with you until you find Anton."

Vera turned so Edith wouldn't see the emotion on her face. When they were together, Vera felt like she and Edith were two girls on a grand adventure instead of orphans alone in the world.

"We can buy presents for Marcus and Paolo and Rosa with the money I've saved." Vera folded the polishing cloth. "If we have some left over, we'll buy stockings and perfume. We can't stroll on the first-class deck of the *Queen Elizabeth* with runs in our stockings."

"Cruise ships are full of famous people. What if we meet Vivien Leigh and she wants me to design her dress for the Oscars?" Edith's eyes sparkled, and she giggled. "Or Gene Kelly asks us to dance?"

Vera followed Edith outside, and an officer crossed the street. He turned and looked at Vera and her heart lurched. The only man she wanted to dance with was Anton.

CHAPTER NINE

Vera stood in the stateroom of the *Queen Elizabeth* and ran her fingers over the oriental armoire. It was all too much: the uniformed stewards who delivered their bags, the paneled walls and velvet furniture, the silver tray holding a box of Swiss chocolates and a handwritten note from the captain.

Vera took off her white gloves and read out loud to Edith:

" 'Dear Miss Frankel and Miss Ban,

" 'The officers and crew welcome you aboard the *Queen Elizabeth*. Please do not hesitate to ask for assistance. Mr. Rothschild has instructed us to make your crossing as pleasant as possible. I look forward to the pleasure of meeting you both tonight at the captain's table.

" 'Warm regards,

" 'Captain Gordon James.' "

"Did you see the shuffleboard court?" Edith sunk onto the loveseat. "And the beauty parlor. I'm going to get my hair cut and my nails painted."

"Slow down," Vera laughed. "We have eight days; we haven't even left the port."

"New York is going to be fabulous," Edith gushed. "I'm going to meet a millionaire and fall madly in love."

"I thought you were done with men," Vera remarked. "You're going to concentrate on your career."

"That was before I saw gorgeous American men," Edith sighed. "Did you see them on the gangway? They all have blond hair and white teeth and American accents."

The horn bleated and the ship swayed beneath their feet.

"We're leaving!" Vera grabbed her gloves. "Let's go on the deck and wave good-bye to Naples."

Edith nibbled a chocolate truffle and consulted a sheet of paper. "I'm going to stay here and read the itinerary. We don't want to miss a shuffleboard tournament or a bridge game."

Vera had never seen so many happy people since before the war. The women were dressed in the latest fashions and the men wore beautifully cut blazers and twill slacks. Little girls twirled in satin dresses and boys slouched against the railing in navy sailor suits.

She inhaled the fresh sea air and thought of Gina and Signora Rosa. It had been hard saying good-bye to Rosa; she had been so good to them. The night before they left, Rosa invited Marcus and Paolo for dinner, and they ate fettuccini Bolognese and drank a bottle of wine Paolo brought from the restaurant, and Vera had to fight back the tears. Rosa had been like a mother to them, and she would miss the front parlor always filled with flowers and Rosa's sunny face in the kitchen. Rosa insisted on packing their suitcases with gloves and stockings, and made Vera promise to send their address when they arrived in New York.

It was just as hard saying good-bye to Gina. Gina was Vera's last link to Anton, and she couldn't think about her without remembering the wonderful food she left for them on the kitchen counter. She recalled the night Gina helped her get dressed for her first dinner with Anton and the way she comforted her when Vera read Anton's letter.

Vera promised to send dolls for Gina's daughters from one of the big toy stores in Manhattan, and Gina insisted she take some of Countess Mezzi's evening gowns. It was even difficult saying good-bye to Paolo. The morning they left, he brought them each a bottle of perfume and said he expected to see them on the cover of *LIFE*, under the headline: TWO HUNGARIAN BEAUTIES TAKE NEW YORK BY STORM. The only one who didn't mind them leaving was Marcus. He waved from the dock and said soon he'd be rich from selling his photographs, and then he would follow them. They would be reunited in New York and have dinner at the Stork Club.

The luxury of the ocean liner reminded Vera of the only time her family stayed at an elegant hotel. In 1941, her parents booked five nights at the Grand Hotel on Margaret Island. Vera was allowed to bring Edith and it was the best five days of her life. But even then, with the war confined to headlines in newspapers and reports on the radio, she could tell that something was terribly wrong.

Vera was familiar with Margaret Island, perched in the middle of the Danube River that separated Buda and Pest. She even spent occasional Sundays there with her mother, listening to music and strolling on the park-like grounds. But to actually stay at the Grand Hotel was an unimaginable luxury. From the outside, the hotel resembled a palace. Their room had a canopied bed and a bathroom with gold faucets.

"Did you see the family in the suite next to us?" Vera jumped on the bed to see if it was soft. "There was a nanny for each child. I wouldn't know what to do with a nanny."

"You could ask her to send love letters to the boy down the hall." Edith sat at the window. In a pavilion below, guests sat in the shade and drank iced coffee with whipped cream.

"Why would we waste our time on boys when there is so much to do?" Vera asked. "The hotel has its own stables and a tennis court. I still don't understand why we came. My parents have never stayed anywhere like this before."

"Maybe they want to set you up with an eligible suitor," Edith suggested. "Did you know that Shirley Temple stayed here after she made *The Little Princess*? She probably sat right there"—Edith pointed at the pavilion—"eating sponge cake and reading love notes from lovesick boys."

Shirley Temple was only a year younger than Vera and Edith, and they dreamed of having her life. Edith even borrowed her mother's curlers and curled her hair in the same way.

"We're too young for suitors! Anyway, my parents want me to go to university." Vera inspected the gold bedspread. "My father must have robbed a bank to afford this."

"There's no point trying to figure out why we came." Edith jumped up. "Let's take a dip in the pool. We'll order drinks and wait for a movie star to say hello."

They had a wonderful time swimming and bicycling, and it wasn't until they were getting ready for dinner that Vera started to worry.

"My parents spent all afternoon in the mineral baths. What if my father is sick and they're afraid to tell me?" Vera frowned, tying the sash on her dress.

"Save your imagination for your stories and let's go to dinner," Edith said as she put down her hairbrush. "I'm starving from all that exercise."

The dining room had a domed ceiling and steps leading up to a raised dining area. There were indoor plants in silver urns and Vera noticed birds fluttering in a cage.

They had only been seated for a few moments when the maître d' whispered something to her father. Her father glanced at a table of German officers and stood up.

"We'll dine in our rooms tonight," he said, then turned to Vera, "You and Edith can order whatever you like and eat in bed."

"But we got dressed up to sit in the dining room," Vera said in surprise. She had seen German officers in Budapest, but no one had bothered them.

"That's a good idea. I have a headache from soaking in the mineral baths." Vera's mother stood up and touched her husband's hand. "Come, we'll be more comfortable in our room."

Edith went back to their room and Vera followed her parents down the hallway.

"I want to know what's going on," she said, entering their room. It was even bigger than the room she shared with Edith, with a separate sitting area and a balcony overlooking the garden.

"You saw the maître d' talking to your father." Her mother took the hairpins out of her hair. "There was an error in the seating arrangements. We'll dine in the dining room another night."

"I mean, what's going on with everything?" Vera fumed, perching on the four-poster bed. "First we stay in a hotel frequented by movie stars, and then we make dinner reservations at the restaurant where everything on the menu costs more than the dry foods section at Moshe's delicatessen, and then we leave for no reason. Did you rob a bank and you're afraid they've come after you?"

"A lady should never comment on the prices on a menu," Alice murmured, wiping the lipstick from her mouth.

"We left because of the German officers at the next table." Vera turned to her father. "But what did they do to you? And why are we on Margaret Island?"

Lawrence took his wife's hand and they sat on the sofa facing the bed.

"The German officers didn't want to eat in the same room as Jews." Lawrence hung his head. "And we came because I have to go away for a while. I wanted to take my family on a special vacation first."

Vera glanced frantically from her father to her mother. Now she was sure of it; her father had some terrible disease. They would pretend he was going away, when really he was being admitted to a hospital.

"Tell me the truth. Are you sick?" she asked.

Lawrence looked at Vera as if was he wondering if she was old enough to know the truth. His shoulders crumpled and he shook his head.

"I'm not sick. I'm being sent to a work camp."

Vera had heard about the work camps. Jewish men in Hungary weren't allowed to serve in the military and were forced to go to work camps instead. They were packed into dormitories as tightly as sardines and made to dig ditches and work in factories without having enough to eat.

"You have a family and a law practice," Vera pleaded. Her voice was tight and her skin felt clammy. Her father was not big and burly; he couldn't carry bricks all day without collapsing.

"I'll be fine." Lawrence moved to the bedside table and handed Vera a book. "I've been making notes in *Ulysses* for you to study while I'm gone."

Vera accepted the book and walked to the door. If her parents saw that she was crying, it would only make things worse.

"I'll start reading it tonight after Edith goes to sleep." She tried to keep her voice light. "Can we really order whatever we like? We bicycled all afternoon and I'm starving."

"Order anything on the room service menu," her father answered. "But watch out for the waiter. I worked as a hotel waiter one summer and the best part was meeting pretty girls."

Vera took the stairs to their floor and flung open the door to the room. Edith was eating hazelnut torte in bed.

"Where were you? I couldn't wait. I ordered dinner," Edith announced, waving at the table set with a white tablecloth. "You were going to say good night to your parents and you've been gone for ages."

"My parents explained everything," Vera said worriedly, sinking onto the bed. "It's worse than I thought. My father is being sent to a forced labor camp. He wanted to go somewhere special before he left."

"Why does he have to go now?" Edith put down her fork.

"He's been able to put it off, but the German army invaded Russia and the Germans need all the men they can get." There was a lump in her throat. "He can't avoid it any longer."

"Don't worry, the war will be over soon and he'll come back."

"Or it will go on for years and my mother and I will be alone," Vera gulped.

"You're not alone; we have each other," Edith assured her.

"We'll come here when we're twenty-one and we'll stay in the finest suite. We'll be married by then and we'll ride horses and go dancing. If we see any Germans at dinner, our husbands will tell them they have to leave," she glowered. "If they refuse, our husbands will pick them up by their jackets and throw them out of the dining room."

"We'll have to learn to walk in high heels," Vera said, slipping off her shoes.

"Why high heels?" Edith asked.

"So we can step on them when we walk back to our rooms. It would hurt more than if we were wearing flats."

Vera sat at the captain's table of the *Queen Elizabeth* and wished more than anything her parents were with her. Her father would love the afternoon chess games and her mother the concerts performed on the upper deck.

"We have five different forks," Edith hissed, interrupting her thoughts. "I can't remember which one we use first."

Vera suppressed a laugh and surveyed the dining room. It was three stories, with a black-and-white dance floor and marble columns. A grand piano stood in the corner and crystal chandeliers dangled from the ceiling.

Edith had convinced Vera to spend the afternoon in the ship's beauty parlor, and they had their hair washed and set. When she caught her reflection in the stateroom mirror before they went to dinner, she couldn't help but smile. She looked like Vivien Leigh.

They were joined at the table by Captain James and several older couples. Men with slicked-back hair talked about the building boom and the stock market. Women wearing diamond chokers chatted about Coco Chanel and the Paris fashion houses. Vera and Edith ate juicy steaks and drank full-bodied red wine.

Edith got up to dance, and a man with light brown hair approached the table. He was in his early thirties with brown eyes and a long nose.

"May I?" He slid into Edith's chair. "Your friend is a good dancer."

Vera nodded. "Edith loves to dance."

"Douglas Bauer." The man held out his hand. "You must be one of the Hungarian refugees sponsored by Sam Rothschild."

"How did you know?" Vera raised her eyebrows.

"No one else at the captain's table is younger than fifty; you're the talk of the ship," he said with a smile.

Vera blushed. "We're very grateful to Mr. Rothschild. I can't wait to meet him."

"Sam Rothschild is a smart man," Douglas mused. "A little charity goes a long way when you're tearing down tenement buildings to build luxury apartments."

Vera chose to ignore his question. It wasn't her business how Sam Rothschild made his money. And how could she object when he paid their fare and was allowing them to come to America.

"What took you to Europe?" Vera inquired.

"I'm a journalist for *Time* magazine." Douglas lit a cigarette. "I'm writing an article on the devastation in the European capitals after the war: Paris, Rome, London."

"It sounds fascinating," Vera murmured. She suddenly wanted to leave, but she couldn't catch Edith's eye. "I hope you had a lovely trip."

"The piece in the *New York Times* said you want to be a writer,"

Douglas continued. "You should write about the war. Readers love stories about beautiful young girls conquering adversity."

"My mother died at Auschwitz and my father never returned from a work camp," Vera bristled. "Edith and I lived in a freezing barn and ate nothing except eggs and broth for a year. I doubt your readers would find it uplifting reading."

Douglas's eyes softened. "I'm sorry. Five years of war headlines and one forgets about individual suffering. I can't imagine what you went through. I come from a small town in Michigan; the only thing I lost growing up was my dog."

"I have to go." Vera pushed back her chair.

"I didn't mean to offend you." Douglas jumped up. "If you change your mind, I'd be happy to read what you write."

Vera stood at the dessert station, watching Edith whirl around the dance floor. Edith found it so easy to be happy.

She remembered what Douglas said and had an idea. She put her coffee cup down and motioned to Edith. She couldn't wait to get back to their stateroom.

"You have to play shuffleboard." Edith stood in front of the mirror, fixing her hair. "Patrick has a friend and he wants to make a foursome."

"How can you play shuffleboard when the ship is rolling like a beach ball?" Vera groaned and looked up from her notepad. "Anyway, I'm busy. Patrick and his friend will have to fight over you."

"You've been cooped up in here for three days." Edith dabbed lipstick on her mouth. "You missed the bridge tournament and the dance contest."

"I'm almost finished," Vera declared. She put the lid on her pen and turned her full attention to Edith. "Aren't you spending too much time with this new man?"

"Patrick is a member of one of the oldest families in Boston. Plus he has the greenest eyes I've ever seen, and I think he's in love with me."

"You don't know anything about him, and in a few days you'll probably never see him again," Vera reminded her.

"It's okay for you to cross the Atlantic to find a man you only knew for four months, but I can't play shuffleboard with a charming man?" Edith demanded.

Vera wanted to say it was different; it was as if she had known Anton all her life. But she never told Edith what happened in Capri and she was afraid Edith might guess the truth.

"Go and have fun. But try not to get seasick," Vera relented. "I don't know how you walk on the deck without wanting to throw up."

Vera entered the dining room and noticed Douglas Bauer standing by the buffet. He balanced a teacup in one hand and a plate of toast and jam in the other.

"This is a lovely surprise," he beamed. "I haven't seen you since the first night's dinner."

"I've been busy," Vera replied.

"Would you like some toast?" Douglas handed her the plate. "I thought I was hungry, but I have the stomach of a debutante. The minute the ship starts rolling I lose my appetite."

"I wonder if you are serious about reading what I write," Vera asked.

"I never say anything I don't mean." Douglas poured milk into the porcelain teacup.

"It's a first draft," Vera said nervously, reaching into her purse for her notebook. "I'd be grateful if you could take a look."

"Why don't you come to my stateroom at six p.m. and I'll give you a report."

"Your stateroom?" Vera raised her eyebrow.

The ship lurched and Vera almost fell against Douglas's shoulder.

"I'm not leaving my cabin again until the sea calms down." Douglas wiped his brow. "Number thirty-two on the Admiral Floor."

"You must join us for dinner," Edith implored. She wore a turquoise silk dress and a strand of pearls around her neck. "Patrick said he has a surprise. Maybe he'll invite us to his home in Boston."

"Where did you get that dress and those pearls?" Vera asked. It was almost six and she was anxious about going to Douglas's stateroom. Maybe she should send him a note saying she was too ill to leave her cabin.

"Patrick bought them for me at the ship's gift shop," Edith sighed happily. She twirled in front of the mirror. "He said the pearls make my skin look like porcelain. And don't say anything about accepting gifts from men." She looked at Vera. "I have a feeling Patrick is the one."

Vera knocked on the stateroom door and glanced at her watch. She debated until the last minute what she should do and now it was almost six thirty. Maybe Douglas had gone for an evening stroll or was having a cocktail in the Captain's Bar. The storm had passed and the sea was finally calm.

Douglas opened the door. "There you are. I was about to give up and go in search of dinner. I'm so hungry, I could eat a horse."

"I can come back," Vera hesitated, suddenly uncomfortable. She had never been alone in a room with a man besides Anton.

"Come in," Douglas said. He moved aside and waved her into the room. "I'll pour us both a brandy. Thank God for expense accounts; the *Queen Elizabeth* stocks the finest cognac."

Vera stepped inside and took in the narrow bed with its quilted gold bedspread. The coffee table was piled with magazines and there was an ashtray filled with cigarette butts.

"I apologize for the bachelor mess." Douglas swept away the ashtray. "The maids come twice a day but I still manage to make a pigsty.

"I read your stories. You have a great eye for detail," he continued, handing her a shot glass. "If I went to Budapest, I could find your apartment from your descriptions."

"Thank you." Vera nodded, perching on an armchair.

"But there's no drama." Douglas rubbed his brow. "It's like a diary entry. You have to show your reader more emotion. Writing has to be larger than life to be appreciated."

"I see," Vera said stiffly. She rose and picked up the notebook. "I was silly to think I'm a writer. Thank you for your time."

Douglas stopped her. He put his hand on her shoulder. "You're a wonderful writer, but every story needs drama. It may be that the story is too hard to write; you have to give it time."

His hand brushed her sleeve and she smelled the liquor on his breath. Suddenly he caught her arm and kissed her.

"What are you doing?" She slapped his cheek and pulled away.

"I'm kissing you." Douglas smiled.

"I don't want to be kissed!" Vera exclaimed.

"Of course you do," Douglas replied. "You came to my cabin."

"Because you said you'd read my story," Vera stammered.

"Relax, if you don't like it I won't do it again," Douglas laughed. "Let me give you some advice. You're beautiful and smart, but you have to be careful of men. No matter what we say, we want to get under your dress."

"I have to go." Vera opened the door.

She ran down the hall to her stateroom and closed the door. Edith was at dinner with Patrick, and the room smelled of perfume and roses.

Just because she accepted Douglas's invitation didn't mean she wanted to kiss him. She remembered knocking on Anton's door in Capri and urging him to make love. That was different; they were engaged and meant to be together.

She gazed out at the sea and recalled the summer she was sixteen and her mother told her about her courtship with her father. Her father had been terribly shy, and if Alice didn't make the first move, they may never have gotten married.

It was the summer of 1943, and Edith and Stefan had been secretly seeing each other for a year. Edith's mother adored Stefan, but Edith worried that Lily would think she was too young. It was Vera's job to distract Lily when Edith and Stefan spent too long at the lake and Edith came home with brambles in her hair.

One night the sun had already set, and Edith and Stefan were nowhere in sight. Lily had gone upstairs, but Vera's mother was sitting on the porch. Vera stood at the window and waited for Edith to appear. How would Edith explain why she was still wearing a swimsuit and had missed dinner when she returned?

"There you are," Vera said to her mother, walking onto the porch. "I cut a cherry strudel. Why don't you join me in the kitchen for a slice?"

Alice put down her sewing. "We already had dessert and you said you were full."

"I couldn't resist Lily's cherry strudel," Vera said quickly.

"If you're trying to distract me for when Edith comes home, it's not necessary," Alice answered. "Lily and I know about Stefan and Edith."

"Lily doesn't mind?" Vera wondered.

"She's happy that Edith is in love," Alice said. "She worries that there aren't any men in Edith's life since her father ran off with the secretary."

"Stefan is wonderful. He treats Edith like a princess," Vera sighed with relief. "We were afraid Lily thought they were too young."

"Age means nothing when it comes to love," Alice countered. "I was barely nineteen when I met your father, and we were married a month later."

"You never told me that." Vera sat down beside her.

"Lawrence and his friends were sitting in a café in Paris after one of my dance performances. They asked a few of the dancers to join them and we drank vermouth and had a few laughs. He walked me back to my room and we had so much in common. The next night, his group was there again but he barely talked to me. That went on for a week. Every night his friends asked us to join them, and every night

Lawrence ignored me. One night, I asked him to walk me home. We were so wrapped up in our discussion we missed my flat! When we finally reached my door, I was sure he was going to kiss me. But he just tipped his hat and left.

"A few nights later, he was with his friends at the café. I said I had something urgent to tell him and asked him to meet me outside. We strolled along the Seine and our hands touched, and it was more thrilling than being onstage. I stopped in the middle of the sidewalk and kissed him. He was so surprised he almost dropped his hat in the river!

"He explained that the first night he walked me home as a dare from his friends. But he's terribly shy and he was too nervous to ask me again. Every night he wanted to say how he felt, but his tongue turned to rubber," she laughed. "I told him he better get over it or he'd never be able to argue in court. A week later he proposed, and a month after that we were married."

"You never told me." Vera tried to imagine her parents sharing their first kiss. She knew they met in Paris, but she never stopped to imagine their courtship.

"My mother would have thought I was terribly fast if she knew. She thought studying dance was a phase and I'd come back to Budapest and marry a boy I'd known since Hebrew school." Alice smiled. "It was better to keep quiet."

"I'm glad Edith has Stefan," Vera said with a nod. "He makes her happy."

"You're only sixteen; you have years to find the right man," Alice counseled. "When you do, you'll know the minute you set eyes on him. That's what's different about love. It doesn't need any history."

"I hope there will be boys left to fall in love with." Vera thought of her father in the labor camp.

"The war can't win over love," Alice said shortly. "The right man will find you."

Vera stood in her stateroom in the *Queen Elizabeth* and pictured Anton in his white dinner jacket in Capri. Anton had been the right man. What if she couldn't find him again? And if she did, would he marry her, or would he insist she wait for a man who could give her children?

CHAPTER TEN

The *Queen Elizabeth* nudged into New York Harbor and Vera leaned against the railing. Pink clouds floated above the skyscrapers, and the sun gleaming on the water was like an impressionist painting. The Empire State Building reached the sky and the Statue of Liberty looked more impressive than she had on any movie reel.

It was only now, when the ship's pursers were checking the other passengers' passports that Vera remembered why they were here. Soon the people they sat with at the captain's table every night would disappear into limousines, and Vera and Edith would have to go through immigration at Ellis Island.

"A lawyer from New Jersey and a doctor from Philadelphia gave me their phone numbers," Edith said as she joined her at the railing.

"What about Patrick?" Vera asked. "You said he was the one."

"I went to say good-bye and there was a telegram in his stateroom. It was from a girl named Barbara. She couldn't wait for him to arrive in Boston, and her mother had already picked out their wedding china. Apparently, Patrick forgot to tell me he was engaged."

Vera squeezed her arm. "You shouldn't waste your time with men anyway. We're in New York now and anything is possible."

The ship's nose nudged into the dock and a giant cheer rose on deck. Vera hugged her chest and thought of her parents and Stefan and their apartment building in Budapest. The future had to be bright; something had to erase all the darkness of the past.

They collected their bags and followed the other immigrants into the Great Hall. The elaborate frescoes and glittering chandeliers of the *Queen Elizabeth* were replaced by an austere room as big as a stadium. People stood in long lines, clutching their papers.

What if the officer saw "Jewish" on their papers and sent them back to Europe? But he simply handed Vera her documents and asked if she wanted to change her name.

"Change my name?" Vera repeated.

"Some immigrants want to fit in more easily," the officer explained. "They want a name that sounds less Jewish."

"I like my name," Vera said stiffly.

After Edith passed the health exam, they were directed to the Kissing Post. They waited while pale men and women were greeted by relatives with pink cheeks and glossy hair. A boy ran into the arms of an older woman in a smart dress and Vera wondered if he lost his parents in the camps and was being claimed by an aunt.

"I hope Mr. and Mrs. Rothschild arrive soon," Edith sighed. They had been standing for hours.

Vera had a queasy feeling. What if Samuel Rothschild forgot his promise? What if he was playing poker at his club or in the mountains with his wife? She and Edith would be put on the next ship back to Italy.

All afternoon they stood in the Great Hall and stared at the entrance. Edith asked one of the officers for a pack of cards and they played a desultory game of twenty-one. Vera reminded herself of the afternoons they frittered away in the last year before the war, reading Lily's movie magazines and dreaming of a time in the future when their mothers would call them in for a delicious dinner instead of plain broth and stale bread.

But this was different; there was no Stefan to keep Edith happy and no German officers roaming the streets that made them grateful to be safe in their apartments. On the other side of the river was New York City. All the Rothschilds had to do was show up at Ellis Island for it to be theirs. Then they would take them to their town house with a view of Central Park, their maid would offer to run hot baths, and beds would be covered with duvets so soft they would sleep for days.

"I'm sorry," an officer said as he approached them. "The immigration center is closed; you must sleep here tonight."

"One of the great philanthropists in New York is waiting for us," Edith assured him. "His name is Samuel Rothschild."

The man shrugged. "He is not coming today. I will show you where you can rest."

"You don't understand." Vera stepped forward. "He paid for our passage on the *Queen Elizabeth*, he couldn't have forgotten us."

"I'm sure he didn't forget you," the man said kindly. "But no one is coming tonight; you'll have to wait until morning."

Vera and Edith followed him to a dormitory with narrow iron cots. They climbed into bed fully clothed and hardly slept all night. Vera thought of the long months their mothers spent in the concentration camp and told herself this was nothing compared to what they suffered. But it was because of Edith that Vera was in New York. Samuel Rothschild had to come; there was nowhere else for them to go.

In the morning they took their positions in the Great Hall and waited. The clock on the wall moved so slowly, Vera wanted to climb on Edith's shoulders and move the hands herself. If only she had an address or phone number where she could reach them, but she only had the article in the *New York Times*.

"Maybe there's been a misunderstanding and they're waiting at their residence," Edith suggested in the afternoon. They had been given a meal consisting of a small piece of ham and canned baked beans, but they were both still hungry. "I'm going to ask the officer if he can let us through. We'll find their address in the phone book and take the ferry and then a taxi to their home."

"I don't think he'll let us through," Vera said worriedly. "The officer in charge said all immigrants must stay in the Great Hall, with no exceptions."

Edith unbuttoned the top button of her dress and fanned out her hair.

"I won't ask the officer in charge; I'll ask that one." She pointed to a young officer with red hair and freckles. "I'm sure I can get him to make two tiny exceptions."

Edith strode across the Great Hall and approached the young officer. He blushed and shook his head. Edith was about to try again but suddenly she picked up something from his desk and hurried through the hall.

"What did he say?" Vera asked.

"He didn't have to say anything. Read this," Edith gasped. "It's yesterday's copy of the *New York Times*."

Vera scanned the headline.

MILLIONAIRE BANKER

SAMUEL ROTHSCHILD COLLAPSES ON VACATION.

Samuel Rothschild, who at the age of thirty became the youngest bank president in America, collapsed while playing tennis at The Breakers, Palm Beach. Mr. Rothschild, sixty-two, was on vacation with his wife, Gilda. Doctors attempted to revive him, but he was pronounced dead at Palm Beach Hospital. Mr. Rothschild has donated millions to the New York City Library and the Jewish Federation. His wife of forty years, Gilda Rothschild, was sedated and is now in seclusion.

Vera put the newspaper down and her heart hammered.

"He can't be dead." Edith's eyes were wide. "There must be someone we can talk to. Perhaps he has a son or a daughter."

Vera pointed to the newspaper. "It says that his wife is in seclusion. I don't think anyone else in his family will care about two Hungarian girls on Ellis Island when the most important person in their world just died."

"What will we do?" Edith asked. "We have to find a way to get out of here."

Vera thought about the things in New York they dreamed of doing together: cocktails at Tavern on the Green, the exhibits at the Met, and boating in Central Park. If they couldn't find a sponsor, they would never get to experience any of that.

Vera paced the dormitory. It was almost dinnertime, which consisted of liver and a potato. For the last two days, she and Edith spent their time shuffling between the Great Hall and the dormitory. But even the red-haired officer said they couldn't stay much longer.

That morning Vera had finally written a letter to Harry Wight. Edith had given the envelope to the young officer, with red lipstick on its front. She whispered that he would receive a similar kiss if he delivered it to the address in the advertisement in the magazine.

Edith dashed into the dormitory.

"You got a letter," she announced. Her face looked pale.

Vera took the envelope and fingered the gold lettering that read "Wight Hotels." Harry Wight had read her letter and replied! He would be arriving at Ellis Island any minute to collect them.

"Read it out loud," Edith breathed.

" 'Dear Miss Frankel,

" 'I received your letter to Mr. Harry Wight, chairman of Wight Hotels. Unfortunately, Mr. Wight is battling pneumonia and has not been in the Manhattan office for several weeks. Upon his return, I will be sure to give him your note.

" 'Sincerely,

" 'Jane Grant

" 'Secretary to Harry Wight.' "

Vera slid the letter in the envelope and sank onto the cot. They wouldn't be allowed to wait for weeks in the detention center. There was no choice; they would have to return to Europe.

"I can't go back to Italy," Edith sobbed, burying her face in the pillow.

Vera stroked Edith's hair and tried to calm her down. Edith had adored Naples. She and Marcus loved going to the cinema and eating gelato and dancing. Would it be so bad to return? And Edith was so talented. Signora Stella would find her work and perhaps Maria would order more dresses.

But there were so many things in Naples that reminded them of war. Vera thought of the bombed-out buildings she passed on the way to the embassy, and the girls who flirted with every boy they met because there weren't enough young men to marry. She remembered Anton's impassioned speeches about rebuilding the city, and the old Italian men who grumbled that they could do it themselves.

Vera opened her suitcase and dug out the Cunard brochure that listed all its destinations.

"There is a ship going to Sydney, and one to Rio de Janeiro, and one to Caracas."

They sat on the cot and studied the brochure. They read about these cities, and Vera had a sense of hope and renewal. They could get jobs and rent a small apartment. On a new continent they would be two hard-working young girls instead of tragic Hungarian refugees.

"They all look good." Vera turned to Edith. "How will we choose?"

Edith closed her eyes and stabbed the page with her fingernail. Her eyes opened and she glanced at the brochure.

"We're going to Caracas."

Vera peered at the photos of busy streets and white buildings and lush foliage. There were palm trees and mountains and exotic flowers. If she couldn't find Anton, she didn't care where she was. She folded the brochure and turned to Edith.

"I'll book our tickets."

CHAPTER ELEVEN

Vera sampled a slice of mango and wiped the juice from her mouth. It was even sweeter than the chestnut purees her mother used to order at the cafés in Budapest. Her mother always laughed that she couldn't possibly finish a whole chestnut puree without ruining her waistline. One of Vera's favorite memories was her mother handing her a long silver spoon and digging into the whipped cream.

They had been in Venezuela for two weeks. At first Vera had worried that they had made the wrong decision; everything was so different. Even though Italian and Spanish were similar, the locals spoke so rapidly she found it difficult to understand. Even the season was different. They had packed clothes for winter in New York. Marcus had given them thick sweaters that Paolo had bought on the black market, and they had spent the last of their savings on winter coats. But it was summer in Venezuela, and the minute they stepped off the ship, the humidity rose to greet them.

The first few days were spent exploring their new city. Churches that dated back to the seventeenth century sat amid the young and vibrant city. Central University was filled with students lounging on the grass and the Plaza Bolívar teemed with office workers enjoying the hot South American sun on their lunch breaks. In parts of the city, music vibrated so loudly Vera could feel it beating in her heart. And Edith loved the garment district, where racks of bright dresses filled the streets.

They spent an afternoon at the Panthéon Nacional, where Venezuela's most prominent citizens were buried. Vera and Edith marveled at the magnificent chandelier that hung above the tomb of the second president, Simón Bolívar. And there were rows of tombs labeled with the names of war heroes and the dates of their battles. Vera flashed on the unmarked graves scattered across Europe and wondered if they would ever be free of death. But then they walked outside to the modern buildings of the Capital District and fashionably dressed men and women, and the clouds of war disappeared.

Everywhere they went, Vera was surprised by the number of immigrants. Hungarians and Poles shopping at the street markets, Romanians playing chess in the squares, and Italians and Germans who hid behind newspapers and avoided the others as if they were personally responsible for the fate of the European Jews.

They had already been invited to a get-together at a private home. A few days after they arrived, a Hungarian woman they met on the ship invited them to tea at her house. Vera had been eager to attend, but the platters of stuffed cabbage and veal schnitzel had looked out of place next to the bowls filled with tropical fruit. And the other guests—widowers who lost their wives, women without husbands or children—were like amputees learning to live without an arm or a leg.

Edith wanted to leave right away, but Vera whispered it wouldn't be polite. So they accepted slices of coffee cake and listened to the others talk about Budapest before the war: the Parliament Building facing the Danube and strolling across the Chain Bridge and browsing in the elegant shops on Váci Utca. Two emaciated women had a long discussion about eating crepes stuffed with walnuts in a café on Castle Hill and shopping at a delicatessen without wondering if it would run out of butter and eggs. Vera knew what was going through Edith's head: Why were they sitting around talking as if they could walk outside and get tickets to the Budapest Opera House when they would never see those places again?

There were also things that made them happy in Caracas: the boulevards flanked by palm trees and the mountains that surrounded the city and were covered with grass as green as emeralds. The Venezuelan women wore dresses in bright colors and the men drove flashy sports cars. Everyone acted as if life was one big party.

And they were lucky to find decent lodgings. When they disembarked, Vera gave the taxi driver the name of a boardinghouse in Ciudad Mariche. The taxi driver took one look at the address and said he wouldn't drive through the suburb, let alone allow two young women to stay there. Instead he took them to a house on one of the most elegant streets in Los Palos Grandes.

The villa stood behind ivy-covered walls and was owned by a widow who let out rooms to help pay expenses. Lola had a soft spot for European refugees and offered them a room at the top of the house. The sloped roof meant that Vera and Edith could barely stand up at the same time, but the view from the window showed the spectacular mountains and the city.

For the first two weeks, Vera worried that Edith would slip into her old ways and spend her days flirting with men and sipping coffee at outdoor cafés. There were more plazas than in Naples, and no one seemed in a hurry to get back to work.

But each morning Edith dressed and rushed off, armed with a list of seamstresses from Lola. She didn't return until dusk, and when Vera suggested they go out and share a passion fruit shake, Edith countered that they both needed a good night's sleep if they wanted to find jobs.

Now, finally, Vera had a job interview and it would be nice to surprise Edith with a treat from the market. The vendor put a whole mango in Vera's hand and she had to laugh. One had to be more careful than at the outdoor markets in Naples. The minute she showed an interest in a basket of nectarines or juicy plums, a man pressed the piece of fruit into her hand and said she was getting a bargain. Vera always shook her head and said she couldn't afford to buy anything; she was just inhaling the sweet perfume.

Vera scooped up a handful of cherries and handed them to the vendor. She dug into her purse for a centimo before he could urge her to add a basket of plums. Then she skipped along the boulevard and opened the gate to Lola's house.

For a moment, she longed to be racing up the steps of the embassy in Naples. Gina would be polishing the staircase and Mozart would be playing on the phonograph. Anton would look up from his desk and his smile would warm her like the sun.

Vera said nothing to Edith about her longing for Anton. How could she explain it without revealing the night in Capri and the feeling that they were joined forever?

Without help from Anton's father, there was no way to find him. It would be pointless to write to Harry Wight from Venezuela. It was different when she and Edith were on Ellis Island. But now they were on another continent. They couldn't afford to return to America.

She pushed thoughts of Anton from her mind; she had more urgent things to think about. The job was at an English-speaking advertising agency, and she had to press her dress and make sure she had a pair of stockings. Working as a copywriter might not be as thrilling as being a playwright, but she could make a living.

The other boarders were at work and Lola was getting a manicure. Lola was almost never home. A widow in her midfifties, she was determined to find a new husband. She spent her days at the beauty parlor and nights allowing new men to admire the candlesticks in the living room and sip her late husband's sherry.

Vera took her shopping bag into the kitchen and heard footsteps in the entry. Edith stood in the doorway wearing a tea dress. It had padded shoulders and a sweetheart collar and was one of the loveliest dresses Vera had ever seen.

"What are you wearing?" Vera asked. "You said you weren't interested in men; you were going to get a job."

"What does this dress have to do with men?" Edith put her purse on the counter. "I made the dress myself, finished it this morning."

"But how?" Vera continued. They didn't own a sewing machine.

"I borrowed Lola's," Edith replied. "It's gorgeous, isn't it?" Edith breathed. "Raw silk made in Colombia. Two bolts of silk cost more than ten bolivares."

"I've never seen anything so beautiful, but how could you afford the material?" Vera wondered.

"I pawned the pearls Patrick gave me." Edith's hands went to her bare neck. One good thing had come out of their voyage to America. "Don't worry, I'll get them back. The owner was quite generous. He said he wanted to make sure I returned."

"But where will you wear the dress? It will be difficult to get a job as a seamstress's assistant if you show up dressed like a princess." Vera frowned. "They'll think you're some bored socialite who doesn't really need a job."

"I'm going to wear it to an important party." Edith handed her an invitation.

Vera scanned it. It was for a black-tie gala at the Hotel Majestic in honor of Mr. and Mrs. Reginald Buchanan of Houston, Texas.

"Who are the Buchanans?" she asked.

Vera couldn't imagine why a Hungarian Jewish refugee would be invited to a gala at the fanciest hotel in Caracas.

"Mr. Reginald Buchanan is one of the richest oilmen in America, and he and his wife just moved to Venezuela. It's their welcome party." Edith twirled the invitation. "A penniless refugee might not be invited to drink champagne and dance to Cole Porter. But the daughter of a well-known Hungarian fashion designer would, and she would be wearing a silk dress."

Vera glanced at the clock. Her interview was first thing in the morning, and if she didn't iron her dress soon, Lola would need the iron to get ready for her date.

"Why should I be a seamstress's assistant and spend my days in a workroom that is so hot and smoky I'll get some terrible lung disease, when I can be a fashion designer and get paid hundreds of bolivares for doing what I love?" Edith continued breezily. "My mother was Lily Ban, with her own salon on Andrássy Avenue, Budapest's finest shopping street. I was sent to Paris before the war to study under my mother's good friend, Elsa Schiaparelli. When Schiaparelli closed her atelier during the war, my mother begged me to go somewhere safe, but the passion for couture was under my skin. I joined the salon of that Spanish newcomer Cristóbal Balenciaga and dressed all the fashionable women remaining in Paris." Edith's eyes darkened. "Then came the news that the Germans confiscated my parents' apartment and they were sent to a concentration camp. After the war, I learned they were never coming back. I couldn't return to Budapest, and Paris was too expensive for a young girl all alone. I saved enough money to come to Venezuela, and Balenciaga allowed me to take the dresses I designed."

Vera smiled at Edith's story. "That's a lovely fairy tale, but it isn't true. You've never been to Paris."

"Do you think anyone tells the truth about their past?" Edith asked. "The doctor at the Hotel Majestic boasts that he was a renowned surgeon in Vienna. Miguel heard him talking at the hotel bar and he flunked out of medical school. He faints at the sight of blood."

"I knew a man had something to do with this," Vera said. "Who is Miguel?"

"He's the porter at the Hotel Majestic; he got us the invitation. There was a whole stack of invitations in the Buchanans' suite; they weren't going to miss one. And don't worry, Miguel isn't attracted to me. He likes full-figured women." She ran a hand over her slim hips.

"Your new friend Miguel is risking his job," Vera warned.

"I promised to make his girlfriend a dress once I get my first commission," Edith admitted. "The party will be packed with women who can afford a wardrobe of evening gowns."

Vera put the cherries in a bowl.

"I can't wait to hear all about it. I'll be home, ironing my dress. I have an interview at an ad agency tomorrow. They want someone who speaks English, so I'm going to reread the books Anton gave me."

Vera kept the small stack of books under the bed: *Tender Is the Night* by F. Scott Fitzgerald and *A Farewell to Arms* by Ernest Hemingway, as well as a poetry collection. When she turned the pages she imagined Anton reading them over his coffee in the morning room of the embassy in Naples.

"Please come with me; I have an extra invitation. A single girl is a sight of pity, but two Hungarian beauties together will be the talk of the ball. Besides, you don't want me to go alone," Edith sighed theatrically. "I don't want to get in a dangerous situation."

It would be fun to go to a party, and Edith knew just what to say to make her reconsider. The last thing she wanted was for Edith to drink too much champagne. "All right, I'll go. But I'll have to wear my black dress; I don't have anything else."

She had sold the gowns Gina had given her to pay their rent while they searched for jobs.

"Yes you do. I'll be right back." Edith turned and hurried up the staircase.

Edith returned holding a breadth of white fabric as gossamer-like as a cloud on a summer day. She unfurled it and it was something Vera had seen Rita Hayworth wear at the movies: a white organza skirt and a fitted bodice with a white sash.

"It's gorgeous! Where did it come from?" Vera breathed.

"I made it for you." Edith held it out to her. "You didn't think I spent all the money from the pearls on myself?"

The ballroom at the Hotel Majestic was even more elegant than the one at the Grand Hotel in Budapest. The parquet floors looked perfect for dancing, and vases of flowers gave off an exotic scent. The American women—friends of the Buchanans'—had diamond earrings as big as birds' eggs, and evening gowns that rustled when they walked. Vera wondered if these were the kind of women Anton met at his country club.

Edith was luminous in a velvet stole and white gloves. She stood in a corner surrounded by men, and Vera had to laugh. How could Edith show off her dress to other women if she was practically hidden by a wall of tuxedos?

"Your friend is a good actress." A man stood next to her. He had a beak-like nose and wore a shabby sports jacket.

"Edith isn't an actress; she's a dress designer," Vera said, watching Edith pull charmingly at her gloves. She looked so young and fresh, like a debutante at a ball.

"She might not be an actress, but I doubt she's spent time at an atelier in Paris." He reached into his pocket for a lighter. "If she had worked for Schiaparelli or Balenciaga, she would have become addicted to cigarettes." He waved at the group. "All those men are smoking and she hasn't once asked for a cigarette."

"I don't know what you mean," Vera claimed. If she didn't go along with Edith's story, they might get kicked out of the party.

"Your secret is safe with me," he said, grinning. "I like watching her, and Mr. and Mrs. Reginald Buchanan can afford to feed two extra guests. They could afford to feed a good portion of Caracas with the sapphire pendant around Kitty Buchanan's neck." He held out his hand. "Julius Cohen."

"Vera Frankel." Vera breathed a sigh of relief. "How did you know?"

"I'm a portrait artist. I'm paid to notice small details," he said. He lit a cigarette.

"Have you been in Venezuela long?" Vera asked, recognizing his Austrian accent.

"Since 1939. My wife and son and I were some of the lucky ones. We were passengers on the *Caribia*," Julius said gravely.

"You were on the *Caribia*?" Vera repeated. She had read about the ship that left Vienna in 1939 as the borders of Austria were closing. It set sail for Trinidad, but when it arrived no one was allowed to disembark because the government didn't want the burden of Jews in their country. After that the captain tried to land at all the British colonies, but no one would accept them. The passengers were afraid they would have to return to Europe, but finally the Venezuelan authorities allowed them entry.

"It was the most nerve-wracking few weeks of our lives," Julius recalled. "I still remember when the port in Venezuela came into view. It was nighttime, and the sea and sky were black, and in the distance I could make out mountains. But there were no lights, and the ship's captain couldn't land without them. Suddenly there was the strangest sight: all along the dock, trucks beamed their lights in our direction.

"When we landed there was a crowd waiting with food and clothing. I even remember a band and people dancing. Venezuela has been our home for eight years and I thank God every day for putting us on that ship. Here it doesn't matter if you're Jewish, the Venezuelans have enough love for everyone." Julius studied his drink and his tone lightened. "Tell me, how did you and Edith end up in Caracas?"

Vera thought of their passage on the *Queen Elizabeth*, when they couldn't wait to arrive in New York and be driven to Samuel Rothschild's Fifth Avenue town house. There were the hours spent pacing under the clock at Ellis Island before they realized he wasn't coming. But there was no point in bringing it up now. The whole idea of coming to Venezuela was to create new lives.

"We wanted to get far away from Europe. Venezuela seemed like the perfect destination," Vera said instead. "Edith lost her childhood sweetheart. I keep telling her he might be alive, but she gave up hope. It's easier to forget when you're somewhere new."

"And what about you? Did you lose anyone?"

Should she tell him about her mother who died because Vera jumped off the train without her? Or Anton, who was lost to her now? But Julius was a stranger.

"There's no one," she answered, pretending to concentrate on the sash of her dress. "I read a brochure and it promised sun-kissed beaches and a city alive with music and color."

"It's even better than what you've read," Julius agreed. "A warm climate and plenty of food, and oil money welling up from the ground." He pointed to where Edith was standing. A young man pressed a champagne flute to Edith's lips. "But be careful, even Caracas has a dark side. When life becomes too easy, sometimes common decency is left behind."

"Thank you," Vera said, but suddenly the sound of Edith's laughter from across the room made her uneasy. "If you'll excuse me, it was nice to meet you. I'm sure we'll see you again."

Edith had finally slipped away from the circle of men and was chatting with two women wearing silk evening gowns and long white gloves. Even from across the ballroom Vera could tell they had money.

Maybe Edith knew what she was doing after all. The band played Perry Como's "Till the End of Time," and Vera remembered dancing with Anton at the Hotel Quisisana in Capri. Her head had rested on Anton's shoulder, and for a moment she wasn't a homeless refugee. She was a nineteen-year-old girl dancing with her fiancé in one of the most romantic spots on earth.

"Would you like to dance?" a male voice asked in English, interrupting her thoughts.

Vera's eyes flickered to a man with dark hair standing beside her. He resembled a movie star in a perfectly cut dinner jacket and white bow tie.

"No, thank you." She shook her head. "I don't dance."

"Everyone is here to dance. And that dress is too pretty to waste." He held out his arms. "I promise I'm a good dancer."

They moved to the center of the ballroom and the man put his hand around Vera's waist. Instinctively she froze. No man had touched her since Anton. But then he twirled her around the dance floor and the dress flared around her knees like a spinning top.

"I told you I was a good dancer," he said when they stopped, and he led her to the punch bowl. He dipped a cup into the crystal bowl and handed it to her. "My mother made me take dancing lessons. I hated everything about it." He smiled at Vera. "Now I send her flowers to thank her. There are few things better than dancing with a beautiful woman."

His eyes were liquid brown and his cheeks were smooth as butter, but something about him made her nervous. Was it just the idea of talking to an attractive man? She remembered Douglas Bauer expecting her to kiss him because she went to his cabin, and took a step back.

"It was fun, thank you," Vera said and sipped the punch. "I have to go; my friend is waiting for me."

The man followed her gaze. "Your friend has more admirers than any woman in the room. Please stay and talk to me." He made a small bow. "Ricardo Albee."

"Vera Frankel," Vera said.

"You speak good English," Ricardo replied.

"I'm glad you think so." Vera smiled. "I have a job interview at an

English-speaking ad agency tomorrow and I've been worried I need more practice."

"Beautiful and a workingwoman, too." Ricardo nodded his approval. "The young women in Caracas rely on their parents to pay for everything until a suitor comes along to take over the task." His eyes ran down Vera's dress. "Not that it would be a burden with you."

"I'm not looking for a suitor," Vera returned. She glanced toward Edith again. "If you'll excuse me, I have to go."

He put his hand on her arm. She looked up and there was an amused expression on his face.

"I apologize if I upset you." He bowed again. "I'm sure we'll see each other. There is only one grand ballroom in Caracas and there are parties here almost every week."

Later that night, Vera and Edith sat in Lola's kitchen and ate chicken broth soup with eggs and carrots that Lola had left for them with black bread. They had been too worried about ruining their gowns to eat at the ball, and now Edith dipped bread into the soup.

"All that flirting must be good for your appetite," Vera observed.

"I barely noticed the men at the party. But Kitty Buchanan complimented me on my gown," Edith replied. "She invited me to a luncheon next week. I'm going to sew a new dress that is so stylish every woman will want a copy."

"Didn't Kitty wonder how you ended up at her party?" Vera asked.

"She thought we met at a fashion show in Paris in 1944, after the liberation," Edith said as she buttered her bread. "Kitty is so crazy about Parisian fashion, she made her husband attend the shows while the rest of Europe was still at war." Her eyes darkened. "While Stefan and our fathers were laboring at the work camps, American husbands were trailing after their wives in Paris, drinking champagne and buying hats."

"You really think she'll help you?" Vera asked.

"Kitty is the kind of woman who loves taking artists under her wing. She'll boast that I studied under Schiaparelli. Enough about me." Edith glanced up from the soup. "I saw you dancing with that man."

Vera shrugged. "It was nothing. He asked me to dance and wouldn't take no for an answer."

"Maybe he's some wealthy Venezuelan who'll take you driving in his convertible and bring you boxes of chocolates."

"The only thing I'm interested in is my job interview." Vera ate a bite of plantain. It was coated with brown sugar and tasted delicious after the spicy soup. "I don't even want to think about men; it only causes heartache." The image of Anton sitting on the ferry to Capri came unbidden to her mind and she walked determinedly to the door. "I'm going upstairs to read until I fall asleep."

It was getting late and Vera closed her book. She was too tired to read. Ricardo was handsome, but when he put his arms around her she felt nothing. She remembered the happiness of making love with Anton in Capri as if her whole body was floating.

It was time to stop holding on to her losses as if they were favorite childhood dolls. She and Edith were in Caracas now. The breeze smelled of flowers and the sun shone all day long. All she had to do was believe anything was possible.

CHAPTER TWELVE

February 1947

Vera sat in the reception area of the ad agency and studied the framed ads on the wall. She had dressed carefully in a floral dress. At the last minute, Lola loaned her a hat and a pair of short white gloves.

It was already hot when she left the house that morning and she had been afraid her dress would stick to her stockings. At least it was the dry season. She heard that from May to October it could rain all evening. It was impossible to walk through the streets without ruining your shoes.

She had to take two streetcars to reach the ad agency, and the streetcar moved so quickly she almost missed her stop. Everything about the city still felt so foreign: the neighborhoods with abandoned cars and dilapidated apartments that were poorer than anything she'd seen in Budapest contrasted with the central business district where banks stood proudly next to buildings that housed oil companies and embassies with flags flying above gold canopies.

Vera adjusted her gloves and hoped she looked older. When she applied for the secretary position in Naples she hadn't worried about her age. She had the letter of introduction from Captain Bingham, and not many women spoke both English and Italian. In Venezuela there had been no war, and more women were able to take secretarial courses and learn languages at the university. There were bound to be applicants with better qualifications.

"Miss Frankel?" The receptionist appeared with her steno pad. "If you follow me, Mr. Matthews will see you."

The woman led her to an office that was completely different from Anton's office at the embassy. The desk was clear except for a framed photograph and a metal in-box stacked with papers. There was an empty ashtray and two chairs covered in orange fabric.

Vera wouldn't be able to impress Mr. Matthews by sweeping away cigarette butts and screwing caps on pens.

"Good morning," Mr. Matthews greeted as he entered the room. He wore black-rimmed glasses and his shirtsleeves were rolled up. "I'm sorry if I kept you waiting."

"You have a very nice office," Vera commented.

"I'm very organized. I learned it in the army," he confessed. "Please have a seat." He waved at the chair. "Tell me, Miss Frankel. What's your favorite kind of car?"

"My favorite car?" Vera gulped. She had practiced responses to all sorts of questions: her necessary salary, her dictation speed—but her favorite car?

"General Motors is building a factory outside of Caracas and in a few months the roads will be full of American cars," he explained as if he had read her thoughts. "J. Walter Thompson has been chosen as the advertising agency tasked with making a GM the only car that Venezuelans want to drive. Everyone on the team—even the lady who caters our meetings—should have an opinion on cars."

149

Vera couldn't even pretend to know anything about the subject.

"I'm from Budapest. My parents didn't drive a car," Vera said. "They kept a car in the country, but I don't remember what it was."

"You don't remember?" he repeated.

"I was sixteen when the war came to Hungary and we stopped going to the country," she answered.

"How do you expect to write ads convincing people to buy cars if you've hardly driven in one?"

"I'm a fast learner. My parents taught me Italian and French and Spanish, and I learned to write in English from reading plays."

"This isn't a university, it's an ad agency," he grunted. "A copywriter is like cupid with an arrow. An ad only has space for a few words, but it has to pierce the heart of anyone who reads it. I'm afraid you don't have the necessary skills for the position."

Vera stood up, but something stopped her before she opened the door.

"I have a letter of recommendation." She pulled a paper from her purse. It was Anton's letter to General Ashe in Rome, asking him to find a position for her.

He scanned the letter.

"Obviously this person felt strongly about your character, but this letter doesn't say anything about your writing experience." He glanced up at Vera, her chin trembling. Vera wondered whether he could see the desperation in her eyes. "I've got to interview half a dozen girls," he announced, taking pity on her. He folded the letter and put it on the desk. "Why don't you come back this afternoon? Frankly, I don't think this is the job for you, but I can give you an answer then."

*   *   *

Vera stood on the steps of J. Walter Thompson and noticed the famous Caracas Cathedral with its bell tower and white turrets on the other side of Plaza Bolívar. But she was too nervous to appreciate it. She had spent the afternoon trying every place that might have an opening. She revisited the bookstore that sold foreign books, and the Italian and British consulates. All she got were polite rejections and offers to let her know if something opened up.

The door to the agency swung open and a girl with a leather purse and matching shoes walked out. She was smiling gaily and there was confidence in her step. The assistant copywriter job was probably hers.

Vera squeezed through the door and approached the reception desk.

"Can I help you?" the receptionist asked.

"Mr. Matthews said I should come back," Vera stammered.

The woman consulted her book. "I'm afraid he's about to leave. He has to meet some clients for cocktails."

Vera turned when the door to the inner office opened. Mr. Matthews emerged, and this time he wore a jacket over his shirt.

"Miss Frankel," he said, straightening his tie. "Please come in."

"You didn't have to wait for me," she responded. "I saw the young woman outside. It seems you made a good choice."

"The woman outside?" he repeated.

"The woman carrying the alligator-skin purse," Vera went on. "I'm sure she'll be a good addition to your team."

"Miss Jores?" He scratched his head. "She'd never do. She's getting married in six months and wanted the job to save money for her trousseau. Do you plan on getting married soon?"

"I don't think about marriage," Vera responded.

He smiled.

"You will someday." His voice was kind. "You're barely twenty years old. Come into my office."

Vera followed him inside and perched on a chair. She was thirsty from looking for a job, but she was too anxious to ask for a glass of water.

"It seems you were too modest," Mr. Matthews said as he sat at his desk. "I have it on good authority that you're a star copywriter."

"I am?" Vera repeated.

"Ricardo Albee visited the office this afternoon. He owns one of the biggest car dealerships in Caracas. He said if we hired you, he'd bring his business." He looked at Vera. "I assumed it was because you are a great copywriter."

Vera tried to think. How did Ricardo know she was applying to J. Walter Thompson? What had he told Mr. Matthews?

"I did some writing in Naples after the war." Vera thought of the letters she helped Anton write to mothers who had lost their sons.

"What kind of writing?"

"For the American army," she said quickly. "The army wasn't popular in Naples because the city was destroyed by the Allies."

"So you were assigned the task of making the Americans more likable?" He inquired. "That must have been difficult."

"It was but I enjoyed it." Vera nodded. If she wanted the job, it was better to let him believe she composed the letters herself. "It's satisfying to do a job well." She recalled the long hours of taking dictation, when her fingers curled from holding the pen.

"Your employer, this Captain Wight, gave you a glowing review, and Ricardo Albee thinks the same," he said thoughtfully. "I suppose we can try you out."

"Oh, thank you!" Vera clapped her hands. "I promise you won't regret it."

"A three-month trial period," he continued. "How does sixteen bolivares a week sound?"

Vera gulped and imagined earning sixteen bolivares a week. They could move to a room on the second floor with its own sink. Edith would be thrilled not to have to wash her face in the communal bathroom, and they'd have room to hang up their dresses.

"You can start tomorrow." He walked to the door. "There are plenty of cars in Caracas. Maybe you can borrow one and practice driving."

Vera stopped at the market in the Plaza Bolívar and bought fruit for her and Edith, and a bottle of whiskey for Lola. Now that Vera had a job, they could afford to explore the city. There were art museums, and the Sabana Grande Boulevard was lined with elegant shops. They could even take a taxi to Cerro El Ávila Mountain for the fresh air. The view was supposed to be breathtaking: Caracas nestled in a green valley and the Caribbean Sea far below. And they could sit at a café in the Plaza Venezuela without being asked to leave. It was Vera's favorite place, but the waiters gave them sour looks if they took up a table without ordering a dish to share or glasses of *chicha*. Sometimes she gazed at the lights glittering in the fountain at night and was reminded of Naples. She could almost smell the mix of gasoline and cigarettes in the air and imagine Marcus crossing the piazza to join them.

A green convertible with a yellow racing stripe was parked in front of Lola's house. Ricardo hopped out as Vera approached.

"Good evening." He greeted her and held out a potted plant. "This is for you. It's an orchid from my mother's garden."

"It's beautiful, thank you. But what are you doing here?" Vera took the plant.

"It is common courtesy in Venezuela to call on a pretty woman you meet at a ball." He bowed formally. "May I come inside?"

"Into the house?" Vera asked.

"I wasn't expecting to be invited into the bedroom. I'm guessing there is a salon." He smiled. "Or even a kitchen where I could get a glass of water."

It was evening and the other boarders were probably at home. It was perfectly safe to invite Ricardo inside.

"Please, come in." She walked up the steps. "We don't need to sit in the kitchen. There's a comfortable living room."

They entered the living room and Vera put a bowl of nuts on the coffee table. Ricardo wore a sports jacket and slacks. She hadn't seen anyone dress like that since before the war. Anton wore casual shirts when he wasn't in uniform, and the young men in Naples showed off leather jackets bought on the black market.

"How did you know which ad agency I applied to and where we live?" she inquired.

"You were applying to an English-speaking ad agency and there are only two in Caracas," he said easily. "I visited the office and your address was written on the information card."

"You copied it down?" Vera repeated. "That's private information."

Ricardo's actions unsettled her, but she didn't want to make more of a fuss. She could hardly accuse him of doing something wrong when it was because of him that she got the job.

"I wanted to see where you live." He looked around the room. "Kitty said Edith's mother was friends with Elsa Schiaparelli in Paris. With that sort of pedigree, I confess I thought your accommodations would be grander."

Vera wished Edith hadn't made up stories about her past. She didn't want to lie, but she didn't trust Ricardo enough to tell him the truth.

"Why did you tell Mr. Matthews that I was a star copywriter and you'd bring him your business if he hired me?" she asked instead. "You hardly know me."

"I guessed you didn't know anyone who could give you a recommendation," he explained. "I hope it was of some help."

She nodded. "I got the job. I wouldn't have had a chance without you."

"You are thanking me by allowing me to sit in your company," Ricardo replied. When he looked at Vera, his brown eyes were large and dark. "What do two Hungarian girls in Caracas do to enjoy themselves?"

"We haven't done anything; we've been busy trying to get jobs."

It seemed too intimate to admit they couldn't afford to sit at a café and order fruit punch with melon slices soaked in rum.

"That will change tonight," he suggested. "We'll go for a drive and celebrate. There is a salsa club that serves the best Caribe rum."

"I can't just get into your car," she laughed. "I don't know anything about you."

"I'll give you a short history," he offered. "All my life I have had a love affair with cars. When I was eighteen, I convinced my parents to take me to the Grand Prix in Monte Carlo. I was determined to be a race car driver. My mother said she hadn't spent twenty hours giving birth to a son to see him die in a ball of flames. Instead, I opened a car dealership. Tonight I am driving my favorite: a British MG."

Mr. Matthews did say she should drive in a car, and the night was so balmy. It would be lovely to sit under the stars and watch the glittering lights of the city.

"I'm too tired for a nightclub, but it might be nice to sit outside and have a cool drink."

"An excellent plan." He stood up and held out his hand. "You will love Caracas at night."

They sat at an outdoor café and Ricardo ordered *cocadas*: coconut pulp with sugar and condensed milk. It reminded Vera of the way her mother made coffee, with two sugar cubes and whole cream instead of water.

The café was on one of the pedestrian-only boulevards near Plaza Luis Brión that were so pretty. Trees arched over the road and couples strolled by, the men in light jackets and the women wearing summer dresses.

Sitting with Ricardo felt different than being with Anton. Everything about Anton had been warm and open. Ricardo was the opposite and completely unpredictable. He went a few minutes without talking and Vera couldn't tell what he was the thinking.

"I have been invited to dinner on Saturday night at the home of the Vasquezes. They own petroleum stations. You and Edith can come as my guests; it would be a good place for her to find a husband."

"Who said Edith was looking for a husband?" Vera sipped her drink.

"Why else would you both have come to Caracas?"

"We came to find jobs and make a life," she answered. "That doesn't have to revolve around men."

"Europe is rebuilding after the war; there must be jobs," he said, studying Vera. "But there might not be so many men."

"No, not so many," Vera faltered, thinking of Stefan and the boys she had known in school. Had any of them returned to Budapest, or were their bodies lying in open graves at the camps?

"There is nothing wrong with wanting a husband." He touched her hand. "It is a man's privilege to look after his wife."

"We're perfectly capable of taking care of ourselves," she answered, moving her hand. "I have the job at the ad agency and Edith is going to design dresses."

His expression grew curious. "Why do you think I suggested Clark Matthews hire you?"

"If it's because you think it gives you permission to take me home and kiss me, you wasted your time." Her cheeks flushed. "I accepted the invitation for a drink because it seemed like a pleasant way to spend the evening."

"That's not the reason. I am a big believer in women," he mused. "My father would be a clerk instead of a member of parliament if my mother didn't write his speeches. At the ball, I could tell you were very intelligent."

Ricardo hadn't done anything wrong, and she was enjoying herself. She wondered why she was irritable. Was it because no matter how hard she tried to forget Anton, she still longed to be sitting with him at a café in Naples?

"I am grateful." She nodded. "You did something nice for me even though I'm a stranger."

"I may not have fought any battles or gone days without food, but

I've seen pain," he continued. "One of my sisters was beaten by her husband, and my younger brother died when I was ten."

"I'm sorry," Vera apologized.

"Life can be bright." He waved at the sky. "We are lucky that in the summer the sun doesn't set until seven p.m. There are many hours in the day to be happy."

"You're right." She lifted her glass. "I'll take another one of these."

After they finished their rum drinks, Ricardo drove Vera home. The MG pulled up in front of Lola's house and Ricardo turned off the engine.

"Perhaps we can do this again and next time you can drive?" Ricardo suggested.

"You'll let me drive your car?" Vera wondered.

"Driving a car is the second most enjoyable thing in life." Ricardo jumped up and opened Vera's door.

The sky was a sheath of stars above the open roof of the convertible. The rum warmed her and she nodded.

"All right, I'd like that."

"You didn't ask me what the most enjoyable thing is." Ricardo helped her out of the car.

"What is it?"

"Spending the evening with a beautiful woman," he said, walking her to the door.

"Where have you been? Who were you with?" Edith asked when Vera reached their room.

Edith stood at the window. She wore a robe that Signora Rosa had given her in Naples and her hair was in curlers.

"How do you know I was with someone?" Vera asked.

"I saw him drive away." Edith pointed at the window.

"It was nothing. I got the job, and Ricardo asked me for a drink to celebrate."

"The man you danced with at the ball?" Edith inquired. "I was right! I told you he was some wealthy Venezuelan who would buy you chocolates and take you driving in his convertible."

"He didn't buy me chocolates, only a plant," Vera laughed, pointing to the orchid. She noticed a bag of buttons beside it. "What are these?"

"Aren't they beautiful?" Edith asked. "I'm going to sew them on my dress for Kitty's luncheon."

"If you spend all the money you got from the pearls, there won't be anything left," Vera reminded her.

"You have to trust in the future," Edith said.

Vera was tired as she crawled into her side of the bed while Edith continued her sewing.

Ricardo had asked why they came to Caracas. She could have said that they came to forget the past. But the truth was that they were afraid of facing a future without the people they loved.

CHAPTER THIRTEEN

March 1947

Vera sat in Lola's kitchen and ate scrambled eggs with tomatoes and onions and peppers. Everything Lola cooked was spicy compared to the creamy sauces in Naples and the potato gnocchi her mother made in Budapest. Lola laughed and said Venezuelans loved spice in their food and in their love affairs.

It had been three weeks since Vera started working at J. Walter Thompson. All day she sat at her desk and thought up catchy phrases to go in newspaper ads and magazines. She took a prepared lunch of bread and beans to save money, and bought a briefcase to carry her notepads and pens.

Ricardo picked her up most evenings and they drove around the city. Sometimes she wondered why she accepted his invitations. But Edith was busy with Kitty's parties and Lola used her living room to entertain suitors. Ricardo was pleasant company. He introduced her to Latin music and showed her parts of Caracas she never would have discovered alone.

She loved the older neighborhoods of Caracas. Colonial houses stood behind iron gates, and the boulevards were shaded by wide oak trees. She adored strolling around Las Mercedes district with its art galleries and international restaurants. Her favorite was a Sicilian restaurant that served risotto and a selection of Italian wines. She scribbled down the names to include in a letter to Signora Rosa.

Ricardo proved to be the perfect tour guide. They spent an afternoon at a coffee plantation owned by an Italian count. Vera remembered drinking Ottie's tepid coffee on the farm and picked some coffee beans to show Edith. One night they drove to a club that played joropo music in the town of Petare. Vera fell instantly in love with the haunting melodies coming from the bandola llanera. The rum warmed her throat and Ricardo's dark eyes twinkled in the candlelight, and she felt like she belonged.

But at other times she missed exploring Naples with Edith and Marcus and Paolo. They had been so glad that the war was over and there was food and drink, they were like puppies tumbling through the streets. Ricardo was more at home at elegant cocktail parties and museum openings. She spent part of those evenings in the powder room making sure her lipstick was perfectly applied and there wasn't a tear in her stockings.

Often she still longed for Anton: the way he had looked at her when she appeared at the top of the staircase in the green evening gown, the serious expression when he wanted her opinion on a letter. She thought she would feel better alone. But then she would gaze out the window of Ricardo's convertible at the blue swath of ocean or stand under the waterfall at the foot of Angel Falls and the pain of missing Anton receded. Venezuela was full of new sights and sounds, and she was determined to enjoy them.

Vera heard footsteps, and Edith rushed into the kitchen. She wore one of her new dresses. This one had a cinched waist and a slit up the skirt. "Look! It's a letter from New York!"

Vera put down her fork. Could it be from Anton's father? Vera had never written to his secretary again, but perhaps she got Vera's address from Signora Rosa. Or the letter was from Anton himself.

"It's from Marcus," Edith said.

"Marcus? What's he doing in America?"

"I'll read it to you." Edith tore it open. "Marcus should be a writer as well as a photographer. He's a very good storyteller."

" 'Bella Edith,

" 'You will never believe where I am writing! The postage stamp will give it away so I will tell you: New York City. How did a boy from a village in southern Italy come to 4 Sutton Place, New York (that's my address: write it down!)?

" 'After you left, I moved to Rome. I took photographs every-where: the Trevi Fountain at night, the Colosseum with the pink sunset creeping through the ruins, and the Vatican. I had never been truly alive until I saw Michelangelo's frescoes in the Sistine Chapel.

" 'Without you posing for the photographs, they were as bland as the soups my mother made during the war. I was so dejected, I con-sidered throwing myself into the Tiber.' " Edith looked up. "Marcus would never have killed himself; he loves to exaggerate."

"Go on," Vera urged.

" 'Then I met Anthony,' " Edith returned to the letter. " 'He was so beautiful, even Vera would have fallen in love with him. He let me take photos of him, and in exchange he stayed in my room at the pensione. At night we'd lie side by side and stroke hands, and it was the life I had always dreamed of.

" 'One afternoon I came home and found Anthony in bed with

another man. Anthony and I got into a raging fight and I kicked him out. But listen to this: an American who owns a gallery in New York saw the photos I took of Anthony. He invited me to visit. I am sitting in his apartment in Sutton Place and tonight I go to a showing of my work.'"

"Don't you see?" Vera frowned. "There's only one reason why this man would pay Marcus's fare and put him up in his apartment."

"The reason is Marcus is a genius!" Edith folded the letter. "I'm sure there are enough pretty boys in New York that he'll never have to return to Italy."

"I still don't like it," Vera said. "Marcus will get hurt."

"Marcus is an adult. He can take care of himself." Edith eyed Vera's plate. "I have to go. I'm meeting Kitty for breakfast at the Hotel Majestic."

"You can't spend all your time with Kitty," Vera urged. "She hasn't gotten you a single commission. You need to be looking for work."

"The meeting is about work," Edith replied. "There's going to be a dinner tonight in the Empire Suite. All the fashionable people will be there, and my dresses are included in the fashion show."

"What are you talking about?" Vera asked. "You haven't mentioned anything."

"An American friend of Kitty's arrived in Caracas a few days ago. His name is Robert Kinkaid. He lives in Manhattan and owns dress shops in New York and Boston. He's in Caracas to buy fabric and loves my designs. He's holding the dinner tonight in my honor."

"A dinner! That's very generous of him." Vera smiled.

"He knows how hard it is to get ahead," she responded. "And before you ask what his intentions are, he's married with a son. His wife looks like Ava Gardner. Why don't you and Ricardo come? It will be nice to have someone there I know, and you'll enjoy it."

"All right, we'll come," Vera agreed. Edith worked so hard on her dresses; all she needed was a little luck. "You know I believe in you. But we can't pay Lola with buttons and thread."

Ricardo looked particularly handsome in a navy smoking jacket when he picked her up from work. Vera glanced down at her own blue dress and thought she should have worn something more elegant.

"You look beautiful tonight." Ricardo jumped out of the MG and opened her door.

"I'll be the only woman there who hasn't spent the afternoon at the beauty parlor." Vera slipped into the passenger seat. "I worry about Edith hanging around with these rich Americans."

"Edith is more capable than you give her credit for," Ricardo said. "She's only been in Caracas for a month and already has her own fashion show."

"In Budapest our parents led simple lives." Vera glanced in the rearview mirror. Her hair needed a good brushing and she should have applied some lipstick. "Once a month my parents attended the opera, but the rest of the time they stayed home. Edith has been going out every night."

"There is nothing wrong with enjoying oneself." Ricardo reached into the glove compartment and took out a flat box. "This is for you."

"For me?" Vera repeated. "You shouldn't give me anything."

"Open it," Ricardo said, placing it in her hands. "I think you'll like it."

Vera snapped it open and inside were silver heart-shaped earrings.

"I wanted to complement your beauty," Ricardo said.

Vera remembered Anton saying she wore the same dress every day and needed to buy herself a present.

"Thank you, they're beautiful," she said, and closed the case. "But I can't accept them."

"It's a small gift. They are only silver," he pleaded.

"I'm not ready to be anything but friends," Vera stammered.

"So it is a gift between friends," he encouraged her. "Take them, be happy."

"I am happy," Vera answered. "I have a good job and a place to live."

Vera remembered when she was sixteen and a boy put a note in her schoolbag. Her mother found it and tucked it into a box. A girl should have a place for her love letters. One day Vera would grow old, and reading them would bring her happiness.

"All right, I'll wear them," Vera agreed. "Thank you, that was very thoughtful."

The Empire Suite was furnished with plush velvet sofas and glass chandeliers. There was a sideboard with platters of fruit and flan—a dessert made of custard with a caramel sauce.

Edith wore a midnight-blue dress with a narrow waist and daring neckline, like something Rosalind Russell would wear in a movie. She was chatting with a man who couldn't have been older than thirty. He had broad shoulders like an American football player and wore a beige suit.

"Vera, there you are! You must meet Robert." Edith took her arm. Ricardo had gone to get champagne and hors d'oeuvres and Vera stood alone. Edith waved at the chairs set up on opposite sides of a gold carpet. "Doesn't it look fantastic? I know the fashion show will be a success!"

"It's a pleasure," Robert said when he shook Vera's hand. "Edith has talked so much about you."

"You two get acquainted; I have to greet our guests." Edith turned to Vera and laughed. "Be nice to Robert; I told him you're overprotective."

Edith left them alone, and Vera found herself searching for something to say to Robert.

"It's so kind of you to do this for Edith," Vera said awkwardly.

"I feel like there's a 'but' at the end of that sentence," Robert chuckled.

"This must have cost a fortune," Vera replied. "I don't want Edith to get hurt."

"You mean, do I have ulterior motives?" Robert asked. "Let me tell you about myself. I was the first in my family to go to college. If I hadn't, I probably would have been blown up somewhere over France. Instead, I married my college sweetheart and had a son." He took out a wallet and showed her a picture of a pretty blonde and a boy with freckles. "When life brings you luck, you have to pass it on."

"You hardly know Edith," Vera countered.

"I know talent when I see it." Robert smiled. "Have a glass of champagne and relax. Edith's dresses are going to be the hit of Caracas."

Ricardo returned with two champagne glasses and small plates of sweet bread stuffed with olives and raisins. The lights dimmed and the guests crowded around the runway.

The first model appeared in a tailored skirt and a matching jacket. The outfit was finished off with a wide hat and two-tone shoes. The second model wore a silver evening gown as light and airy as a meringue. And then the last model started down the runway in a crepe pantsuit, and even Vera was surprised.

Edith never told her she had designed pants! They were smart and elegant and the whole room broke into applause.

Vera started across the room to congratulate Edith when a woman carrying a glass of champagne bumped into her. The champagne spilled on Vera's dress.

Robert appeared beside her. "You'd better dab that in soapy water or it will stain. Come with me, you can use the bathroom."

Vera followed him through the suite's bedroom. A robe was flung over a chair and Vera froze. The lettering above the pocket read WIGHT HOTEL, BOSTON.

"Where did you get that robe?" she gasped.

Vera remembered the ad she had seen for Wight Hotels in Marcus's *LIFE* magazine.

"I collect robes when I travel," Robert said in amusement. "The Wight is my favorite hotel in Boston. It's like being invited into an elegant home."

Vera's face grew hot and she thought about the letter she sent to Anton's father. She had been so hopeful that he would come for them at Ellis Island.

"Are you all right?" Robert asked. "You look like you've seen a ghost."

"I'm fine; I have to go." She turned back to the living room.

He stopped her. "What about the stain?"

"It's not even a good dress. I might not wear it again."

*   *   *

Vera sat in the passenger seat of Ricardo's convertible and concentrated on the road. Usually after a dinner party, they made comments while they drove. But she couldn't think about anything except the robe.

"What happened in the bedroom?" Ricardo asked.

"What are you talking about?" Vera turned her attention to the driver's seat. Ricardo was clutching the steering wheel and driving too fast, even for him.

"That Kinkaid fellow took you into the bedroom and you came out white as a sheet," Ricardo said through gritted teeth. "If he tried anything, I'll go back and put a pistol to his head." She was surprised by the anger in his voice.

"Don't be silly. He wanted to get the stain out of my dress."

"The stain is still there." Ricardo pointed to her skirt. "Something must have happened."

Vera had never told Ricardo about Anton. Ricardo said he gave her the earrings out of friendship, but she could sense he wanted more. Vera was afraid of hurting his feelings and didn't know how to discourage him. But if he got that jealous over a stranger leading her through his bedroom, what would he say when she revealed she had been engaged?

"It was my fault. I was reminded of the past," Vera explained. "All I wanted was to leave."

"The suites in the Hotel Majestic are furnished in a European style." Ricardo reached over and squeezed her hand. "You are very brave. Time will make the ghosts go away. In Venezuela we have a saying: 'life is for the living.'"

"I'm sure you're right," Vera said, and wondered if it was different when one of the ghosts was still alive.

*   *   *

Vera took off the silver earrings and placed them on the dresser. She shouldn't have accepted them; Ricardo might expect something in return. But it would have been rude to refuse when Ricardo had been so kind, buying her dinners and escorting her to the fashion show.

"Look!" Edith burst into their room.

Vera noticed the pieces of paper in her hand.

"More letters from Marcus in New York?"

"Something better!" Edith exclaimed. "Orders for dresses from the fashion show."

"That's wonderful!" Vera hugged her.

"I got the idea for the pantsuit from Kitty's magazines." Edith sat on the bed. "You should see the fashions in America: gowns with billowing skirts because there is no shortage of fabric. You can wear the next dress I design; it will have shoulder pads and a fitted jacket and it will be perfect for the office."

"It would be my pleasure." Vera smiled. "I'll tell everyone it's an Edith Ban original."

"Tomorrow Robert is taking me to lunch." Edith took off her earrings. "We're going to meet a fabric supplier."

"Doesn't Robert have his own work?" Vera was suddenly wary. He was good-looking, and his wife and child were thousands of miles away.

"You still think he's trying to seduce me?" Edith demanded. "You work with men, why can't I do the same?"

Edith was right. Besides the receptionist and the woman who brought sandwiches, Vera was the only woman in the office.

"I'm sorry," Vera apologized. "He's lucky to know someone so talented."

"This is just the beginning. One day, my dresses will be in department stores in Philadelphia and New York."

"What about London and Paris?" Vera asked gaily.

"So some German can come in and try on my gowns? I'd rather stab myself with a pair of scissors." Edith's eyes darkened. "I'm never going back to Europe. Our lives are in South America."

CHAPTER FOURTEEN

May 1947

Vera sat at her desk at J. Walter Thompson and studied a sketch of a boxy yellow car. A blond in a bathing suit was draped over the hood, and the background showed the green of the Cerro El Ávila and the blue of the Caribbean.

She was happier at work than she could have imagined. The small office had plenty of friendly people. Besides Mr. Matthews, there was an account executive named Mike from New York. Mike was stationed in Scotland during the war and accepted the position in Caracas because of the warm climate. The head copywriter, Harold, was in his thirties and had a thick Boston accent. Only the art director, Juan, was from Venezuela. His office was lined with movie posters; he thought creating ads for cars was his ticket to Hollywood somehow.

Vera often wished her mother could see her name on the plaque on her desk. She would have been so proud to read her English copy: EXPLORE VENEZUELA IN A CAR AS THRILLING AS THE SCENERY, under the photo of a red car parked in front of a colonial building in the town of El Hatillo.

There was a tapping sound, and Mr. Matthews stood outside her cubicle

"Come in," Vera said. "I was going to ask your opinion on this sketch. The model is blond, but most of the women in Venezuela have dark hair." She handed him the piece of paper.

"Juan thinks all the models should look like Lana Turner. I'll ask him to fix it." Mr. Matthews picked up the ad. "A gentleman called earlier; he wanted to speak to you."

"A gentleman?" Vera repeated.

"A Captain Bingham?"

She couldn't keep the surprise from her face. How had he found her? What did he want? Perhaps it was about Anton. Maybe they had been in touch since he'd disappeared.

"Why is he here?" Her voice was a whisper.

"He wouldn't say over the phone." Mr. Matthews looked uncomfortable. "He wanted to tell you in person. He's here."

"Here in Caracas?" Vera couldn't have been more shocked if Mr. Matthews announced he'd come from the moon.

"Here, outside the office," Mr. Matthews said gently. "He said it couldn't wait. I wanted to check with you first."

"Please, bring him in."

Mr. Matthews glanced around the small space. "Why don't you use my office? This is a private conversation and these walls are thin as paper."

Vera sat in Mr. Matthew's office and Captain Bingham appeared in the doorway. He looked older than she remembered. There were deep lines on his forehead.

"Vera!" He took off his cap. "Look at you. So lovely and grown-up. I wouldn't have recognized you."

"I wouldn't have recognized you, either," she waved at the orange chair. "Please sit down. It seems much longer than fourteen months."

"A lifetime." Captain Bingham nodded soberly. "Mr. Matthews said you're a wonderful addition to the team. I'm so happy to see you thriving."

"What are you doing in Caracas?"

"As you can see, I'm still in the army." He waved at his uniform. "I've been promoted, got a purple heart and everything."

"A purple heart?" Vera asked quizzically.

"I was driving in a jeep near Dusseldorf when a landmine exploded," he replied. "I wasn't injured badly. Just enough to be sent home."

"I'm sorry, that's terrible," Vera gasped.

"I met a pretty nurse at the rehabilitation hospital, and we got married last month." He pointed to his gold wedding band. "Serena and I are in Caracas on our honeymoon."

"Your honeymoon." Vera tried to hide her disappointment. It wasn't about her mother or Anton. Captain Bingham happened to be in Venezuela and decided to look her up.

"How did you know where to find me?" she asked.

"I didn't," he said slowly. "I got a letter and started looking."

"A letter?" Vera's heart hammered so loudly she was certain he could hear it.

Vera reached up for a glass of water.

"From Budapest." He looked at her. "From Alice Frankel."

Her hand slipped and the glass fell to the floor. Captain Bingham bent down to pick up the pieces and Vera steadied herself on the armrest.

"I'm sorry," she said. "I was sure you said there was a letter from my mother."

"There is. Somehow it made it to my desk in Washington." He smiled, and for a moment the haggardness disappeared. "It's funny how the army works. It could as easily have been buried under dinner invitations for some general. Instead it came to me," he said. "I cleared my schedule to find you."

"What kind of letter?" Vera asked. She still couldn't get her hopes up. Maybe her mother had written it in a concentration camp before she died.

"Your mother is alive. Your old neighbor, Miriam Gold, is a smart woman. When your mother returned from the camps, you had disappeared. Miriam recalled my visit and suggested Alice write to me. There is no American embassy in Budapest, so she contacted a relative in London. The relative got my address and forwarded your mother's letter." His voice caught. "I decided to deliver it in person. It's not the sort of thing a twenty-year-old girl should have to receive in the mail."

"Tell me what's in it," Vera said quietly.

Vera couldn't quite grasp that her mother had survived. All the days and nights she had longed to see her again, and now her dreams were coming true. She felt guilty that she had given up hope. If she had searched harder, perhaps they would have been together sooner.

Captain Bingham drummed his fingers on the chair as if he needed courage to tell the story.

"Alice and Lily weren't sent to the gas chamber, they were only moved to a different part of the camp. But in January 1945, they were part of the death march."

Vera had read about the terrible death march. The Germans knew the Russians were coming, so they rounded up prisoners and forced them to march thirty-five miles to Wodzislaw.

"The object was to shoot the prisoners so the Russians wouldn't discover the dead bodies at the camps. One day Edith's mother collapsed and was shot on the spot," Captain Bingham continued. "Alice was made to keep walking. Eventually she was put on a train to Flossenbürg in Germany."

"And from there?" Vera had heard of the concentration camp in Germany where thousands of Jews had died.

"Flossenbürg was liberated in April 1945. The Germans made the prisoners leave before the Americans arrived. The SS fled, and your mother and hundreds of other Jews escaped. She hid in the forest and another escapee helped her to a village. After that she got sick and the next months were hazy. When she finally returned to Budapest you were gone, and she didn't know how to contact you."

"And my father?" Vera said, hope and grief mingling in her chest.

"He survived, too." Captain Bingham nodded. "They are together."

Vera sat up straighter and the room seemed to spin. It wasn't the Venezuelan sun that made patterns on the rug; it was the sun at their country house outside of Budapest. She saw her mother waving them in for dinner, Edith and Stefan stealing a kiss, their hair wet from swimming. It was her fault that she and her parents were on different continents. If only she had returned to Budapest, they would all be together.

"How did you find me?" Vera asked.

"I wrote to the American embassy in Naples but it was closed. Then I tried the embassy in Rome and got nothing. Last week I got a letter from a woman named Gina."

"Gina?" Vera's eyes widened.

"She was still employed to clean the embassy in Naples," he said with a smile. "In her letter she said to tell you the tomatoes from the garden are particularly sweet and she's going to send you a jar of tomato sauce."

"I never wrote to Gina," Vera commented. "How would she know where I was?"

"She didn't. When she discovered my letter she went to your landlady, a Signora Rosa," Captain Bingham finished. "Signora Rosa had your address."

Vera felt as exhausted as if she were the letter traveling from Budapest to London to Washington to Naples and then to Caracas.

"All these people went to so much trouble to find me?" she asked in wonderment.

"You and Edith made quite an impression." He acknowledged

"They are still in Budapest?" she asked. "I wouldn't ask for your help, but I must bring them to Venezuela." Vera's mind was racing. She couldn't go back to Budapest. It would be too painful for Edith, and she wouldn't go without her. Their lives were here now. Vera had a good job and Edith's career was blossoming. She had to go down to the ship offices and find out the cost of two tickets to Caracas.

"I don't know how to thank you." She leaned forward and kissed his cheek.

He rubbed his cheek and grinned. "My wife wanted to see South America. It seemed like the perfect excuse to come on honeymoon."

Vera sat in the streetcar and looked for the stop of the shipping office. She had thanked Captain Bingham and made him promise he would bring his wife to Lola's for dinner before they left Caracas.

The letter from her mother was folded in her purse, but she didn't want to take it out in public. What if she started crying like she had at the office? She would read it in her room after work.

Her heart broke for Edith. How could Vera share her miraculous news when the same letter described how Edith's mother had been shot and left for dead? And what about Stefan? Vera hadn't asked if there was any news of him. Edith was sure Stefan was dead, and Vera was beginning to believe her.

She had to find the money to bring her parents to Caracas. Her wages barely covered their lodging, and Edith hadn't been paid yet for her commissions. Ricardo would lend it to her, but it was bad enough that she accepted the silver earrings. If she asked Ricardo for anything, she'd have to acknowledge their relationship was more than a friendship.

The Cunard office was decorated with posters of huge cruise ships. There was a poster of a ship sailing under the Sydney Harbour Bridge. The sky was pale blue and the harbor was a sheet of glass. And there was another of a ship docked at some tropical port. The passengers stood on the deck in floral shirts, and waiters carried drinks in carved-out coconuts.

"Can I help you?" the woman behind the counter asked.

"How much are two tickets from Budapest?"

The woman consulted her book. "The closest port is Venice. What date did you have in mind?"

"The soonest date you have," Vera said.

"The next ship leaves in three weeks, but it's fully booked."

"Fully booked?" Vera repeated.

"We still get thousands of European immigrants a month," the woman said pleasantly. "The next available berths are in two months."

"Two months!" Vera exclaimed, disappointment settling over her.

"The *Mauretania* is our latest ship; it was refitted and returned to service this year," The woman flipped a page. "The price for two berths is a hundred bolivares."

"I didn't mean a first-class cabin," Vera responded. "Third class will do."

The woman closed her book and looked at Vera expectantly. "That is for a third-class cabin."

Vera stepped off the streetcar and walked back to the office. One hundred bolivares was two months' salary. She could ask Mr. Matthews for an advance, but what would she and Edith live on?

Ricardo's green MG was parked in front of the office.

"Ricardo? What are you doing here?"

"I came to pick you up." He was wearing a blazer and a boater hat. "Tonight is the opening of Alberto's new nightclub. We promised we'd be there."

"I'm sorry, I completely forgot." Vera shook her head. "Please, tell him another time."

"I don't like letting friends down," Ricardo said with a frown. "How will it look if his nightclub is empty?"

"I can't tonight; I have a headache," Vera said. "Besides, I didn't bring anything to wear."

Vera wasn't ready to tell him that her parents were still alive. She had hardly spoken to him about her parents. She didn't know how she could bring them to Caracas, and she didn't want Ricardo to offer to pay their fare. If he did, she would feel like she owed him something.

"I'll take you home so you can change." Ricardo opened the passenger door. "The nightclub is supposed to be fantastic. It will be good for you. You can't work day and night."

Vera was too hot and tired to argue. It was better just to go. She could always say her headache was worse and excuse herself.

"All right." She slipped into the passenger seat. "But if my head keeps throbbing, you'll have to take me home."

They drove out of the city and reached a villa set in the middle of lush tropical grounds. The private home had been turned into a night-club, and from the terrace there was a view of the Cerro El Ávila. A bartender mixed drinks in a silver shaker and the stars seemed close enough to touch.

"Ricardo, you came!" A man wearing a white dinner jacket greeted them. "And you brought the lovely Vera." He kissed Vera's hand and turned to a woman wearing a silver crepe dress. "This is Elena. She is pretending to be in love with me, but I suspect she's only dating me for the free food and cocktails."

"Alberto think he's funny, but he has the sense of humor of a school-boy." Elena pecked Vera on the cheek. "It's a pleasure to meet you."

Ricardo wandered off with Alberto to see the nightclub and Vera stood on the terrace with Elena.

"I've only met Alberto once; have you been dating long?" Vera asked, leaning against the balcony and admiring the sparkling lights below them.

"Long enough to learn to put up with his jokes," Elena said with a smile. "Alberto can be childish, but he has a good heart." She shrugged and nursed her drink. "And a woman needs a man in Ven-ezuela. Without one, she'd have to eat all her meals at home. And I'm a terrible cook."

"What do you mean?" Vera wondered.

"You haven't been in Caracas long. It's not like America, where it's becoming more accepted for a woman to ask for a table for one at a restaurant or dine out at night with a friend. Here it's frowned on for a woman to dine in public without a man. And a married woman would never go out without her husband."

Vera was puzzled. In Naples, she and Edith ate at restaurants by themselves. And her mother had described the smoky cafés she practically lived in when she was a dance student in Paris.

"But it's the 1940s," Vera protested. "And lots of women work in Caracas. I'm a copywriter at an advertising agency."

"The workplace has changed since girls started attending university," Elena conceded. "But society in Venezuela is very traditional. If a woman is out at night, it seems like she's looking for something."

"Looking for something?" Vera repeated.

"You know, hoping to find a man." Elena finished her drink. "But you don't have to worry. From the expression on Ricardo's face, I can see he'll never let you out of his sight. You're lucky, he's one of the best catches in Caracas."

Vera was about to protest that they weren't involved, when Ricardo and Alberto appeared.

"I hope Elena has only been saying nice things about me and the nightclub," Alberto said, taking Elena's arm. "I need as many customers as I can get."

Alberto and Elena drifted off to meet other diners, and Ricardo led her to a table.

The waiter handed them two menus and Ricardo smiled at Vera.

"Please allow me to order for both of us. Alberto told me all the best dishes."

The waiter took their order and Vera sat back in her chair. Every course the waiter brought looked delicious: the arepas stuffed with beef and corn, the braised pork chops, and the silky caramel flan. But Vera barely managed a bite of each without feeling as if she was choking.

"You haven't tried the dessert." Ricardo pointed to her plate.

Vera took a bite. "Everything tastes wonderful. I'm sorry; I'm just distracted."

"Was it the American officer who distracted you?"

"What are you talking about?" she wondered.

"I stopped by your office at lunch and saw you with an American officer." Ricardo waved his hand.

"That was Captain Bingham; we met in Austria after the war."

"An American captain who came all the way to Venezuela to see you?" Ricardo demanded.

"Captain Bingham got married last month and he's here on his honeymoon," she continued. She looked at him seriously. "But what would it matter if he wasn't married? You and I agreed to be just friends."

"You accepted my silver earrings."

Vera looked at Ricardo sharply. She wanted to jump up, but it was five kilometers to Caracas, and she didn't have money for a taxi.

"I'd be happy to give the earrings back."

"I don't want them back. I want to know why an American captain was visiting you. He seemed very familiar."

"Please take me home." Vera stood and snatched up her evening bag.

"There is something you're not telling me," Ricardo said stubbornly. "I'll take you home when you tell me what it is."

"All right, I'll tell you," she relented. "But not here. In the car."

They found Alberto, and Ricardo offered his apologies for leaving early. Alberto thanked them for coming and made them promise to stay for the dancing next time.

"Captain Bingham brought a letter from my mother," she said when they sat in the car in front of the nightclub. The night air was warm, and Vera fiddled with her earrings. "My mother and Edith's mother, Lily, were in a concentration camp at Auschwitz during the war. Weeks before Auschwitz was liberated, the Germans began moving the inmates out of the camp," she continued. "Edith's mother collapsed and was shot. My mother was put on a train to Flossenbürg and is alive."

Vera's hair had been tossed by the breeze and fell across her cheek. Ricardo picked it up and tucked it behind her ear. The glass of *ponche* with rum she had at dinner and Ricardo's gentle touch caused her defenses to fall away.

She laid her head on the dashboard and sobbed: She cried for Stefan, who would never stand in a synagogue and see Edith in a lace wedding dress. She cried for her mother, who witnessed her best friend shot like a dog, and for Edith and her father and every other Jew who lost parents or children. She cried for the Budapest she had loved and might not see again.

"Vera, *querida*, my darling. I am so sorry. You're the bravest girl I have ever met. Let me help you. Let me make it better for you," Ricardo said.

Vera lifted her head and there was a depth to Ricardo's eyes she hadn't seen. He leaned forward and she met him halfway. She tipped her face up to his and he kissed her.

"Please forgive me," Ricardo whispered. "I acted like an oaf."

"I should have told you right away," Vera answered. "I wasn't ready to talk about it."

"So young and the witness of so much evil." He stroked her cheek. "In Venezuela we protect our women. If any man tries to hurt you, I will cut out his heart."

Vera stood by the window of Lola's living room and waited for Edith to arrive. The room was arranged for when Lola returned with her beau: a bottle of brandy with two glasses, a bouquet of flowers in a vase, and a selection of pralines from Lola's favorite chocolate shop.

Ricardo had offered to keep her company, but Vera wanted to see Edith alone.

"You're home!" Edith entered the room. She wore a pleated skirt and carried a bundle of fabrics. "We had dinner with a fabric supplier." She dropped the fabrics on the table. "Peruvian wool and cotton from Argentina. See this green linen! It's for a dress for a well-known model. She's going to wear it with emerald earrings that match the linen."

"How did you pay for this?" Vera asked. "Don't tell me you've been back to the pawnshop."

"Don't worry, I didn't pawn Lola's candlesticks." Edith smiled. "Robert loaned me the money. It's called 'buying on credit.' I'm going to pay him back when I deliver my first dress. I even insisted on paying him interest."

"It makes me nervous." Vera frowned. "All the money goes out, but nothing comes in."

"That's how you start a business." Edith sat on the sofa. "Maria taught me in Naples. She borrowed fifty thousand lire from her ex-husband. She had to promise to take him back if she couldn't repay him," Edith laughed. "He was still in love with her, but she despised him. She paid him back with interest in the first six months."

"If you're sure," Vera said doubtfully. She didn't want to make Edith more unhappy now.

"I've never been more certain of anything," Edith replied. "What are you doing home so early? I saw Ricardo speeding off. Don't tell me he tried something. Robert was a boxer in college. He can pay Ricardo a visit."

"Ricardo is fine," Vera said. "I had the most unexpected visitor. Captain Bingham."

It took a moment for the name to register.

"Captain Bingham?" Edith repeated. "From Austria?"

"He's in Caracas on his honeymoon," Vera continued. "He brought a letter."

"If it's official documentation that Stefan is dead, he could have saved himself the trip," Edith retorted. "I've known he's been dead for years. I don't need a letter of condolence from an American GI who spent the war shuffling papers while Stefan dug graves for his fellow inmates."

"We don't know that's what Stefan was doing. It could have been anything."

"We've heard enough accounts to guess," Edith said. "Regardless, Stefan was rebuilding bombed railroads so the Germans could transport more Jews to their deaths. Either way, he died knowing he was helping the murderers who killed him."

"The letter wasn't about Stefan. It was from my mother."

"Your mother?" Edith gasped, her eyes wide as saucers. "But our mothers are dead."

"They weren't sent to the gas chamber. Instead they were made to do forced labor. They were part of the death march before Auschwitz were liberated." Vera looked at Edith and the words caught in her throat. "Your mother was very weak. She collapsed on the way; she didn't make it."

Edith stiffened and her face turned pale. She picked up one of Lola's pralines and put it back on the plate. When she looked back at Vera, her cheeks were hollow and she had bitten her lip until it bled.

"You mean she was shot," Edith said coldly. "We read the reports in the newspapers. The Germans didn't simply let the weak die. They helped them along."

Edith's eyes were bright as candles, and Vera had never seen her in so much pain.

"I'm so sorry," Vera whispered. "My mother was sent to Flossen-bürg. She's alive."

"I'm happy that Alice is alive, but how many times in this war does someone have to die?" Edith railed. "I've known my mother was dead for almost two years. Do I have to learn it again? How can we begin to live if we keep hearing our loved ones have died like a broken record on the phonograph?" She picked up her fabrics and opened the door. "If you get a letter saying Stefan is dead, I don't want to hear it."

"Where are you going?" Vera warned. "It's dangerous to walk around Caracas at night."

"It's not dangerous," Edith said. "What's dangerous is to lie in bed and wonder why the people we love are now dirt used to make flowers grow. Because if I think about that, I don't want to live."

CHAPTER FIFTEEN

June 1947

It had been two weeks since Vera received her mother's letter and her relationship with Ricardo had changed. They were spending a lot more time together. It wasn't quite love, but Ricardo was polite and she enjoyed his company. She was grateful to be able to experience Caracas with someone. And she loved strolling along the Guaire River that flowed through the city and reminded her of her beloved Danube.

Every night when Ricardo brought her home, they sat in his car and kissed. It was only then, with the top of the MG down, that she longed for Anton. She kept her eyes closed and tried to blot out the image of Anton standing in Anacapri, telling her that new artists and philosophers would rise from the dust of Hitler's Europe.

"How do I look?" Edith entered Lola's kitchen and interrupted her musings. It was Sunday morning and Lola and the other borders were at church.

"You're dressed formally for a Sunday." Vera noticed Edith's two-piece suit and matching hat. "Don't tell me Robert convinced you to go to church."

"Of course not. He's there now." Edith shook her head. "Robert goes every Sunday; it makes him feel closer to his wife and son in Boston when they pray at the same time."

"He would feel closer if he went home," Vera muttered, pouring two cups of coffee.

"He can't go home; all his suppliers are in South America." Edith accepted the cup of coffee. "I came to tell you my news. I finished my first dress and Robert is going to help me deliver it."

"That's wonderful," Vera agreed. "But why would Robert need to help you with that?"

"The client's name is Edna Burrows and she spends half the year in Venezuela and the other half in Boston." Edith sipped her coffee. "She and her husband have a stud farm five hours from Caracas. They invited us to be their dinner guests."

"Five hours! It will be late by the time you finish dinner," Vera started. "And Venezuelans are terrible drivers. It's not safe to be on the road late at night."

"Robert agrees with you. He thinks all Venezuelans should have their licenses taken away," Edith laughed. "That's why we're going to come back tomorrow."

"What did you say?" Vera asked.

"It was Edna's idea." Edith put down her cup. "They have a guest wing and a separate hacienda in the back. I'll sleep in the guest wing and Robert will stay in the hacienda. There won't be any chance of bumping into each other in the corridor on the way to the bathroom at night."

"How will that look?" Vera wondered nervously. "Robert is married. Even if he wasn't, you can't go away with a man."

"You went to Capri with Anton," Edith reminded her.

"That was different," Vera said, her cheeks turning scarlet.

"You stayed in the same hotel," Edith pointed out.

"Anton's parents took him to the Hotel Quisisana before the war. He wanted to show it to me," Vera responded. "We had rooms on different floors."

Vera still hadn't told Edith the whole truth: that she knocked on Anton's door and begged him to let her in. That she urged him to make love to her because they were engaged and going to be together forever.

"You called him Captain Wight, but you were in love with him even then. I saw it in your eyes."

"Of course I called him Captain Wight; he was my boss," Vera exclaimed. "I didn't realize I had feelings for him, they just grew."

"We keep talking about Robert when there is nothing to say," Edith went on. "You're the one who sits in Ricardo's car in front of the house. Twenty minutes last night."

"How do you know?" Vera asked.

"I counted. I was standing by the window," Edith said. "If it hadn't been a convertible, the windows would have been steamed up."

"You couldn't see anything in the dark," Vera responded.

"Why shouldn't you see Ricardo?" Edith asked. "He's charming and he looks like Clark Gable."

"Ricardo would look ridiculous with a mustache," Vera giggled. Suddenly they were two young women swooning over actors in American movie magazines.

"He's obviously in love with you," Edith insisted.

"I do enjoy his company, but he's just moving fast," Vera said tentatively. "He wants me to meet his mother."

Vera thought about how quickly her romance with Anton moved, but that was different. From the moment Anton said he was falling in love with her, she felt like she had known him forever.

"She will adore you," Edith assured her. "When will you meet her?"

"Today," Vera sighed. "We're going to lunch at his parents' villa."

Ricardo's parents lived in one of the huge colonial-style houses near the Plaza Venezuela. The entry was as imposing as the Palazzo Mezzi in Naples. There was a sweeping staircase and tall French doors leading into an inner courtyard.

"You look like you're waiting for the schoolmistress," Ricardo chuckled, leading her into the living room. Ceiling fans turned overhead, and white sofas were flanked by palm trees in clay pots.

"Does your mother know I'm Jewish?" Vera whispered, noticing the collection of gold crosses on the mantel. Why hadn't she asked Ricardo before? But meeting his parents had been so sudden; she didn't have time to ask questions.

"Of course she knows you're Jewish," Ricardo responded. "I told her everything about you: you're a star copywriter and so beautiful that a famous philanthropist sponsored you to come to America."

"You shouldn't have said that. She'll think I have a big head."

"You don't have a big head." He laughed at her English. "But you have a bright mind. My mother is a great admirer of intellect; you'll get along wonderfully."

A door opened and Ricardo's parents entered the living room. Ricardo's father was an older version of Ricardo. His dark hair was streaked with gray and his cheeks were tan from the sun. He wore a white suit and the most polished shoes Vera had ever seen.

But Ricardo's mother was younger than she expected, and quite beautiful. Alessandra Albee had the face and figure of a model. She wore a form-fitting crepe dress and smelled of jasmine perfume.

"Vera." She kissed Vera on the cheek. "Ricardo told us so much about you."

"It's wonderful to meet you. You have a beautiful home," Vera answered.

"I can't take much credit; it's my husband's childhood home." She patted the sofa. "Come sit next to me."

Ricardo handed them pink cocktails with paper umbrellas.

"Please go help your father choose a bottle of wine," Alessandra said to Ricardo. "Vera and I are getting to know each other."

"It's normal to be nervous," she said after Ricardo left. "I had to take a sleeping drought when I met Pedro's mother, then I almost fell asleep in my soup. But I promise we're harmless. Pedro and I want Ricardo to be happy."

Vera's eyes traveled to the marble fountain in the courtyard and vases filled with roses. "Ricardo never mentioned you had such a beautiful house."

"From when he was a boy, I taught him the true value of money is to take care of the people you love." She pointed to her wedding ring. "My ring belonged to Pedro's grandmother and this house is inherited from Pedro's parents. But every centimo that comes into it has to be put to good use. The reason we have household help is so that Diego, the gardener, and Valeria, our cook, can afford to feed their own children. Plus, I'm terrible in the kitchen." She smiled and then turned serious again. "My grandparents were so poor, their house didn't have a floor. And Pedro's ancestors fled the Spanish Inquisition with what was in their pockets."

Vera nodded. "My parents lost everything in the war. I'm hoping to bring them to Caracas."

"The world has not seen anything like what happened in Europe. I may be Catholic, but what Hitler did to the Jews was the devil at work. But where there is life, there is hope." Alessandra stood up. "Come, let's eat. Ricardo and his father are similar. They both get cranky when they are hungry."

Lunch was served at the oak table in the dining room. Ricardo's father poured glasses of red wine and Alessandra led a lively discussion about female enrollment at the Central University of Venezuela.

"My wife is a fervent supporter of education," Ricardo's father said, smiling. "She would like to see all young people attend university."

"My parents wanted me to go to university, but the war interrupted everything," Vera said. "I was going to study languages and possibly writing. I wanted to write plays."

Alessandra picked up her wineglass. "The war is exactly why the young must attend university. Do you know what the most important human trait is? It is not piety, as our Catholic priests would wish; it's not honesty or even loyalty. It is empathy. If we don't have empathy for others, we are finished. How can we learn empathy without studying history and geography and literature?"

"That's enough of a lecture; it's time for dessert," Pedro said fondly. "Our cook makes the tastiest dulce de leche in Caracas. You must try it."

After lunch, the men smoked cigars in the library and Vera and Alessandra sat in the living room.

"I take it you are very close to your parents," Alessandra said, sipping a cup of dark coffee.

"How did you know?" Vera asked in surprise. The dulce de leche had been delicious—condensed milk and caramel spooned onto thin slices of toast. But the coffee was too strong, and Vera left her cup on its saucer.

"I can see it in your eyes when you talk about them," Alessandra commented. "My children are the best thing I've ever done. I was lucky to have four. Ricardo has two married sisters." She paused. "Tragically, my youngest son, Enrico, was run over by a tractor and died when he was eight."

"Ricardo told me. I'm so sorry." Vera nodded.

"It is the worst thing that can happen to a mother." Alessandra was somber. "Do you have brothers or sisters?"

"I'm an only child. I suppose that's why I've always wanted a large family," Vera answered. "My friend Edith and I were born three days apart at the same hospital; she's always been like a sister."

"It's important to have someone to talk to, especially with everything you've gone through." Alessandra put down her cup. "Ricardo said you just turned twenty. I can't imagine the hardships you've had at your age. To lose your home and your country is unthinkable."

"Edith and I turned twenty in April." Vera replied. "At least this year I know my parents are alive. Last birthday, I thought they were both dead."

"I was barely sixteen when I married Pedro," Alessandra said thoughtfully. "He was an old man of twenty-five. Ricardo is twenty-seven, and people wonder why he's not married. Ricardo is old-fashioned; he believes in love." She leaned back against the cushions. "I taught him two things: to love and respect his parents, and then to love his wife even more."

*   *   *

Ricardo drove Vera home and they sat in his car in front of the house.

"Your mother is wonderful," Vera said. "She looks like a movie star and she's so intelligent."

"My mother is a modern woman and she's not afraid to speak her opinions," he chuckled. "I told you she would like you."

"How do you know she liked me?" Vera asked. "I didn't even finish high school, and my Spanish isn't that good."

"She called you *mija* when we said good-bye." He leaned forward and kissed her.

Vera put her fingers to her mouth and gulped. Even she knew that *mija* was Spanish slang for "my daughter."

CHAPTER SIXTEEN

June 1947

Vera looked up from her notepad and glanced at the clock in Lola's living room. Ricardo was picking her up in half an hour, but she was still sorting numbers into two columns. No matter how she arranged them, she simply didn't have enough money to bring her parents to Caracas. And she didn't want to return to Budapest with them; they all needed a fresh start.

She had written to her parents telling them how overjoyed she was that they were alive, giving them news of her and Edith. But she felt guilty that she couldn't promise when she would bring them to Venezuela. She had to find a way to afford their passage.

She tried everything: asking Mr. Matthews if she could bring work home from the office, begging Lola to let her do the ironing. But it would be months until she could afford the tickets.

"You look glum for a Saturday night," Edith said as she breezed into the room. She had a silk cape draped over a turquoise dress.

"I've been doing sums and my head is about to split open," Vera moaned. "If I iron Lola's tablecloths for three months, I still won't be able to pay the ship fare. Mr. Matthews can't give me any more work.

Until the rollout of the GM cars, the New York office is watching every centimo."

"I could ask Kitty for the money," Edith offered. "She spends that much on a new purse."

"You can't ask Kitty for money. She's already done so much for you."

"Ricardo would lend you the money," Edith said. "I heard a rumor that he's going to ask you to marry him."

"Where did you hear that?" Vera asked.

"From a friend of Kitty's," Edith giggled. "A few of the women are heartbroken that he'll be off the market."

"That's ridiculous. We've only known each other for a few months," Vera said.

"Ricardo isn't young, and he's already introduced you to his parents."

"He did say he had a surprise for me tonight," Vera said uneasily. "We're going to the opening of the new wing at the Museo de Bellas Artes."

"What if he drops to his knee and proposes in front of a naked marble statue?" Edith giggled.

"It's not going to happen." Vera shook her head. "And I would never marry Ricardo to bring my parents to Caracas."

"Of course not, that would just be an extra perk," Edith suggested. "Like having a husband who is a great chef. Every marriage needs perks." Edith adjusted her stole. "Besides in the bedroom, of course."

"That's no way to talk," Vera said.

She noticed the diamond pendant around Edith's neck.

"Where did you get that?" she asked, pointing to it.

"Don't worry, it's fake. It's made of paste." Edith's eyes danced. "Robert and I have a meeting with the general manager of the Majestic. Robert thinks I should rent a little space to showcase my dresses. Wouldn't it be wonderful if every woman who enters the hotel lobby sees an Edith Ban design?"

"Why do you need a diamond pendant?" Vera asked.

"It's the best way to negotiate the price. As if I'm doing the hotel a favor by allowing them to show my designs." She ran her fingers over her neck. "I feel richer just wearing it."

"You're going to be a fashion mogul and I'll still be an assistant copywriter working ten hours a day to afford a pair of shoes," Vera said fondly.

"Not if you marry Ricardo." Edith hugged her and walked to the door. "Then you can buy shoes all day long."

Vera stood at her bedroom window and heard a car pull up outside. She rubbed her wrists with perfume and hurried downstairs.

"You smell wonderful tonight." Ricardo kissed her when she opened the door. "But I'm afraid they're not going to let you in the museum."

"Why not?" Vera wondered if her dress was too revealing. Edith had insisted Vera wear one of her designs: a red dress with a scooped neckline and narrow skirt.

Ricardo smiled.

"Because every eye will be on you in that dress." He took her hand. "How will the donors give money if no one looks at the exhibits?"

Vera laughed and grabbed her purse. She was used to Ricardo's flattery, but it was still nice to be admired.

"What's that?" Vera asked. A royal-blue convertible was parked in front of the house. The seats were cream-colored leather and the steering wheel was walnut.

"That's the surprise!" Ricardo said eagerly. "It's a 1940 Lagonda, I saw one at the 1939 New York Motor Show. It just arrived by boat; it's the only one in Venezuela."

"It's gorgeous." Vera admired the spoked wheels and silver emblem on the hood. "But what about your MG?"

"A man is allowed to have two cars." He opened her door and smiled. "As long as he devotes his time to only one woman."

Vera slid into the passenger seat and ran her hands over the dashboard. The gears were as shiny as one of Lola's brass candlesticks; she could smell the polish.

The surprise wasn't an engagement ring; it was a new car. She glanced at Ricardo and felt a twinge of disappointment. Would it be fun to be married? To drive a beautiful car and never worry about money? To eat Sunday dinners with Ricardo's parents and one day have a houseful of children? She had told Mr. Matthews she wasn't thinking about marriage, so why did it come to mind now?

Yet, hadn't she and Edith always dreamed they would marry for love? True love happened only once, and she would never experience what she had with Anton again. But what was love, except a feeling that made you happy? There were other ways to be happy: a night of dancing or a piece of art that took her breath away.

"You look like you're having a wonderful dream." Ricardo leaned close to her.

Vera started out of her thoughts, and tipped her face up to the sky. The stars were notes on a sheet of music and she was reminded how lucky she was to be in Caracas.

"I'm enjoying the night air," she answered. Why was she even worrying about marriage? Ricardo hadn't proposed.

"I brought a bottle of champagne." He pointed to a basket on the backseat. "We will pay our respects at the museum and then take a drive in the car."

Vera stood near the Bellas Artes entrance and searched the vast space, a beautiful neoclassical structure designed by the famous architect Carlos Villanueva. The interior had mosaic floors and marble columns and a ceiling so high, Vera had to crane her neck to admire the domed frescoes.

Ricardo had gone to say hello to the director, but Vera had needed to use the powder room and said she would catch up with him. Now he had disappeared.

"You look like you lost something." A man with stooped shoulders stood near her. "I hope it wasn't a valuable piece of jewelry. With the number of people crammed in here, you'd be lucky to see it again."

"That's not likely, I hardly own any jewelry." She turned and recognized the Austrian portrait artist she met at Kitty's party.

"Julius Cohen." He held out his hand. "We met at the Majestic."

"Vera Frankel." Vera shook his hand. "It's nice to see you again."

He gestured at the men in tuxedos and women wearing evening gowns. "I knew two beautiful Hungarian girls would get swept up by Caracas society. Is your friend in a corner drinking champagne and making all the married men wish they were single?"

"Edith is at a work event; she's become a dress designer," Vera said coolly. "And I'm a copywriter at J. Walter Thompson."

"They must pay you well," he whistled. "This is an expensive invitation. I'm only here because I work part-time at the museum."

"I'm here with someone," she admitted. "Ricardo Albee."

"Ahh, the Albee family." Julius said with a slight smirk.

"Do you know them?" Vera asked, curious about his mocking tone.

"Everyone in Caracas knows the Albees," he replied. "Pedro Albee is in politics and his wife supports all those intellectual causes."

"Alessandra Albee believes in education," Vera returned. "That's a good thing."

"You're right," he agreed. "I'm being rude. I just didn't expect to see you at something like this."

"Because I'm a Jewish Hungarian refugee?" Vera wondered.

"Not at all. Your radiance outshines any woman's in this room." Julian made a small bow. "It's just that most of these women are married to men as rich as pharaohs."

"You're right." Vera noticed a woman wearing a sapphire-and-diamond tiara that belonged on a princess. "I've never seen so many fabulous jewels, as if every woman raided the Egyptian pyramids."

"Appearances can be deceiving. Most of the jewels aren't real." He pointed to a dark-haired woman wearing a ruby choker. "That's Esme Puentas. Her husband is head of transportation and he receives more money in bribes than we'll ever see in our lives. He gave his wife the choker after he got the maid pregnant. Five carats of rubies from Brazil."

"It's stunning," Vera agreed.

"Except the one around Esme's neck is fake. The real one is locked in the family safe," Julius corrected. "Jewel thieves in Caracas can bribe a policeman with a stack of bolivares. It's too dangerous to wear expensive jewelry."

"It seems a shame to lock up all those jewels," Vera responded.

"On the contrary, it creates business for the makers of paste jewelry. The insurance companies are happy and the husbands can still apologize for their peccadilloes with a well-placed diamond or sapphire." He grinned mischievously.

"Venezuelan society seems complicated," Vera laughed.

"All societies are complicated, but at least in Caracas there is work for everyone." Julius's eyes darkened. "If I'd stayed in Europe, I'd be selling my paintings on street corners and washing windows to survive."

"You're right." Vera thought of her mother, who was cleaning houses to eat. She spotted Ricardo in the crowd, his eyes scanning the room, presumably for her. She didn't want Ricardo to be jealous of her talking to Julius. "I think I see Ricardo; it was nice to see you again."

"Perhaps Ricardo will commission a portrait of you," Julius said hopefully.

"I doubt that." Vera turned and smiled. "But you never know."

After she and Ricardo left the museum, they drove leisurely back to Lola's house. The air was sweet like persimmons and Vera thought Julius was right. She was lucky to live in a country where there was work and plenty to eat.

"I had a wonderful time," Vera said when Ricardo stopped the car.

"I knew when I saw her in 1939 that she'd drive like a dream." Ricardo ran his hands over the steering wheel. "I've been waiting for eight years to feel her under my hands."

"Perhaps I should be jealous," Vera said playfully. She had drunk two glasses of champagne and felt light-headed and bold.

Ricardo turned to her. "You have nothing to be jealous of. In fact, there's a present for you in the glove box."

"For me?" she repeated.

"Open it, you'll see." He motioned to the glove box.

She clicked it open and inside was a black velvet case. "I don't need more jewelry. I have my silver earrings."

"It's not just a piece of jewelry." He took out the case and held it open. "It's something I have never given a woman."

Vera glanced down and saw a square-cut diamond on a gold band.

"I'm afraid it doesn't have historical value, since my mother wears the family heirloom," Ricardo said with a smile. "I had it made by a local jeweler, and he assured me it's one of the finest diamonds in South America."

He took Vera's hand and brought it up to his chest.

"Vera Frankel, I fell in love with you the moment I saw you at the party at the Hotel Majestic. I have waited all my life to meet a woman with such intelligence and grace." He looked into her eyes. "Nothing would make me happier than if you did me the honor of becoming my wife."

Vera's cheeks turned red. "You can't ask me to marry you; we haven't known each other long,"

"I fell in love the night we met. Do you remember? You said you weren't interested in suitors; you could take care of yourself. I'm used to strong women, but there was also a vulnerability about you that you couldn't hide." He touched her chin. "I love you and I want you to be my wife."

"It's so sudden; I don't know what to say," Vera stammered.

"All you have to do is say yes." Ricardo's voice was steady.

If she said yes, all hope of being with Anton would disappear. But if she didn't, the things she envisioned for her life—the intimate dinners and conversation, the hope of one day having children—would be lost like Cinderella's glass slipper at the stroke of midnight.

"Can I think about it?" she asked.

Ricardo put the velvet case in the glove compartment and handed Vera the car key.

"What are you doing?" she said in alarm.

He smiled at Vera and his expression was warm and understanding.

"I'm going to catch the streetcar home. In the morning, you can drive the car to my house and give me your answer."

"I've never driven a car like this! What if I get in an accident?"

"I trust you with the car." He leaned forward and kissed her. "And I trust you to make the right decision about our future."

Vera sat at the small desk in her room and stared at the velvet case. She couldn't leave it in the car; it might get stolen. But it didn't feel right having it in her room, as if she had already given Ricardo her answer.

How could she decide the most important question of her life by morning? Then she remembered her dinner with Anton at the Quisisana. He asked her to marry him and she answered "yes" before her seafood ravioli got cold.

What would Edith do if she got married? And what about her parents? She still couldn't ask Ricardo to pay for their passage; he might wonder why she agreed to marry him. And she didn't want to start the marriage by owing Ricardo something. But he was also traditional, and if he didn't allow her to keep working, she would never afford her parents' passage.

It seemed simple with Anton; she loved him and couldn't imagine life without him. With Ricardo, she weighed her feelings as carefully as the butcher weighed her mother's meager purchases during the war.

She remembered pacing around her hotel room in Capri and wondering what life would be like without children. Ricardo would give her as many children as she pleased, along with nannies and family holidays. Ricardo's parents would be doting grandparents. Her life would overflow with ease and happiness.

So what was holding her back? She pictured the first time she saw Anton at the embassy. He had answered the door in his uniform and her life had changed. But even saying no to Ricardo wouldn't bring Anton back.

Her eye caught the case for Edith's pendant on the nightstand.

She couldn't.

But the more she thought about it, the more it took root, like the flowers in the Austrian Alps in springtime.

What if she agreed to marry Ricardo and took his ring to the pawnshop Edith told her about and had a paste replica made in its place? She could pay for her parents' fare and even get them a small flat. Eventually she would find a way to buy back the ring, and Ricardo would never know.

It was an impossible plan, but wasn't that how Vera's mother felt when she devised the plan to jump off the train to Auschwitz? How could she let her parents stay in Budapest when she could bring them to Venezuela, where there were jobs?

Julius had offered to paint her. She could pay Julius a small sum and give Ricardo a portrait of her as a wedding present. In return, Julius would find someone who would make a paste diamond ring fabulous enough to deceive her prospective husband.

Her mother had risked her life for her. Vera could gamble her own happiness. Under the circumstances, how could she do anything else?

CHAPTER SEVENTEEN

October 1947

In two hours, Vera was going to collect her parents from the RMS *Mauretania*. She wanted to write down the date, like the other important dates she had noted at the end of the war: April 30, when Hitler committed suicide; May 6, when Goering surrendered to the US Army; and May 8, when Winston Churchill announced on the radio the fighting was over.

It hadn't been over for Vera then; there were the long months on the Dunkels' farm waiting to learn anything from the concentration camps. There was Captain Bingham bringing news of their mothers' fates, and Edith's insistence that Stefan was dead.

Even in Naples, with the delicacies Paolo procured on the black market, there were signs of war everywhere: shops run by widows because their husbands and sons never came home, babies with new last names because their fathers were dead and their young mothers would marry any man willing to raise their children.

But this afternoon, when the RMS *Mauretania* docked at the port in La Guaira, it would be like when Edith cut the last thread on a dress before delivering it to a client. Europe, with all its beauty and heartache, wasn't Vera's any longer; everyone she loved would be in Venezuela.

Ricardo offered to drive her to the port, and at first she refused. She was afraid she would break down in front of him. But he asked again, and she agreed. After all, they planned to marry the next week, and she needed to introduce her fiancé to her parents.

In the four months since Ricardo had proposed, he had been everything she could wish for in a fiancé. He took her to meet friends and relatives, but made sure they left before it became overwhelming. He gave her free rein in planning the wedding, only insisting that he was in charge of the honeymoon. When she laughed and said she wouldn't know what to pack, he whispered she'd look beautiful in anything.

They agreed on a civil ceremony at the Albees' villa followed by a dinner dance at the Majestic. Edith made two wedding dresses. The dress for the ceremony was patterned after the dress Princess Elizabeth wore to announce her engagement to Philip Mountbatten. Edith studied the photo of the royal couple on the balcony of Windsor Castle until she could count the pearls in Princess Elizabeth's necklace from memory.

Edith entered the room and searched for her gloves.

"I have the best news!" she said to Vera. "Kitty wants four evening gowns for New Year's Eve. When her friends find out, they'll order dresses, too."

Edith was picking up Robert at the airport at the same time that Ricardo was taking Vera to greet her parents. Robert had only been gone a month, and he had found a new supplier in Venezuela who was offering him and Edith the finest raw silk at half the usual price. Vera couldn't help but worry that Edith was overextending herself.

Bolts of fabric were already stacked so high in her workroom that she couldn't see the ceiling.

"Are you sure you need more fabric?" Vera wondered. "You already owe more money than what has come in."

Edith smiled. "Don't worry. I write every amount down: the cost of the fabric and the overhead for the workroom and even the mousetraps I had to buy for the mice."

"I don't know how you keep it all straight. The only numbers I've been working on are the guest list for the dinner dance," Vera sighed. "The Albees know everyone in Caracas."

"I still can't believe you're getting married. Look at that ring." Edith pointed at the square-cut diamond. "Don't you remember when we made rings out of daisy chains at the house in the country?"

Vera followed Edith's gaze and winced. She had decided not to tell Edith her plan, so Edith wouldn't have to lie to Ricardo. The pawnbroker gave her enough money for her parents' passage, and rent for a small bungalow. Julius found someone who would make the paste ring and Vera told Ricardo that an organization that helped Jewish refugees paid for her parents' fare.

"You are happy, aren't you?" Edith noticed Vera's expression.

"Of course I'm happy." Vera pulled her mind back to what Edith was saying.

"You don't have to get married so soon," Edith warned, fiddling with her gloves.

"We've been planning it for almost four months!" Vera smiled. "I'm going to be the most elegant bride since Carole Lombard married Clark Gable."

"I heard something today . . ." Edith said hesitantly.

"Heard what?" Vera asked.

"Just gossip, probably, but I can't keep it from you." Edith shrugged. "I had a dress fitting for a woman whose niece dated Ricardo a few years ago. They were practically engaged."

"Engaged?" Vera said sharply. Ricardo never mentioned he had been engaged. But then again, neither had she.

"Not officially," Edith corrected. "The niece was nineteen and studied at the university. Ricardo became jealous of one of her professors, and she broke it off."

"What do you mean jealous?" Vera asked uneasily.

"Ricardo began appearing at the university without warning," Edith continued. "Once he burst into the professor's office because he thought they were together. The professor was giving dictation to his fifty-year-old secretary."

"Maybe she gave him reason to be jealous," Vera suggested. "I've spent hours alone with Julius, and Ricardo hasn't said a thing. He can't wait to see the portrait."

"Julius has a nose like a hawk and he's thin as a scarecrow," Edith retorted.

"Ricardo is very understanding." Vera picked up a hairbrush. "He doesn't even mind if I keep working for a year after the wedding."

"A year is nothing!" Edith exclaimed.

Vera remembered the conversation when Ricardo suggested Vera would be happier furnishing their new house and preparing for a baby. "I don't mind putting my professional aspirations aside for a while. Ricardo and I want to start a family."

"You're only twenty," Edith reminded her. "You're too young to spend your days knitting baby booties and holding tea parties for Venezuelan matrons."

"There's plenty of time to discuss it; we're not married yet." Vera hugged Edith and laughed. "I'm going to have the life I dreamed of, with a husband and a good job and a family."

"This isn't the life we dreamed of," Edith said, turning away. "That was going to be in Budapest with apartments on the same floor and a shared house in the country. Stefan and your husband would have chess tournaments, and on Saturday nights they'd take us dancing."

Vera touched Edith's shoulder. "Stefan would be so proud of you."

"I don't need anyone to be proud of me." Edith walked to the door. "All I need is every woman in Caracas who can afford Dior's New Look to buy an Edith Ban design instead."

Vera stood at the port in La Guaira and waited for the RMS *Mauretania* to dock. The ship's decks were filled with men and women wearing coats and hats. Little kids crammed their faces between the railing and Vera heard a band playing.

"I see a couple waving at you." Ricardo pointed at the ship.

"Where?" Vera asked. Suddenly the crowd on the dock lurched forward and Vera felt as if she was in the cattle car to Auschwitz. She remembered the women clutching their children, as if at any moment the guards might take them away.

"Are you all right?" Ricardo asked. "You look like you might faint."

"I'm fine; the sun is so bright." She waved at the sky and then gasped. She saw them! Her father was almost bald and his arms were thin as matchsticks. But her mother looked miraculously the same. A navy dress peeked out from her coat and her hair was curled around her shoulders.

"It's them!" Vera said excitedly. She grabbed Ricardo's hand and pulled him toward the gangplank.

"They haven't started disembarking!" He laughed at her enthusiasm. "We might stand here for hours."

"My mother will be so anxious and I haven't seen my father since I was fourteen. What if he doesn't recognize me?" Vera moved to the side. "I want them to see me when they arrive."

The first-class passengers appeared, and Vera was reminded how elegant Europeans could be. The women wore crepe dresses and she could smell their perfume when they walked by. The men wore dark-colored suits and carried leather briefcases.

Her mother's face bobbed behind a man, and Vera stepped forward. For a moment Alice disappeared, and then her arms were around Vera.

"Vera, *kedves*, *dragam*, Vera, Vera, darling, darling Vera," Alice said in Hungarian. "*Itt vagyunk, itt vagyunk*. We are here, we are here."

Vera looked up at her mother. Alice's eyes were bright and tears rolled down her cheeks.

"*Mindannyian egyutt*. We are all together," Vera said in English and Hungarian, hugging her tightly.

Her father stood beside her mother and he was so thin she almost cried out. But he put his arms around her and held her gently.

She turned to Ricardo and her voice was thick with emotion. "This is Ricardo. These are my parents, Alice and Lawrence Frankel."

They all shook hands and Ricardo collected their suitcases and led them to his car.

"Who can afford this? Only movie stars drive such a car," Alice said as they approached the royal-blue Lagonda.

"I told you, Ricardo owns a car dealership," Vera answered, as Ricardo stored the suitcases in the trunk. "It's his new car."

"It will be Vera's when we get married," Ricardo said, and his eyes danced. "She looks much better than I do behind the wheel."

Ricardo dropped them off at the bungalow and said he would return for Vera later. The bungalow was in an outer suburb of Caracas and nearby there were farms with chickens. Vera led her parents through the tiny living room with its two armchairs and felt slightly guilty. Ricardo had offered to pay for furniture, but Vera worried her parents were too proud to accept.

"It isn't much," Vera said in English. She decided they had to speak English even when they were alone. Her parents' Spanish wasn't as fluent as their English, and if they fell back into Hungarian when they were with Ricardo, he might feel excluded. "I'll get a bonus soon and then we can afford a sofa and a rug."

"It's lovely." Alice inspected a photo of Vera and Edith on the wall. "We couldn't ask for more."

Vera led the way into a space that held the icebox and a small table. "I stocked the kitchen. There's coffee and milk and sugar."

Her father went to lie down in the bedroom, and Alice heated milk on the stove. She poured two cups of coffee and Vera was transported back to the apartment in Budapest. How many mornings had she hovered in the kitchen so she could taste her mother's coffee? Her mother would finish and leave the best part for Vera: the coffee at the bottom of the cup, which was all milk and sugar and hardly any coffee at all.

"Is he all right? He's very quiet." Vera motioned at the bedroom door where her father had disappeared.

"When your father arrived at your uncle Tibby's house, he was so thin, his skin was transparent." Alice handed Vera a cup. "It was spring, but he was so cold he wore every layer I could find: coats and scarves and sweaters. Your father sat for hours staring into space. He never finished a book, and when someone played a record, he left the room."

"Why?" Vera asked. Her father loved classical music and reading. Her mother used to laugh that she never met a man who found law books exciting until their courtship, when he reeled off cases as they strolled around Paris.

"He was dying in front of my eyes, trying to finish off himself what the Germans started." Alice sipped her coffee. "Finally I told him I was leaving him unless he told me what was wrong."

"Leaving him?" Vera raised her eyebrows.

"I never would have done it, but I had to try something to snap him out of it," Alice chuckled, and then her voice softened. "He finally told me about a Hungarian boy he met at the labor camp. They became quite close. His name was Sandor and he was twenty, with golden hair and big brown eyes. Sandor had been studying opera in London and was engaged to a British girl, but he returned to Budapest when his mother became ill. Every night your father went to sleep with a song ringing through the dormitory, and it lifted his soul. But Sandor came down with tuberculosis and was sent to the infirmary. For weeks your father waited for Sandor to return, and when he did, he was very weak. Even then, Sandor whispered the songs and your father strained to hear them. One night, there were no songs." Alice paused. "The Germans had not only murdered the son of a loving family, they took a girl's fiancé, and silenced a voice that could have made thousands of people happy. Your father didn't want to live in a world where there was no beauty and no love and no music."

"What did you say to him?" Vera asked.

"I poured him a shot of my brother's brandy and said he could stay in this house sitting shiva for thousands of strangers or he could join his wife for a stroll in the garden. If he was lucky, I might kiss him." She smiled at the memory. "He sat silently for so long, I was afraid I was too harsh. Then he asked for his hat."

"His hat?" Vera wondered.

"Your father is a gentleman. He would never go for a walk with a lady without his hat."

Vera took in the story and wanted to hear more.

"I shouldn't have let you push us off the train. We should have stayed together," Vera said finally. "The whole time we hid at the farm, I blamed myself that you were at Auschwitz."

"It's because of you I survived," Alice began. "From the minute I arrived at Auschwitz, they started taking things. First they took my suitcase with the photographs and pieces of jewelry sewn into the dresses." She tried to smile. "What was I thinking? That I would be allowed to wear a favorite dress when they were preparing us for the gas chamber? Then I was taken to the dormitory with nothing but the prisoner uniform, and I thought, they can't hurt me anymore, they have taken everything that is dear to me. But every day they took something more: the gold fillings in my teeth, the flesh that covered my bones. They took everything except the breath that kept me alive, and I wondered if they would take that, too," Alice said slowly. "But they couldn't take my thoughts. Every night I went to bed and imagined you somewhere safe. That's all I needed to survive."

Vera's eyes misted and she remembered Anton saying her mother would have wanted her to be safe.

"Miriam Gold told Captain Bingham that you prayed for me at every meal," Vera said. "You talked to God, and he listened."

Alice looked up in surprise. "I didn't talk to God when I was at Auschwitz."

"You did. Someone heard your prayers, and then you weren't at the next meal. I thought you had been sent to the gas chamber."

"God wasn't anywhere near the concentration camps," Alice said firmly.

"Then why did you pray for me?" Vera asked.

Alice gazed at Vera as if she was trying to find the right words. "Just because God was absent, didn't mean I stopped believing in him. I knew he wasn't close enough to Auschwitz to help me, but I had to pray for you. I couldn't let him desert you, too."

Alice put the coffee cups in the sink, and they moved to the living room.

"I don't want to talk about the war anymore." Alice said as she sat on one of the armchairs. "Tell me about your life."

Vera twisted her engagement ring. She had written about her work at the American embassy in Naples and meeting other refugees in Caracas. She described her job at J. Walter Thompson and Lola's boardinghouse and even Ricardo's parents. But she never mentioned Anton or her feelings for Ricardo.

"You know everything," she said evasively. "Ricardo and I are getting married next week."

"So you are in love and Ricardo makes you happy?" Alice prodded.

Vera gazed at her mother's face, a face she thought she would never see again, and nodded. "I am happy."

There was a knock at the door and Vera answered it. Edith stood outside holding a box of chocolates.

"I wanted to come earlier but it took longer than I thought to pick up Robert at the airport," she said as she walked into the living room. "He didn't want to intrude. He's waiting in the car; I said I'd only be a little while."

Edith saw Alice and stopped. Edith's eyes glistened and she handed the box to Alice.

"These are from Robert," she said shakily. "To welcome you to Venezuela."

Alice set the box aside and took Edith in her arms. She waited until Edith's tears subsided and then she motioned her to sit down.

"The day your mother died was one of the hardest of my life," Alice began. "It was so cold on the death march, we longed to lie down and let the snow cover us. But the Germans kept prodding us with their guns; we weren't given the luxury of going to sleep and not waking up." She smiled weakly. "Lily had been sick for days, but she didn't want to call attention to herself. She was afraid if she fell behind, I would stay with her and we would both be shot. So we made the time go faster by reliving our memories. We were talking about the play you put on when you dressed up like Greta Garbo." Alice looked at Edith. "You were the last thing she thought about before she died. She loved you very much."

Edith's chest heaved and Alice hugged her.

"The years since your father left were hard for Lily, but she was the best friend I could wish for. I think about her every day and I would do anything to have her here." Alice's voice caught. "You and Vera have always been sisters. Now Lawrence and I will be your parents."

* * *

Her mother went to lie down, and Edith left with Robert. Vera opened the front door and breathed in the fresh air. Her mother's story about Auschwitz had made her feel ill; she could almost smell the stench on her clothes.

It felt odd to be standing here while her parents were inside. As if her mother should ask her to run down to the delicatessen and get a schnitzel for dinner. How could her parents start over when everything that mattered—the offices where her father practiced law, the apartments of her mother's friends—were all erased by the war?

She remembered the winter she and Edith spent on the Dunkels' farm. Each day was so strange and different; it was impossible to imagine there was a better life waiting for them.

It was November 1944 and Vera had never been so cold. The walls of the barn couldn't keep out the freezing Austrian air, and she and Edith slept huddled under Ottie's blankets. The days weren't much better. They fed the chickens and milked the cows, only stopping for lunch. And yet, Vera knew that Ottie and her husband were lucky. The German officers assigned to the village took pity on them because their son Emil was killed fighting in the battle of Kursk, and let them keep two cows and a small number of chickens. There was cheese to go with the bread they ate for dinner, and milk that Ottie heated before bed.

The worst part was not knowing when the war would end and what they would do afterward. The longer the fighting dragged on, the more afraid they were that there would be nothing for them in Budapest.

"I can't do this any longer." Edith pulled the blanket over her legs.

"In the morning I can't feel my feet because they're frozen, and at night I can't move my hands because they're raw from working."

"The war can't last forever." Vera closed her eyes. Even though she was tired, it was too cold to sleep.

"The Russians win every battle, but Hitler keeps calling up more men," Edith moaned. "When the war is over, there won't be a single male under the age of forty in Europe."

"Stefan and our fathers aren't fighting in any battles," Vera reminded her.

"You think they have a better chance of surviving in the labor camps?" Edith asked. "We listen to Ottie's radio. How do you think they make the ammunition? The men in the camps must be working harder than ever. And what about Budapest? It will be like a dollhouse when it's over. Just windows and doors and a roof with nothing inside."

"Let's play a game," Vera suggested.

"What kind of a game?" Edith asked.

They were curled up, facing each other to keep warm.

"Let's imagine our lives after the war," Vera said. "I'll go first. I'll move to Paris and get a job as a translator, and in the evenings I'll write plays. I'll meet a handsome man who'll be doing important work, perhaps finding homes for war orphans. Just as my job is up, he'll ask me to marry him. We'll buy a chateau in the French countryside and fill it with children and dogs." Vera paused. "When the children are older, they'll perform my plays like we did for our mothers."

"What does he look like?" Edith asked dreamily.

Vera thought for a moment. "He has a kind smile like Robert Taylor in *Camille* and a sexy French accent."

"You should have a cow so you can make your own milk." Edith joined the game.

"We'll have a cow," Vera laughed. "Now it's your turn."

"I don't see anything." Edith turned on her back

"It's a game, make up something."

"The only future I could see is with Stefan." Edith stared out the window at the night sky. "And now all I see is black."

Vera shielded her eyes from the Venezuelan sun and noticed Ricardo's car rounding the bend. The top was down, and the sun gleamed on the walnut dashboard.

What Edith said about Ricardo had been gossip; perhaps the woman was jealous that Ricardo was marrying Vera instead of her niece.

Vera was going to have a wonderful future and she would make sure Edith and her parents did, too. She would take her father to one of the Hungarian refugee get-togethers at Ruth Goldblum's and find him a chess partner. She could ask Alessandra to include her mother on one of her committees. She could even ask Ricardo to find someone for Edith to date. Edith hadn't been able to get enough of love in Naples; she couldn't spend all her time planning her business with Robert.

There wasn't only one perfect life. If one set one's mind to it, there were many ways to be happy.

CHAPTER EIGHTEEN

November 1947

The morning of Vera's wedding, she sat at the dressing table in her suite at the Majestic. Her suite contained a sitting room with gold sofas and a thick red carpet. The bedroom held a massive four-poster bed and a dressing room with a velvet stool and a table where Vera laid out her hairbrush and the diamond earrings Alessandra loaned her for the dinner dance.

Edith stayed with her in the suite last night, but tonight Ricardo would join her. She tried not to think about the wedding night. What if Ricardo discovered she wasn't a virgin? She couldn't tell him about Anton.

There were other things that made her anxious: after they returned from the honeymoon, she was moving out of Lola's home and into Ricardo's house. What would it be like to live with Ricardo when she was used to seeing Edith's stockings hanging in the bathroom and hearing Edith's voice when she came down to the kitchen?

There was a knock at the door and her mother stood in the hallway. "Please, come in. How is your room?" Vera ushered her inside.

"Ricardo insisted it be in the back of the hotel so you'd have a view of the gardens."

"It's beautiful. I feel like the Empress of Hungary," Alice said as she entered the suite. She wore a beige dress that Edith had made her for the ceremony. "Where's Edith?"

"She had to deliver a dress to a customer." Vera walked into the sitting room. "Can you believe Edith is working on my wedding day?"

"I can't believe any of this." Alice pointed to the tray of bonbons and bouquets of flowers. "Your father and I got married in a synagogue in Paris with two witnesses and a rabbi who was so old, he was practically deaf. We had to repeat our vows twice before he said we were married."

"Do you think it's too much?" Vera asked worriedly. "Ricardo is the last child to get married, and the Albees want it to be perfect."

"I like Ricardo's parents," Alice said as she sat on the sofa. Ricardo's father had loaned Lawrence a tuxedo and Alessandra had offered Alice anything in her closet for the wedding. "They are good people."

Their parents had met three days ago. At first Vera's parents were uncomfortable in the Albees' luxurious villa. But Alessandra made sure they felt welcomed. She included Hungarian dishes on the dinner menu. Pedro mentioned that they had visited and loved Budapest before the war. By the time they moved to the living room for brandies, they were all friends.

"I hoped you'd think so." Vera let out a sigh of relief. "I like them too."

"Your father told me he would like you to do something this morning. He was too anxious to ask you himself," Alice crossed her hands. "He would like you to speak to the rabbi."

"Which rabbi?" Vera asked.

"Rabbi Gorem," Alice said. "Lawrence met him a couple of days ago. He leads a Shabbat for European immigrants."

"You went to a Shabbat?" Vera said in surprise. "I would have come with you."

"Rabbi Gorem is going to be Lawrence's new chess partner." Alice smiled. "Thank God he has someone to play with. I was afraid I might have to learn."

"Why would I meet with the rabbi on my wedding day?" Vera asked. "Ricardo and I already agreed on a civil ceremony."

"It's not about the ceremony, it's about children."

"We haven't discussed how we'll raise our children," Vera offered. "Ricardo was raised Catholic, but his parents are open-minded. And I—"

"How you raise your children is up to you," Alice interrupted.

"You don't mind if they aren't raised Jewish?" Vera's eyes widened.

"Of course I would like them to know the history of the Jews," her mother said slowly. "But there are many ways to teach them. Did you know when you were five we had a Christmas tree?"

"A Christmas tree?" Vera was shocked.

"You saw it in a department store and thought it was the prettiest thing in the world: it was decorated with gold ornaments and a star like the Star of David. Your father didn't mind; it was something pretty to look at—like the set decorations in *The Nutcracker* ballet.

"But when you came down with diphtheria, I made a pact with God not to have a tree again if you lived." She paused. "You always envied your school friends with Christmas trees lit up like a million fireflies. But if the war showed us anything, it is that being Jewish isn't about what you study in synagogue—it's here." She pointed to her heart. "You were born a Jew and nothing can change that."

"Then why does he want me to talk to the rabbi?" Vera wondered.

"Let Rabbi Gorem tell you." Alice stood up. "He's waiting in the lobby."

Rabbi Gorem reminded Vera of a clothes hanger. His coat hung on his gaunt frame and his almost-bald head had gray tufts of hair.

"You must be Vera." He stood up and held out his hand. "Your father said you would be the prettiest woman in the hotel lobby."

"Thank you." Vera shook his hand. "It's nice to meet you."

He smiled at Vera. "The pleasure is mine. There's nothing lovelier than a girl on her wedding day."

"Where would you like to talk?" Vera asked. It was almost noon and the lobby bustled with activity. Bellboys carried steamer trunks, and well-dressed men and women sat in high-backed chairs sipping coffee and reading newspapers.

"Let's walk in the gardens," Rabbi Gorem suggested. "I spent the last fifty-five years battling Polish winters; the Venezuelan climate is still a pleasant surprise."

The Majestic's gardens had manicured lawns and lush oak trees. Flower beds flanked stone pathways and a fountain trickled.

"My family and I arrived from Poland last July," he began. "We were lucky; my wife's cousin settled in Caracas before the war. At first I didn't want to come. We are from a small town in Poland called Krosno. At the beginning of the war the Germans installed a *Judenrat*—a small group of Jewish leaders who were in charge of the community. We didn't have it easy; the Germans destroyed the glass-blowing factory and by the time the fighting ended, the Russians had bombed the rest of the town.

"Our house was near the graveyard where there are gravestones commemorating my parents and our son Josef. Josef died at Bergen-Belsen." He paused. "After the war, my wife wanted to take our three surviving children somewhere new. I argued that the town needed its rabbi. She looked at me and said it's easier to care for the souls of the dead than the conscience of those who survived."

"What do you mean?" Vera asked curiously.

"Human beings are tricky. In Krosno, when we learned of those who died in battle or in the camps, we could mourn knowing there was nothing we could have done to save them.

"But it was different for the survivors of the concentration camps. Their lives were like a spin of the roulette wheel. Why did my friend Avram go to the gas chamber and not me? Why did a young boy like Sandor die from tuberculosis and I survived?"

"My father told you about Sandor?" Vera gasped.

"Lawrence is intelligent, and intelligence can be a burden when you've witnessed so much pain. It makes you ask questions that have no answers." Rabbi Gorem went on. "Your father thinks that as a survivor he must have something to teach others, or why else was he spared? But he tried listening to Mozart and reading Plato and Sartre and came up with nothing. That's why he wanted to ask you a favor."

"A favor?" Vera repeated.

"If you have a son, he would like his middle name to be Lawrence."

Vera looked up sharply. Jews never named their children after living parents. They used their ancestors' names only to honor the dead.

"Don't worry. He convinced me he's not planning on dying anytime soon." Rabbi Gorem noticed her expression and chuckled. "He doesn't think he will be able to pass on any wealth or wisdom to his grandchildren, but he would like to give them something." He looked at Vera. "All he could think of was his name."

"I see." Vera's eyes welled up. "Why a son's middle name and why didn't he ask me himself?"

"He didn't want to break tradition completely by calling your son Lawrence; the middle name will be enough." He paused. "And he wanted my permission first. I told him God has grown a bit more lenient, like the air stewardess on a transatlantic flight who allows you to use the restroom when the 'fasten your seat belt' sign is still on."

"I've never flown in a plane," Vera laughed.

He rolled his eyes. "It's a terrifying experience. There's a reason only God lives in the clouds; the rest of us are more comfortable on earth."

"Tell my father that Ricardo and I would be honored to give our son his name," Vera said.

They walked back to the lobby together and Rabbi Gorem rested his hand on Vera's arm. "Children are the greatest blessing. May you have a happy home filled with boys and girls."

Vera sat in the study in the Albees' villa and tried to stop her heart from racing. A hotel car had transported her from her suite at the Majestic to the villa and now she waited for the ceremony to begin. The wedding guests were already gathered in the Albees' living room. Ricardo and the judge were sequestered in the library, going over the judge's speech.

All brides were nervous; it didn't mean anything. And Ricardo had been so kind: sending more roses to her suite with a box tied with a gold ribbon. Inside was a pair of long white gloves with the note:

For my bride. You will be the most beautiful woman at the ball.

A knock sounded at the door. She answered it.

"Is it all right to come in?" Alessandra stood in the hall. She wore a mauve dress and her dark hair was coiled on the top of her head.

"Please do," Vera said. "Ricardo insisted I wait in here. It's bad luck for the guests to see the bride."

"I've never seen Ricardo so excited." She smiled at Vera. "I didn't come to offer advice or tell you how nervous I was on my wedding day. Brides get too much advice these days. I only came to tell you how happy we are that you're joining the family."

"Thank you." Vera nodded. "I'm very lucky."

"We're all lucky." She gave Vera a quick hug. "I'll have a daughter-in-law and hopefully soon more grandchildren. Venezuela is like Europe: family is everything."

Alessandra left and there was another knock on the door. Edith appeared in a stunning aquamarine dress with a matching hat.

"Can I come in?" Edith asked.

"Come quickly." Vera peered into the hallway.

Edith entered the room and studied the ivory dress and pearl necklace.

"A bride really does have a special glow." Edith nodded her approval. "You're more beautiful than at the fitting."

"I'm so nervous, I can't breathe. I keep worrying about how Ricardo likes his coffee and if I'll be able to read in bed after he goes to sleep. Will I have to ask Ricardo for money or will he give me a household allowance?" She paused. "But those things will work out. What scares me most is being without my best friend." She looked at Edith. "I don't know how I'm going to survive without you every day."

Edith hugged her and stifled a laugh. "Who said I'm going anywhere? I'm a terrible cook. I'll be over for dinner twice a week."

"I hope so, how else will I improve my recipes? Alessandra offered to lend me her cook, but I want to learn my way around the kitchen myself," Vera joked, and her tone softened. "I love you more than a sister. You're my other half."

Edith returned to the living room and Vera touched up her hair. She heard footsteps outside, and her father stood in the hall. His suit jacket hung on him and his head looked too big for his body.

"*Gyönyörű* Vera, my beautiful Vera," he said in Hungarian. "We must go; they're waiting."

"I'm ready." She replied, grabbing the bouquet of violets. It was only after a few steps that she realized her father wasn't next to her. She found him hovering at the door to the study.

"I was fixing my tie," he said, but there were tears in his eyes.

"Your tie is perfect." She examined it.

He took her arm and smiled weakly. "Then I suppose I have no more excuses."

Vera stood in the ballroom of the Majestic and sipped a glass of champagne. Her back ached from dancing and her head throbbed from the music, but she didn't want her wedding day to end.

Ricardo had looked so handsome standing at the altar. Her doubts had dissolved when she saw the love in his eyes. And seeing her parents sitting in the Albees' living room when just a few months ago she thought they were dead, made her heart swell.

The smile Edith gave her when their eyes met was almost too much to bear. They had been through so much together—how could Vera abandon her? But during cocktails, Ricardo introduced Edith to his cousin, Jorge, who had just returned from a screen test in Hollywood. Edith whispered to Ricardo that she wasn't looking for a man, but Ricardo seated them at the same table anyway.

When the doors of the ballroom opened, Vera couldn't believe her eyes. Every inch of carpet was covered with elegantly set tables, and there were more orchids than in the botanical gardens in Budapest. The orchestra played a medley of Frank Sinatra songs. She had to crane her neck to see the top of the six-tier wedding cake.

The best part was having the people she loved in the same place. Her father was too weak to dance, but her mother danced with Ricardo and his father. Julius looked elegant in a new jacket, and Lola stayed briefly with her beau. Pedro gave a moving speech, and Ricardo spun Vera across the dance floor to the sounds of Louis Armstrong and Glenn Miller.

"Here's the bride." Robert approached her. "I haven't been able to get close enough to the bride and groom to say congratulations."

"There's quite a crowd," Vera laughed, waving at the tables. "Ricardo keeps introducing me to people, but I can't remember so many names."

"It's a beautiful night," Robert said. "I'm happy for you."

"Thank you. It's been wonderful." She searched the dance floor. "Where's Edith?"

"Trying to ignore the advances of Ricardo's cousin," Robert said with a grin. "He keeps telling her he can set her up with a screen test and she keeps saying she's a dress designer."

"You've been so kind to help Edith with her career," Vera said. In the last few months, Vera had finally acknowledged that Robert's interest in Edith was purely business.

"Don't you remember when we met at Kitty's fashion show, I told you Edith had real talent?" Robert sipped his champagne. "I keep telling her she should come to New York. You and Ricardo should come too. You can stay at the wonderful Wight Hotel on Fifth Avenue. My wife, Daisy, is a proud New Yorker; she loves to show off her city."

Vera remembered all the things Anton was going to show her in New York: his parents' club and Tavern on the Green. They were going to take carriage rides in Central Park and go ice-skating in Rockefeller Center.

"Excuse me," she said, her heart beating faster. "I need to use the powder room."

She walked halfway across the ballroom when she felt a hand on her arm. She turned and Ricardo stood in front of her.

"Are you all right?" Ricardo asked. "You're white as a ghost."

"I must have drunk too much champagne; I have a terrible headache."

"Are you sure it doesn't have anything to do with Edith's friend Robert?" Ricardo asked.

"What are you talking about?" Vera wondered.

"I saw you talking to him and then you hurried away," Ricardo said.

Vera ran her hands over the glorious white chiffon gown. Today was the most wonderful day of her life. She couldn't let her thoughts of Anton or Ricardo's small jealousies ruin their happiness.

"I'm only hurrying to find you." She kissed him. "I don't want to be apart from my new husband."

The dinner dance finally ended and Vera and Ricardo went up to their suite. Vera entered the dressing room and closed the door. She peeled off her gloves and studied her reflection in the mirror.

Ricardo rustled around in the bedroom and she tried not to panic.

Would he be naked when she appeared? There was nothing to be afraid of. Making love couldn't be so different, even if it was with a new man.

She changed into the silk negligee that Edith made for her and dabbed her wrists with perfume. When she opened the door, Ricardo was sitting against the pillows. There was a bottle of brandy on the bedside table and he wore a white undershirt.

"My darling Vera," he said. "Come here."

Vera crossed the room, hoping he didn't notice the trepidation in her eyes. Her hair fell loosely to her shoulders and her feet were bare.

"We've had enough champagne, perhaps some cognac instead?" He pointed to the brandy snifters.

"Nothing for me." She was afraid he'd notice that her hands were shaking if she picked up the glass.

"You're cold and you're shaking." He took her hand and she sat on the bed.

"It was a long day; I'm just tired."

Ricardo leaned forward and kissed her. His mouth was warm from the brandy and he smelled of aftershave. "Not too tired, I hope?"

Vera took a deep breath. She had found the courage to board a ship and start a new life in Caracas. Surely she could go to bed with a man she had feelings for.

"Not too tired," she whispered, and kissed him back.

Ricardo untied the string on her nightgown. He peeled back the bedspread and waited while Vera lay down. Then he took off his shirt and covered her body with kisses.

Vera closed her eyes and let herself be carried away. Ricardo was slow and thoughtful, whispering between caresses that he adored her. Then suddenly he was on top of her and she felt the same piercing pain she remembered with Anton.

"Vera, *tu eres mia*, you are all mine," he whispered, and then moaned and collapsed against her breasts.

Vera lay perfectly still until Ricardo's eyes closed and his breathing was even. She wriggled from underneath him and pulled on her negligee.

For some reason, her mind went to the final scene in *Gone with the Wind*. She remembered Rhett Butler running down the staircase and flinging open the door, and Scarlett O'Hara wondering if he would ever return.

Vera felt like Scarlett. It was because of Vera that Anton went away. If only she had shown him she loved him enough not to need children, they would be together.

Vera poured a shot of brandy and curled up in an armchair. She couldn't lie to herself; she still loved Anton. Tomorrow Ricardo would load their suitcases into the royal-blue Lagonda and they would set out on their honeymoon.

But tonight she would nurse the tear in her heart from missing Anton. After all, she knew from Edith that a tear could easily be repaired. All it took was a piece of thread and a few stitches.

CHAPTER NINETEEN

December 1947

The sun streamed through the window of Vera's new dining room and she admired the linen chairs and the sideboard with its silver punch bowl and brass candlesticks.

She and Ricardo returned from their honeymoon a week before, and Edith was coming for lunch. Vera spent all morning making the house perfect. She took out the china they received as a wedding present and bought lilies because they were Edith's favorite flowers. She even asked Alessandra's cook, Valeria, for her recipe for coconut cookies.

It was silly to go to so much trouble. At the Dunkels' farm, she and Edith ate bread and cheese with their hands and drank milk moments after it came from the cow because they were too hungry to wait. But she wanted to show Edith that she was good at her new role as Ricardo's wife.

Vera and Ricardo spent their honeymoon at a hotel on Choroni Beach. For three hours they drove through the mountains on winding roads so perilous, Vera was tempted to close her eyes. But Ricardo laughed that she would miss the best parts and he was right. She couldn't believe the scenery flying past their car: waterfalls and rushing rivers; tropical birds and a huge, short-haired animal that Ricardo called a tapir.

The hours of gripping the dashboard were worth it when they arrived in Choroni. The town featured colonial buildings and a bay where fishing boats bobbed at the dock. There was a cove for swimming in water the shade of aquamarine.

During the day they took walks on the white sand and at night they danced under the moonlight. Vera enjoyed their lovemaking. Ricardo was skillful, and when she closed her eyes, her body responded to his touch.

There was the time when Ricardo picked up her hand to admire her engagement ring and she was terrified he knew it was fake. But he only kissed her fingers and said her beauty outshone any diamond. There was the evening they played bridge with another young couple. The husband sat close to Vera and afterward Ricardo was in a terrible mood. Vera made sure the next night they played cards with an older couple celebrating their twentieth anniversary.

There was a knock at the door and Vera hurried to open it.

"You're here." Vera hugged Edith. "I've been so nervous I already polished the silver twice."

"Why are you nervous?" Edith walked into the living room. The portrait Julius painted of Vera hung above the fireplace and there was a wool rug and matching sofas.

"You're used to Kitty and her friends in their fancy villas; I wanted to show you I could keep house."

"It's beautiful." Edith pulled off her gloves. She sat on the sofa and took a pack of cigarettes from her purse. "Do you mind?" she asked.

"You don't smoke." Vera frowned. She didn't even comment on the portrait, which she had never seen. Something was off.

Edith had the same misery and fear in her eyes as when they jumped off the train to Auschwitz.

"What's wrong?" Vera sat beside her.

"It's Robert . . ." Edith lit the cigarette shakily.

Vera's breath caught. "If he touched you, I'll have Ricardo go see him."

"It's worse." She inhaled the smoke. "He's disappeared and I'm broke. I'm completely finished."

"But I thought Robert wasn't invested in your business? He was only giving you advice."

"He explained it all to me in a letter," Edith answered. "He had some business troubles before we met and couldn't get any credit to buy fabric. Every time a supplier sold me fabric on credit, Robert asked for more fabric without telling me and kept it for himself. He did the same thing when I borrowed money from the bank. He borrowed fifty thousand American dollars, but I only received twenty-five thousand."

"You borrowed money from the bank," Vera repeated. Edith had never told her.

"I had to come up with the rent for the space at the Majestic. The bank wouldn't lend money to a woman, so Robert signed with me." Edith looked at Vera. "I trusted him completely."

"What happened?" Vera asked.

"Everything was going well until he opened a dress shop in Philadelphia. It did poorly from the start, and he couldn't pay his rent. At the same time, sales in the shops in Boston and New York dropped and he got deeper in debt. He used the money I cosigned for to pay back his creditors, but it wasn't enough. They came and took back all his dresses. Since I was the one who bought the fabric on credit, the suppliers are threatening to call in my debt, too."

"Robert can get another loan," Vera suggested. "Or perhaps his wife's family can help."

"I called Marcus and asked him to go to Robert's apartment in Manhattan. It was one of those fancy doorman buildings in Park Avenue," she gulped. "The superintendent said they moved out. The keys were on the counter and the furniture was gone. They didn't give a forwarding address."

Edith's shoulders shook and Vera comforted her.

"You have all the fabric in your workroom. When you deliver those dresses, you can pay off the creditors."

"The orders haven't come in yet," Edith replied. "Any minute they'll take the fabric, and I'll be left with an empty worktable and some hungry mice."

"I'll ask Ricardo to lend you money. It would be strictly business; we'll have a lawyer draw it up."

"You can't tell Ricardo anything." Edith clutched Vera's arm. "If Kitty and her friends find out, I'll be finished in Caracas forever."

"What will you do?"

Edith stood up and Vera was reminded how beautiful she was. Even with her smudged mascara, Edith had the poise of a model.

She smiled. "First I want to admire my best friend's mansion. Then we're going to have lunch and come up with a plan."

"It's not a mansion," Vera giggled. They had five rooms downstairs, and two bedrooms upstairs. "What kind of plan were you thinking?"

Edith put the cigarette case back in her purse. "A plan that won't let any man take advantage of me again."

Vera showed her Ricardo's study and the kitchen outfitted with the latest appliances and Vera's office where she kept a typewriter.

Upstairs there was a guest room that could be a nursery and a bathroom with a porcelain bathtub.

"You bedroom is bigger than Signora Rosa's top floor!" Edith said when they entered. The king-size bed took up the middle of the room; a silk armchair and an ottoman sat opposite. A balcony overlooked the garden. Doors led to separate dressing rooms.

"Ricardo is used to having his own space," Vera said, embarrassed. "He didn't want us to get in each other's way."

"What's it like?" Edith asked.

"What do you mean?"

"You have to tell me," Edith said. "What's it like to make love to a man?"

Vera looked up and there was a quick flash of pain in Edith's eyes. She remembered the month before Stefan was put on the train to Strasshof. Edith had slumped in her room with an anatomy book, and Vera had been certain Edith was pregnant.

In April 1944, an early spring arrived in Budapest. Vera wore her yellow star on her school dress because it was too warm to wear her coat. Edith and Stefan used the warm weather as an excuse to linger in the botanical gardens. When Edith came home, her hair ribbon was often missing.

Vera knocked on the door and poked her head in Edith's bedroom. Edith was sitting on the floor. Her schoolbag was open and books were scattered on the rug.

"What are you doing?" Vera entered the room. "We just finished dinner, your mother asked where you were."

"Stefan and I were studying." Edith gestured at the books.

"Then why do you have grass stains on your skirt?" Vera raised her eyebrow. "It's all right if you and Stefan stay out late during the summer, but we have school now. You won't pass if you don't do your homework."

"What does it matter, soon we'll be sent to the ghetto or worse," Edith replied. "Stefan's neighbor, Len Rabinovitz, was sent to the labor camps. He's only seventeen, but they came for his older brother and took him, too."

"We don't know when we're going; it could all be a rumor." Vera noticed a textbook with a picture of the human body. "What's this?"

"I found it at a used bookstore."

"Since when are you interested in female anatomy?" Vera flipped through the book. "Don't tell me you're pregnant!"

She had been so moody lately and spent all her time with Stefan.

"I'm not pregnant," Edith insisted. "I just want to know how the female body works."

"Our mothers can tell us what we need to know." Vera studied Edith closely. "Do you promise you're telling the truth?"

"I swear on the life of Anastasia." Edith tugged a brush through her hair.

Anastasia was the beloved cat that lived at the house in the country. Vera and Edith named her after the tragic Russian princess.

Vera nodded. "All right, I believe you."

A week later Alice asked Vera to go to the delicatessen and plead for an extra ounce of gnocchi. Vera had lost weight in the last two months and Alice worried she wasn't getting enough to eat.

"You lied to me." Vera entered Edith's bedroom without knocking. "I knew you were pregnant."

"What are you talking about?" Edith sat on the bed.

"I was at the delicatessen and saw you huddled in the alley with Golda Peskowitz."

"So?" Edith asked.

"She's a midwife!" Vera exclaimed. "You were asking how to get rid of the baby."

"I wanted to know if she had anything for my mother's cramps. They've gotten worse and my mother was too embarrassed to ask," she answered. "It would be a miracle if I was pregnant. Stefan and I haven't had sex."

"All those evenings you stayed out at the lake . . ." Vera said uncertainly.

"We did lots of things, but never that," Edith responded. "We had a long talk last summer and agreed to wait until we were engaged. Then a few weeks ago I changed my mind. I told Stefan I didn't want to wait, and we got in a fight."

"You got in a fight?" Vera repeated.

"Stefan said the only reason I would change my mind is if I thought he was going to be sent away and wasn't coming back."

"That's not what you were thinking," Vera soothed her. "You're young and in love. Lots of girls think about that sort of thing."

"No, he was right." Edith's voice caught. "All I thought about when he kissed me was what if he was sent to the camps? I'd live the rest of my life having missed out on truly knowing the boy I love."

"You've never made love?" Vera asked curiously, folding Ricardo's robe that lay on the bed.

"I told you Stefan and I never had sex," Edith replied.

"I thought perhaps with Marcus before . . ."

"Before I saw him kissing Leo at the jewelry store?" Edith smiled. "Marcus would never do more than kiss me," she sighed.

"There's plenty of time," Vera assured her. "You're only twenty."

Edith shrugged. "I don't mind; my career makes me happy. But now I'm ruined. I'll be a poor spinster renting a room in Lola's boardinghouse when I'm forty."

"Come on, we said we'd think of a plan during lunch." Vera took her arm and led her to the staircase.

Edith stopped her. "First you have to tell me. Is it as painful as our sixth-grade teacher warned, or is it the most exquisite feeling in the world?"

"It hurts in the beginning, but then it's nice," Vera answered truthfully.

"It's not about the kissing and moaning, it's sharing the most intimate act with the man you love," Edith said thoughtfully. "That's what I longed for with Stefan, so I would never forget it no matter what happened."

"You're right." Vera flashed on the night in Capri with Anton. "When you've had that, you never forget it."

Vera and Edith sat at the dining room table and ate.

"I forgot—you have a letter." Edith reached into her purse and gave Vera an envelope.

"It's from Captain Bingham." Vera opened it. "He congratulated me and hopes our marriage is full of happiness." She noticed something stuck to the back of the envelope. "This is for you." She handed it to Edith. "It's a cable."

Edith tore it open. "It's from Marcus! He's coming to Caracas! He says he has a surprise for us."

"What kind of surprise?"

"He doesn't say." Edith stood up.

"Where are you going? I was about to bring out cookies, and we haven't thought of a plan to save your business."

"It will have to wait." Edith kissed her on the cheek. "I have to ask Lola if she has an extra room and get to the airport. Marcus arrives tonight!"

Vera was fixing a milk punch—rum and mango juice and condensed milk—when the front door opened.

"You're home early." Vera looked up. It was still a surprise to see Ricardo enter the house, as if she was acting in one of the plays she and Edith used to perform.

"This is the dream of every man." Ricardo kissed her. "To come home and see my beautiful wife standing in the living room."

"I fixed cocktails." She handed him a highball glass. "Don't be too harsh; it's my first try."

Ricardo had introduced her to the recipe on their honeymoon.

He took a long sip and smiled. "It's just what I needed. A customer refused to pick up his car because he claimed he ordered beige upholstery. I showed him the order and he accused me of changing the color. It's a Citroën. I can't send it back to France."

"I'm sorry if you had a hard day," Vera said. "Edith came over for lunch. You'll never guess—our friend Marcus is coming to Caracas."

"Is Marcus the photographer Edith dated in Naples?" Ricardo wondered.

Vera nodded. "He lives in New York now; he's quite successful. He sent Edith a cable. He's arriving this evening."

"We should invite them to dinner," Ricardo suggested. "Maybe that's why Edith isn't interested in men. She's still in love with Marcus."

Vera had told Ricardo about the photograph in *LIFE* magazine, but she hadn't mentioned that Marcus liked men. Ricardo was opinionated on certain subjects, and she worried he might not approve of her having a homosexual friend.

"Tomorrow I have to deliver a car to a customer in Valencia. I won't be home until midnight," he continued. "We'll do it the next night. It will be our first dinner party."

Ricardo went upstairs to change for dinner and Vera took their glasses into the kitchen. It felt wrong to keep secrets from Ricardo: her past with Anton, the fake engagement ring, and now Marcus's homosexuality.

She peered into the oven and checked that the empanadas she had made were rich and fluffy. Wasn't the point of marriage to make each other happy? It was better to keep some things to herself, especially if they would only cause trouble.

CHAPTER TWENTY

The day after Edith came for lunch, Vera drove to her parents' bungalow. Mr. Matthews had suggested she take three weeks off after the wedding, and she was glad she had agreed. There was so much to keep her busy.

She was bringing her parents an extra serving bowl she and Ricardo had received as a wedding present, and tonight she was meeting Edith and Marcus for drinks. Marcus's news was so exciting he wanted to tell Vera himself.

"Look at you, all independent and driving that beautiful car." Alice kissed Vera when she hopped out of the car. "I can't believe you're my daughter."

"I couldn't accept the Lagonda, but Ricardo can't drive two cars at once," Vera laughed, admiring the green MG. "I never realized it was so freeing to drive. I can go wherever I like."

They walked inside. Alice had an apron tied over her dress and the scent of tomatoes and paprika wafted from the kitchen.

"The house smells wonderful," Vera continued.

"I found the ingredients to make *lecsó* at the market," Alice said.

"I haven't seen your father so excited since Arthur Rubenstein performed Chopin in Paris in 1920."

Lecsó was a Hungarian vegetable stew, her father's favorite dish.

"Where is he?" Vera handed Alice her packages. "I brought the bowl and a pipe. Ricardo received a pipe as a wedding present, and he already has two."

"Lawrence went to the barber."

"The barber? But he doesn't have any hair."

"It's not about the haircut, it's the pleasure of sitting in the barber's chair with hot towels on his cheeks," Alice answered. "For five centimos Lawrence can put his feet up and listen to the barber compliment him on his beautiful daughter."

"The barber doesn't know me," Vera responded.

"All daughters are beautiful to a clever barber," Alice chuckled. "A shave gives Lawrence confidence, and he has a job interview this afternoon."

"What kind of a job?" Vera asked.

A cloud passed over Alice's face and she moved to the kitchen. "Rabbi Gorem's cousin owns a construction company. Lawrence is going to be a clerk."

"A clerk! But he had one of the most respected law practices in Budapest."

"He can't practice law in Venezuela without a degree from a local university," Alice explained as she chopped onions. "And he has to improve his Spanish. I found work, too. I'm going to take on sewing." She wiped her hands on her apron. "Lawrence is getting stronger and we need money. The law degree isn't free, but our situation is only temporary."

"You've both been through so much," Vera wavered. "I wanted you to rest and lead a good life."

"Sit down." Alice pointed to the chair. "I haven't told you about when I escaped from Flossenbürg. Eleven thousand Jews arrived in Flossenbürg from Auschwitz in January 1945, and the conditions were horrendous. Lily was dead and I had no one." Her eyes darkened. "The sick and the healthy all slept in the same dormitory. By the spring, you couldn't go to bed without a dead body being carted away. I developed a cough, but I hid it. I didn't want someone taking my cot because they thought I wouldn't need it." She wiped her hands. "Then in April the guards seemed distracted; we could tell something was wrong. One day, they took us from the camp and said we were being moved to Dachau, two hundred kilometers on foot." She looked at Vera. "By the second day my forehead was on fire and I could hardly swallow. Suddenly guards started running and I was sure the fever made me hallucinate. I learned later that the Allies had surrounded the forest and the guards fled. Can you imagine? We were finally free but I was so weak, I couldn't walk another step."

"What happened?" Vera asked.

"I fainted and another prisoner carried me to a house in a village," Alice said. "I don't even know his name; he left me and kept going. I was in and out of the fever for four months. When I recovered, the war had been over for months."

"The house was owned by a cobbler, Gunther, and his wife, Marie. They were German, but they were good people. Their son, Hans, was part of the White Rose resistance when he was a student at the University of Munich. The Gestapo put Hans on trial for treason. He was executed in 1943," Alice said somberly. "The first day I felt well enough to get out of bed, Marie invited me to join them for dinner. Potatoes were the only food still plentiful in Germany, and Marie used it in everything: potato in vegetable soup when there were no vegetables, and cabbage rolls with potatoes instead of meat, and potato with applesauce for dessert. But all Marie put on my plate was a boiled potato."

"A boiled potato?" Vera repeated.

"Marie knew if I put too much food in my stomach, I would relapse," Alice said. "For two weeks she wouldn't let me eat anything but a boiled potato. No butter and no sauerkraut and no horseradish. It was the best thing I ever tasted.

"Sewing is my boiled potato. It's the simplest activity, but it brings me great joy," Alice finished. "There is nothing more satisfying than pulling a needle and thread through a shirt or pretty dress. I would happily do it every day for the rest of my life."

"Why can't things stay the same?" Vera asked. "Why can't we be in the apartment in Budapest? Father would come home from the office and there would be cherry soup and cheese noodles for dinner. Edith and Lily would join us and bring Lily's chimney cake, and afterward we'd play cards."

"Because you're now a young wife with a good husband, and because I'm making *lecsó*." Alice went back to chopping onions. "Lawrence is crazy for my *lecsó*."

Edith and Marcus were seated at a table at the bar when Vera arrived at the restaurant. The sun was setting and the air was warm and sweet.

"There's the new bride!" Marcus jumped up and hugged Vera. He wore tight white pants and a yellow sweater. His dark hair curled around his ears and his green eyes danced with excitement.

"Don't tell me you didn't bring the groom?" Marcus demanded. "How can I know if he's worthy if I don't meet him?"

"Ricardo is working tonight, but he invited you and Edith to dinner tomorrow night." Vera hugged him back.

"I love dinner parties; it's the best way to get fed in Manhattan." Marcus sat down and picked up his drink. "I'm a growing boy and I'm always hungry."

"Marcus is the new 'It' boy in New York art circles," Edith chimed in, her cheeks glowing from the pleasure of being with Marcus. "Everyone wants him at their table: he dined at the Knickerbocker Club with the Vanderbilts."

"That was almost a disaster," Marcus laughed. "The attendant slipped a note with his phone number into my coat and Preston found it. I had to swear I didn't say two words to him; it was completely one-sided."

"Preston is the owner of the gallery where Marcus shows his work," Edith said. "He owns the apartment where Marcus is staying."

"Not for much longer," Marcus announced. "After the next sale, I'm buying my own place in Gramercy Park. It's only a studio apartment, but I'll have a key to the park. Can you imagine?" He grinned. "Marcus Sorrento strolling in a private park!"

"We're so proud of you." Vera smiled. "Only the most talented make it in New York."

"The critics write that I have a 'special eye.' But the truth is I fall in love with my subject." Marcus gazed at Edith.

"You were never in love with me," Edith retorted.

"Of course I was in love. Perhaps not with my body, but here." He touched his heart and sighed. "If only the heart and all the organs could agree on everything, life would be perfect."

"Don't worry; I got over it," Edith laughed. "I hope Preston treats you right. You don't need him; you'd do fine by yourself."

"Preston has his own side adventures, and what he doesn't know won't hurt him." He reached into his pocket and took out two envelopes. "We're not here to talk about my romances. I have a surprise for both of you."

Vera opened it and inside was a check for ten thousand dollars.

"What's this?" she asked.

"The photographs of you and Edith in *LIFE* magazine were bought by a member of the Astor family," Marcus said. "I decided we should split it three ways."

"We can't take this." Vera handed it back. "It's *your* photograph."

"If it wasn't for those photographs, I'd be lugging my camera around Naples and working part-time in Paolo's restaurant," Marcus responded. "Instead, I'm living in New York and being fed steak and baked Alaska."

Vera remembered sitting at the outdoor cafés in Naples with Anton, and her heart constricted. He'd be wearing his khaki uniform and asking if she'd like a strawberry or lime gelato.

"Don't look sad; we all get nostalgic for the time we spent together," Marcus said, noticing her expression. "Life is simple when it's about having enough to eat and seeing a roof over one's head instead of the stars. Now we have to grow up and prove ourselves."

"Look who turned into a philosopher." Edith grinned.

"I'm only saying what's true," Marcus replied. "I get letters from Paolo and Leo. The black market has dried up because people can find things in the shops, and men aren't buying jewelry for their girlfriends because they're not afraid of going off and getting killed. They both have to work hard for a living. Because of that photograph, I get to do what I love. You both deserve part of it."

Vera picked up the check. She could buy back her diamond ring and Edith could pay off the creditors.

Vera looked at Edith and Edith nodded.

"All right, we accept," Vera beamed.

"I knew I could make you see it my way!" Marcus exclaimed. "We must have dinner tonight to celebrate."

Vera had mentioned to Ricardo that she was meeting Edith and Marcus for drinks, but she didn't say they were having dinner. But Ricardo wouldn't be home until midnight. Why shouldn't she stay? She was already here and she was hungry.

"I'd love to." Vera nodded happily. "As long as we split the check three ways."

"That might not be fair." Marcus glanced at the door. "I invited a friend to join us."

Vera followed Marcus's gaze and saw a boy of about twenty with dark hair and narrow cheekbones. His shirt was unbuttoned and a blazer was slung over his shoulder.

"Where did you find him?" Edith wondered.

"I met Philippe on the airplane." Marcus waved him over. "If all men in Caracas look like Philippe, I'll have to stay longer."

They moved to a booth and ordered shrimp cocktail. Philippe sat next to Vera, with Marcus and Edith across from them.

"Philippe is an art student at the university and he models for some of the art classes." Marcus dipped his shrimp in sauce. "I offered to photograph him, but he refused."

"First Marcus has to prove that photography is real art." Philippe looked at Marcus mischievously. "Then I'll let him take my picture."

A shadow loomed over the table and Vera looked up. Ricardo stood at the end of the booth. His brow was knotted together and his eyes were black as thunderclouds.

"Ricardo! What are you doing here?" Vera exclaimed. She pointed at the two men. "This is Marcus and Philippe."

"I see that I surprised you." Ricardo's voice was tight.

"I didn't expect you back so early," Vera stammered. "Please join us."

Ricardo's eyes stayed on Vera. "I don't think so. It seems the table is full."

"We'll make room," Vera said, but Ricardo had turned toward the door.

She squeezed out of the booth and hurried after him. The door to the restaurant closed and he stepped onto the street.

"Ricardo, wait! I can explain." She ran after him.

Ricardo got into his car and turned on the ignition. His face was red and he raised his voice. "There's nothing to explain. I'm sorry I interrupted your dinner."

The car raced down the avenue and Vera stood frozen on the sidewalk. She didn't know whether to go back inside or go home. She thought about the look of distaste in Ricardo's eyes and felt a pit in her stomach.

Vera stood in the living room of her new house and peered out the window. She had made her excuses to Edith and Marcus and driven home. But it was ten p.m. and she hadn't heard from Ricardo. He hadn't come home.

If only she had told Ricardo that Marcus liked men, he would have realized that Philippe was there for Marcus. Instead he thought he interrupted a romantic dinner and didn't give her a chance to explain.

She picked up the phone and dialed his parents' phone number.

"Hello, its Vera," Vera said when Alessandra answered.

"Vera, why are you calling so late? Is everything all right?"

"I wondered if Ricardo was there." She clutched the phone.

"No, he's not." Alessandra paused. "Should he be?"

Vera took a deep breath. Alessandra was the only person who understood Ricardo well enough to know what to do.

"We got into a fight and I don't know where he went," she admitted.

The phone was silent and then Alessandra's voice came over the line. "Why don't you come over and talk?"

"I told Ricardo I was meeting Marcus and Edith for drinks, but I didn't know we were going to have dinner," Vera said to Alessandra. They sat in the living room of the Albee mansion. The chandeliers were dim and the house was quiet.

"Ricardo came into the restaurant and saw us in the booth—" She fiddled with her teacup. "There was another man at the table. Marcus met him on the airplane; he was very attractive."

"An attractive man?" Alessandra repeated.

"Marcus likes men," Vera said uncomfortably. "I should have told Ricardo, but I thought he wouldn't approve. Now he thinks I was with another man."

The expression on Alessandra's face changed and her shoulders relaxed.

"I see. That explains everything. You have to understand why

Ricardo was upset. In Venezuela, it's not done for a married woman to dine in public without her husband," she said thoughtfully. "Naturally he thought something was going on."

"It was perfectly innocent, but I've never seen Ricardo so angry. He drove off without letting me explain." Her eyes widened. "What if he got into an accident?"

"Don't worry. Ricardo has been driving since he was fourteen," Alessandra assured her. "Ricardo loves you very much, but sometimes love comes with many emotions. Pedro is the same. When we were first married, Pedro didn't like me talking to men at parties unless he was standing beside me. He still treats me like one of his family's racehorses: he's proud of my accomplishments, but he's afraid of anyone stealing me away."

"That doesn't upset you?" Vera wondered.

Alessandra nodded. "It did at first. I attended lectures and read books that men and women should be equal. But even if that's true, marriage is about making each other happy. Sometimes that takes work."

"What should I do?" Vera asked.

"You tell Ricardo the truth," Alessandra said simply. "And then you forgive each other."

The light in the living room was on when Vera arrived home. She walked down the hallway and found Ricardo sitting on the sofa.

"Would you like a brandy?" He raised his glass. "Or have you had enough? It's midnight, you must have had quite a few."

"I've been at your mother's," Vera replied. "I should have called to see if you were home."

"What were you doing at my mother's?" Ricardo asked suspiciously.

"Marcus likes men," she began. "Philippe was his date."

Ricardo sighed.

"Why didn't you tell me?" Ricardo asked. His voice sharpened and he grabbed her wrist.

Vera felt the weight of his hand on hers and shifted uncomfortably. "I thought you might not approve of him."

Ricardo let go of her wrist, then stood up and walked to the bar. His back was to Vera and she couldn't tell what he was thinking.

"In South America, a wife doesn't dine in public without her husband. You don't know what it was like to enter that restaurant and see you all together." He turned around. "How would I keep my wife if the first night I'm away, she's with another man?"

"I hadn't planned on staying for dinner, and I would never be with another man," Vera responded. "You're my husband and I love you."

Ricardo took her in his arms. "My darling Vera, please forgive me."

Vera thought about the time Ricardo got so angry with her at Alberto's nightclub because he had seen Captain Bingham entering her office. A chill ran down her spine. But Alessandra said they should tell the truth and then forgive each other.

She kissed him.

"I cannot live without you," he whispered. "I promise I won't doubt you again."

Ricardo held her hand and they walked upstairs. He undressed quickly and kissed her again, undoing the buttons on her dress.

Vera peeled off her stockings and joined him on the bed.

"*Mi gran amor*," he whispered. "You're everything to me."

She started to answer but he was already on top of her. She closed her eyes and his hands moved skillfully over her body. Then he was inside her and his moans became one long, final groan.

Vera waited until Ricardo was asleep and then padded downstairs and poured a glass of water. Alessandra said that love came with many emotions, but was that always true? She and Anton had been in love, and it simply meant that they wanted to spend all their time together.

The war made her appreciate the importance of family and security. If Ricardo couldn't control his small jealousies, it was up to her to put him at ease. She finished the water and walked back upstairs. Ricardo was her husband, and she would do everything to make it a happy marriage.

CHAPTER TWENTY-ONE

December 1947

Vera sat at her desk at J. Walter Thompson and studied the sketch of a young woman sitting in the driver's seat of a yellow convertible. Underneath was her English copy: *Give her the keys to a GM car and win the keys to her heart.*

Her own green car was parked outside, and she was meeting Ricardo at the Plaza Altamira for lunch. It was wonderful to be able to go wherever she pleased. And since she started driving, the ideas for ad copy came so fast she kept a notepad and pencil in the glove compartment.

After her dinner with Edith and Marcus, she resolved there would be no new secrets in her marriage. She used Marcus's check to buy back her engagement ring. She even debated telling Ricardo about Anton.

Ricardo had been solicitous, arriving home with a pretty bracelet or a box of bonbons. In return she learned to cook his favorite recipes and took his shoes to the shoeshine. Ricardo inherited his love of fine shoes from his father, and he liked to have them shined to perfection.

There was a knock. Mr. Matthews stood in the doorway.

"It's wonderful having you back." Mr. Matthews entered her office. "Your copy is excellent, and the office smells of perfume instead of the chicken Juan ate at his desk for lunch."

"I love being married, but I missed working," Vera agreed. "It's nice to think about something other than how many spoonfuls of sugar to use in a *quesillo*."

"The ad campaign aimed at women is brilliant," Mr. Matthews said approvingly. "You've opened up a new market."

"You were right. You can't describe the thrill of driving until you get behind the wheel." Her eyes sparkled. "Now I'm like Joan Crawford in her Lincoln. There's nothing better than flying down the road wearing leather driving gloves and the wind in your hair."

"There's something I want to talk about." Mr. Matthews sat opposite her. "Harold is moving back to Boston and I need a head copywriter. I was going to start interviewing but you could save me the trouble. I wondered if you'd like the job."

"You want me to be head copywriter?" Vera gasped.

"There would be more responsibility and you'd work longer hours, but you'd get a raise and an expense account." He grinned. "Clients love to be taken to lunch by our star copywriter."

If Vera got a raise, she could help her father earn his law degree. But how would Ricardo feel if she worked later? Would he approve of her dining with strange men?

"Thank you, it's a tremendous opportunity." Vera reached over to shake his hand. "I'm meeting Ricardo for lunch. Do you mind if I ask him first?"

"I'm sure Ricardo will say yes." Mr. Matthews shook her hand and stood up. "He was the one who suggested I hire you in the first place."

*   *   *

The Plaza Altamira was an elaborate square in the middle of the city, with an obelisk taller than Caracas Cathedral and a stone fountain. Couples shared picnics under oak trees and tourists strolled past flags from different countries.

"It was a great idea to come here," Vera said to Ricardo when he spread a blanket over the grass. He carried a picnic basket with a loaf of pan de jamón, cheese, and fresh fruit.

"Arthur Kahn designed the Plaza Altamira a few years ago." Ricardo handed her a plate. "He had a vision of Caracas resembling Paris with its wide boulevards and elegant squares. I thought you'd enjoy it; it's one of my favorite spots in Caracas."

"I have exciting news," she began. "Mr. Matthews came into my office this morning. The head copywriter is leaving and he offered me the position. I'd get a raise and an expense account."

Ricardo peeled a grape and looked at Vera. His eyes were dark. "I don't think that's a good idea," he said in a clipped tone.

"I thought you'd be pleased. After all, it's because you gave me the car," she said gaily. "I love to drive and it shows in my work."

"You don't have to work. We agreed you'd give it up after a year."

"We said we'd talk about it," Vera responded. "I want a family, too, but these days women can do both."

"You sound like the lectures my mother attends at the university." Ricardo's voice was sharp.

"What if I do?" Vera asked. "Alessandra supports them."

"With her donations. Not by working herself," Ricardo said, and then his voice softened. "My mother understands her place in Venezuelan society, and you will too. Why should we change things?

There's no one I'd rather have lunch with than my beautiful wife. I don't want to share you with businessmen. And you don't need more money. You can spend what you earn now on yourself and help your parents."

Vera opened her mouth to say something, but Ricardo leaned forward and kissed her.

"Let's talk about it tonight. After we eat, we can stroll around the fountain." He sliced a peach and gave it to her. "It's a beautiful day and you only have an hour for lunch."

Vera accepted the peach and felt deflated. She had hoped Ricardo would have been more supportive. But there was no point in spoiling their time together. She would try to convince him later.

"All right, we'll talk about it tonight."

All afternoon Vera watched the clock and hoped Mr. Matthews didn't return from his client meeting until five o'clock. She needed to talk to Edith but she couldn't see her until after work.

Finally, Vera waved good-bye to the receptionist and jumped into her car. She drove to the building in the Las Mercedes neighborhood and hurried up the stairs to Edith's workspace.

"Look at you," Vera said, admiring Edith in her black dress with her blond hair tied in a bun. "You look like the magazine photos of Coco Chanel in her atelier before the war."

"We're hardly the same," Edith grunted. "By the time Coco Chanel was twenty-five she owned an apartment building on the rue Cambon in Paris. I'm already twenty and I can barely afford the rent on a tiny workroom that smells of black beans and garlic because it's too hot to close the window," she said. Her face broke into a smile.

"But I'm so grateful to Marcus for bailing me out. I'm happiest when my fingers are flying over the fabric."

Edith had used Marcus's check to appease the creditors and make a payment to the bank. She gave up the boutique in the Majestic and traded a more spacious workroom for a small space above a restaurant.

"Kitty ordered four dresses for the holidays and paid for two in advance." Edith stretched a piece of taffeta over the worktable. "If I'm careful and don't buy any more thimbles, I'm going to make it after all."

"You need thimbles. What will you do if you prick your finger?" Vera laughed. "I have some news." She paused. "Mr. Matthews offered me the head copywriter job."

"That's wonderful!" Edith hugged her.

"Ricardo doesn't think so." Vera frowned. "He doesn't want me to accept it."

"But the whole point of working is to be successful," Edith responded.

"I'd have to work longer hours and entertain clients."

"I thought Ricardo promised to trust you," Edith giggled. "Though I can't blame him for being jealous of Philippe. Philippe was so beautiful; I would have slept with him if he asked."

"Of course Ricardo trusts me," Vera answered. "We don't need the money, and we're going to start a family soon."

"Maybe you could do both. Venezuela is conservative, but the whole world is changing since the war," Edith said. "And remember Marie Curie. She won the Nobel Prize in 1903 and in 1911 and raised two children."

"I love my job, but I want children more than anything," Vera mused.

"You might need to think about it sooner than you planned." Edith looked at Vera curiously. "That dress fits you differently; you're thicker around the waist."

Vera glanced down at her dress. "I bought the dress before the wedding, when I was so nervous I could barely eat a bite."

"It's not the dress." Edith walked around her. "Look at your breasts."

"What are you talking about?" Vera wondered.

"Do you remember the female anatomy book I read during the war?" Edith asked. "When was your last period?"

Vera flushed. "I don't remember. Before the wedding."

"That's two months!" Edith said. "And you've always been regular. Even when we stayed at the Dunkels' farm and there was never enough to eat, you never missed a cycle."

Vera's heart pounded. She remembered their honeymoon, when they made love every night. Ricardo covered her with kisses and whispered she was the most beautiful woman in the world.

"I can't be pregnant!" Vera's eyes widened.

"Many brides come back from their honeymoon already fat." Edith pulled the fabric tighter. "Except you'll be beautiful. You'll blossom like the flowers in Naples when we first arrived."

Vera remembered sitting in the piazza in Naples and watching teenagers zoom by on Vespas. Less than two years ago they were young girls in a new country, wondering whether they should spend Vera's salary on stockings or plates of spaghetti. Now Vera was married and going to have a baby.

"What should I do?" Vera asked.

"You find a doctor," Edith declared. "And then you get used to the idea of becoming a mother."

*　　　*　　　*

Vera parked a few blocks from the new house and turned off the engine. She needed time to think before she went home to Ricardo. A doctor would only confirm what Edith suspected. Vera's body had changed; she had just been too preoccupied to notice.

Her chest constricted. She pictured the dinner when Anton proposed and told her he was sterile. She had gone back to her room and tried to imagine a life without children. How would she feel if she was married to Anton and discovered she was pregnant so soon after the wedding? But that was an impossible idea.

If it were a boy, Ricardo would take him fishing and teach him about cars. Vera would buy a girl books and pretty dresses. There would be horseback riding and dinners at the Albees' with Vera's parents.

Being part of a family was the best feeling in the world. She remembered when she was a child and her parents took her to *The Nutcracker* ballet at the Budapest Opera House. There was nothing more thrilling than sitting between her mother in her fur stole and her father with his top hat and watching the dancers pirouette across the stage.

It was December 1937 and Vera was ten years old. That night was the Kirov Ballet's performance of *The Nutcracker*, and Vera couldn't be more excited.

The opera house resembled an illustration in a storybook, with gold frescoed ceilings and crystal chandeliers. Just entering the horseshoe-shaped concert hall made Vera feel like a princess. Everything seemed draped in opulent fabrics: there were red velvet seats and burgundy silk curtains covering the stage.

The stage was set with a Christmas tree and a fireplace hung with stockings and a table piled with so many presents, they threatened to topple on the floor. Dancers dressed as toy soldiers marched across the stage, and the ballerina who played Clara was impish and graceful at the same time.

A bell chimed for intermission and Vera followed her parents into the lobby.

"I want to go every year," Vera sighed, adjusting her party dress. "The girl playing Clara can't be much older than me, and she's better than Anna Pavlova."

Anna Pavlova had died in 1931, but she had been her mother's favorite ballerina. Alice told Vera all about Anna Pavlova's career as the prima ballerina of the Imperial Russian Ballet and Ballet Russes.

"No one danced better than Anna Pavlova," her mother replied. "But the ballerina playing Clara is very good. The Kirov has the best dancers in Europe; we're lucky to see them in Budapest."

"Your mother would have been just as good if she kept dancing," her father said, nodding at a family that strolled past. "I saw her onstage in Paris. She was an exquisite Giselle."

"It was a student performance," Alice said modestly. "When I was a little girl I used to pray every night that I would be a great ballerina."

"Why did you quit if you loved it so much?" Vera wondered. "You could still dance after you were married."

"Being a ballet dancer can make it hard to have children. I didn't want to spend years performing and discover too late that we couldn't have a child."

"But you prayed that you wanted to be a ballerina." Vera was puzzled. "Weren't you disappointed that your prayers didn't come true?"

Alice hugged Vera against her evening gown. "Sometimes God answers your prayers even when you don't ask him. I wouldn't trade having you for all the pointe shoes in the world."

Vera ran her hands over the steering wheel and imagined the baby growing inside her. Her mother said that when she was at Auschwitz she prayed for Vera because she didn't want God to desert Vera too. Perhaps God was watching over her. A baby was just what she and Ricardo needed, so that she could forget Anton and Ricardo could stop his small jealousies.

She drove the few blocks to the new house. Ricardo's car was in the driveway and she ran upstairs to their bedroom.

"Where have you been?" he asked, fastening his cuff links. "We have a dinner party tonight."

"I'm sorry, it won't take me long to get ready," she apologized. "I'd like to talk about something first."

"It's not polite to be late." Ricardo frowned. "Can we talk about the copywriter job after the party?"

Vera shook her head. "It's not about the job."

"What is it?" he asked.

Ricardo looked so handsome with his dark hair and white shirt. He was her husband and they were going to be a family.

"I haven't been to the doctor, but I'm quite sure"—she touched her stomach and took a deep breath—"I'm pregnant."

Ricardo dropped a cuff link and his face crumpled. For a moment she thought he was still angry that she had dinner with Edith and Marcus without asking his permission, and she felt a tremor of fear. Then he walked to the bedside table and took out a velvet box.

"This is for you." He handed it to her.

Vera opened it and inside were diamond earrings as delicate as snowflakes.

"I was going to give them to you for Kitty's holiday gala, but I want you to wear them now." He kissed her. "You've made me the happiest man in the world."

Ricardo fastened them on and she turned to the mirror. The diamonds glittered in her ears and she recalled Anton slipping the diamond engagement ring on her finger.

"We're going to have a baby," Ricardo whispered, circling his arms around her waist.

Vera touched her dress and realized it was wet with her tears. It was normal to cry; pregnant women were always emotional. She wiped them away.

CHAPTER TWENTY-TWO

January 1948

It had been three weeks since the doctor confirmed Vera's pregnancy and she already felt different. It was silly, of course; she was barely three months pregnant. It was too soon to wear the bright tunics Edith sewed for her, and it would be months until she could use the cotton baby blankets Alessandra had saved.

But things were different; she and Ricardo had become closer. He brought her warm milk and they discussed baby names and the paint color for the nursery. Even their lovemaking had changed. Ricardo was as attentive, but there was a new softness about him.

Vera declined the promotion and Ricardo agreed to let her keep working until she couldn't fit behind her desk. Alessandra showed her a photo of herself when she was pregnant with Ricardo, her stomach as round as a watermelon, and Vera laughed that she would never be that big.

It was midafternoon and she parked her car in front of her parents' bungalow. Her mother was in the kitchen, stirring milk into coffee.

"I brought you flowers." Vera handed her a bunch of lilacs. "Ricardo brings flowers every night. If it's not flowers, it's something for the baby. Last week he brought a toy train set and yesterday it was a doll to show he'd be just as happy having a girl."

"Ricardo is going to be a wonderful father." Alice nodded, pouring two cups of coffee and handing one to Vera.

"I've never seen him so excited." Vera sat at the kitchen table. "He used to read car catalogs, but he got his hands on the childcare book by Dr. Spock that is the rage in America."

"Men are made for different things. Your father is even happier being a law student than he was being a lawyer." Alice smiled. "He spends all his time at the university library. The only thing that would please him more would be if he spoke Spanish well enough to teach the classes himself."

"That reminds me, I have a check for you." Vera took an envelope out of her purse.

"You can't give us all your money." Alice shook her head.

"There's nothing else to do with it. Ricardo insists on paying for everything." She put the envelope on the table and noticed a blue envelope with an airmail stamp.

"What's this?" Vera asked.

"It's a letter from Gina in Naples. I asked Captain Bingham for her address so I could thank her for finding you," Alice said. "It arrived yesterday."

"What did she say?" Vera asked, wondering if there was any news of Anton.

"I haven't opened it." Alice tore it open. She read the letter and handed it to Vera. "You should read it too."

Vera picked it up and scanned the scrawled writing.

Dear Alice,

It was wonderful to receive your letter. Since Captain Wight closed the embassy, I haven't had much chance to practice my English.

When I learned that you have been reunited with Vera, I broke down in tears. I have two girls and there is nothing like the bond between mothers and daughters.

Vera and Captain Wight worked so well together. When they fell in love and got engaged, I was as delighted as if Vera was my own child.

If only it could have worked out, but one can't fault Captain Wight. He cherished Vera more than any man could love a woman.

Please give Vera my love and tell her she and Edith must visit. Louis still tends the garden at the embassy, and there is no one to eat his oranges.

Warmest regards,

Gina

The paper fluttered to the table and Vera met her mother's eyes. "You were engaged?" Alice asked.

"Captain Wight was my boss at the embassy." Vera began. "At first I tried to ignore my feelings, but he was so kind. I told him all about my past: how I felt responsible that you were at Auschwitz, and that Edith and I lived for a year with the parents of a soldier who fought in the German army, and he still loved me." Her eyes were bright. "And he understood about the war. He said one day new philosophers and artists will rise out of the Nazi ruin. No man can wipe out the light in the world forever."

"Don't tell me he went back to America and forgot about you," Alice cut in.

"It was nothing like that." Vera shook her head. "The night Anton proposed he told me he had mumps as a child and was sterile. I was devastated; you know how much I've always wanted children. But I still said yes. I loved Anton and I couldn't imagine life without him."

"What happened?" Alice asked.

"He bought tickets to America. We were so excited." Vera folded her hands. "One morning, I arrived at the embassy and he was gone. He left a letter saying he couldn't marry me. I deserved children and he would never forgive himself for ruining my happiness."

Alice folded the letter and put it in the envelope. "What does Ricardo say?"

"Ricardo doesn't know about Anton. You can't tell him about Gina's letter," Vera said frantically. "Ricardo gets terribly jealous and I don't want to upset him," she sighed. "None of it matters anyway. Anton disappeared and I'll never see him again."

"Love arrives and leaves on its own schedule," Alice commented. "But sometimes a great love affair can last the rest of your life."

"What do you mean?" Vera wondered.

"Let me tell you a story." Alice refilled her coffee cup. "After the war, I stayed with Gunther and Marie in Bavaria for eleven months. At first I was too weak to travel, and then it was too cold. By the time I left for Budapest, it was March 1946. It was still cold, but Marie gave me warm clothes and a little money. One night I stopped for dinner at an inn in the village of Mistendorf. It started snowing and I didn't know what to do. I couldn't afford lodging but if I started walking, I'd freeze.

"The woman at the next table offered to share her room for the night. Her husband and sons weren't arriving until the next morning.

"I moved to her room and stayed up talking all night. Her name was Helen Gottfried. She was born to a wealthy Jewish family in Berlin. She married a furrier and they had two sons, Nathan and Samuel.

266

"In 1943 her husband was detained at Buchenwald, and she was left in their apartment with the boys. There was a bombing raid and the apartment and its contents were destroyed while she and her sons were out shopping. She took the opportunity to obtain forged papers saying she was Anna Hoffman, whose husband was a captain in the German army stationed near Minsk. Then she installed herself and her sons in a vacant flat." Alice paused. "One day there was a knock and two Gestapo officers stood in the hall. They asked for her papers. It was the longest five minutes of her life. The officer was about to hand them back when he remarked they were almost the same age and from the village of Oberstdorf in Bavaria. But he didn't know anyone with the last name of Hoffman.

"For her birthplace, Helen had written the name of a ski village she and her family visited as a child. If the Gestapo officer discovered that she had lied, she and her sons would be shot. Helen smiled and said she remembered him; she had a crush on him since the sixth grade. Then she whispered that if he came back that night, she would show him how she had loved him.

"The two Gestapo officers approved her papers, but she couldn't stay in the apartment. She threw clothes in a suitcase and for the next two years she and her sons kept moving. She took whatever work she could find, and whenever someone suspected she wasn't Anna Hoffman, she moved on.

"I asked where she found the courage to keep going. She said whenever she gave up hope, she could hear her beloved Dietrich in her head, encouraging her to keep going.

"The next morning, Helen insisted I have breakfast with her husband and sons when they arrived. A dark-haired man appeared with two teenage boys. I shook the man's hand and said: 'You must be Dietrich; it's a pleasure to meet you.' He gave me an odd look and said his name was Josef. Then he introduced me to his sons and said he was the luckiest man. For eighteen years he had been married to the most beautiful woman in Berlin and they had a wonderful family.

"Helen and I went to her room to gather my things and I apologized for getting her husband's name wrong. She said I had heard her story correctly. Dietrich was her great love, but her parents separated them twenty years ago because they wanted her to marry a Jew. Helen thought that because she was able to survive without the love of her life, she could survive the war." Alice looked at Vera. "But she still made her husband happy and was a good mother to her sons."

"What are you saying?" Vera's voice was shaky.

"You may never love the same way as you did with Anton, but you can still lead a fulfilling life with many rewards." Alice pointed to Vera's stomach. "Soon you will know a love greater than you can imagine. After I pushed you off the train to Auschwitz, you could smell the desperation in the air. Women whispered in low voices and the elderly prayed aloud they'd die before they arrived. In comparison, I was as light and carefree as a girl. It didn't matter what happened to me; my only daughter was going to survive."

Vera hugged her mother so tightly she could feel Alice's heart beating.

"Is it all right to want a girl?" Vera asked. "Because Gina is right, there is no bond greater than that between mothers and daughters."

Vera left her parents' bungalow and drove through the colonial town of El Hatillo. Music spilled onto the streets and it was as if a weight had been lifted off her shoulders. It was all right if Anton kept part of her heart; she could still make Ricardo happy.

Tonight she would ask Ricardo if they could go dancing. Afterward they could stop by the Albees' for a nightcap.

She pulled up in front of Lola's boardinghouse and skipped up the front steps. Edith sat in the living room and there was a small box on the coffee table.

"You called and said it was important." Vera hugged her. "I just came from my parents' house. My mother received a letter from Gina; she insists we come to Naples and eat Louis's oranges. I'll have to tell her to come and eat the oranges in Caracas," she laughed. "I won't be going anywhere with a baby."

"I received something in the mail too." Edith pushed the box across the table.

Vera opened it and inside was a diamond-and-ruby engagement ring.

"You're engaged! But you haven't been seeing anyone," Vera exclaimed. "Don't tell me it's from Marcus. You can't move to New York to keep Marcus's mother happy."

"It's not from Marcus." Edith's eyes were rimmed with black. "It's from Stefan."

"What?" Vera's eyes widened. Her heart hammered and she was overwhelmed with shock and happiness.

"It came with a letter." Edith pointed to a sheet of stationery. On the top was printed:

From the office of Dr. Henry Abrahamson
Montreux, Switzerland

" 'Dear Miss Ban,' " Edith read out loud.

" 'You don't know me, but that's the thing about war. It scatters families around the world and unites complete strangers. Before the war, I practiced medicine in Budapest. In May 1944, I was put on a train to Strasshof. When we arrived, the inmates were divided into two groups. The young and healthy were placed in one barracks and those who were sick or too weak to work were crowded together. Many men were so weak, they died in their beds, and illness spread through the dormitory like wildfire.

" 'I possessed the one thing a doctor craves: opium. I smuggled it into the camp. I'd had a heart defect since I was a child, but I used the opium to bribe the intake doctor to write me a clean bill of health. Soon I realized that wasn't enough. The physical labor was too demanding and I grew too weak to even swallow a piece of bread.

" 'Every mealtime I sat next to a young man from Budapest named Stefan. We became friends quickly. After the first week, Stefan noticed I couldn't keep up with the work and started doing it for me. He'd carry his bricks and then come back and transport mine. He even offered me his daily bowl of soup.

" 'In June 1944 we had visitors to the camp. They were passengers on a train bound for Switzerland and had been delayed at Strasshof. I recognized one of my patients, Frederic Goldberg, and he told me the story. A Hungarian Jewish lawyer named Rudolf Kastner had made a deal with Adolf Eichmann to allow a thousand Jews to travel safely to Switzerland in exchange for money and jewels paid to the Gestapo.

" 'Frederic offered to smuggle me on the train and I accepted as long as Stefan could come too. It was the most unusual journey. The passengers were chosen by a committee, and they included scientists and rabbis and artists. Each passenger was allowed to bring two changes of clothing and enough food for ten days.

" 'On the journey there were several illnesses, and I was able to cure three cases of pneumonia. On the second to last day, a woman named Riva came down with scarlet fever. Riva had a small daughter named Rose; they were headed to stay with Riva's sister in Geneva. I gave Riva what medicine I had, but I couldn't save her. After Riva died, none of the passengers would go near Rose because they were afraid she was contagious. But Stefan and Rose had become friends and he insisted on delivering Rose to her aunt. I can still see Rose on Stefan's shoulders, crossing the train station to meet a woman holding a teddy bear.

" 'The aunt gave Stefan a diamond-and-ruby ring as a thank-you, and then Stefan and I traveled to Montreux. If you've never been to Switzerland, you are missing the most picturesque landscape: snow-covered mountains and castles perched on the edge of lakes. We found lodging and Stefan started making plans. He was going to join the resistance and go back to Hungary to find you. Then he would bring you to Switzerland.

" 'One night he called me to his bed and I knew before he told me. He had all the symptoms of scarlet fever: the cough and the chills and the dreaded rash on his chest and back. He made me promise that if anything happened to him, I would find you and give you this ring. Stefan died three days later.

" 'I started looking for you after the war, but I got busy and gave up. My wife, Bella, joined me in Montreux and I became a junior doctor in a medical practice. A few months ago, Bella traveled to Caracas to visit friends and returned with a dress with the label "Edith Ban." I asked if she met the designer and when she described you, I was certain I found Stefan's great love.

" 'People think doctors are only concerned with prescribing penicillin and mending broken bones, but medicine is a mystical science. I have always had a strong belief in fate. I recently met the psychiatrist

Carl Jung. Jung lives in Zurich and for decades he has been working on a theory called "synchronicity," which is a series of meaningful coincidences that change your life forever. Receiving this letter from a complete stranger on another continent might seem odd, but Jung would say it was inevitable. I believe I was meant to find you as strongly as Stefan believed that you and Stefan would be together forever.

"'I have enclosed your ring and I hope you will come to Montreux as our guest. It is because of Stefan that I draw breath every day, and I will never forget him.'"

Edith folded the letter and the air in Lola's living room was perfectly still.

"I knew Stefan was dead," Edith whispered. "I knew as clearly as my own name."

Vera took Edith in her arms and let her sob. She tried to think of something to say, but there weren't words big enough for Edith's grief.

She recalled her mother saying that having one great love affair was enough to last your whole life. Perhaps this time God could make an exception. Edith was young and she had suffered so much. She deserved to experience true love again.

CHAPTER TWENTY-THREE

February 1948

Vera opened her drawers and searched for her evening bag. Ricardo would be home soon and she wasn't quite ready. It had been two weeks since Edith received Stefan's engagement ring, and Edith had thrown herself into her work. Tonight Kitty was hosting a fashion show, and Vera promised she and Ricardo would be there.

Her hands touched a smooth object and she took it out. It was a pistol with a silver handle. Since when did Ricardo own a gun?

Vera placed it on the bedside table and tried to think. Many men in Caracas owned firearms. Alessandra mentioned Pedro kept a revolver in case of intruders, and Julius often said Caracas was dangerous at night; it was safer to carry a gun.

But what was it doing in her drawer? Perhaps Ricardo took it out to clean it and returned it to her drawer by accident. She put the pistol back and kept searching for her evening bag. She'd ask him about it tomorrow.

*　　*　　*

Kitty's driveway was already filled with cars when she and Ricardo arrived. Men and women filtered into the villa and the air smelled of flowers and perfume.

"I'm glad we came," Vera said to Ricardo when they entered the living room. French doors opened onto the terrace and waiters passed with trays of champagne. "Edith has been working so hard on her new designs."

She noticed a familiar man standing at the bar. She tried to remember where she'd seen him. He nodded at her and crossed the room.

"Vera Frankel," he beamed. He was in his early thirties and wore a dark suit. "I was hoping I'd find you here."

"I'm sorry, have we met?" she asked.

"On the RMS *Queen Elizabeth*," he said pleasantly, and held out his hand. "Douglas Bauer."

"Of course." Vera turned to Ricardo. "Douglas is a journalist for *Time* magazine."

Ricardo studied Douglas's American good looks and his jaw tightened.

"It's Vera Albee now. Vera is my wife."

"You did better than me," Douglas chuckled. "I tried to kiss Vera and got my cheek slapped." He sipped his drink. "It wasn't entirely my fault. I told her if she goes to a man's cabin alone at night, she can expect to be kissed."

The veins in Ricardo's forehead protruded.

"What are you doing in Caracas, Mr. Bauer?" Ricardo inquired. "It can't be a coincidence that you appear at the same society event as my wife."

"Not at all. In fact, Vera is one of the reasons I'm here. I'm doing a piece for *Time* on European immigrants who were turned away from

Ellis Island. I remembered the two Hungarian girls who were sponsored by Sam Rothschild before he died. I always wondered what happened to them. I found your names on the *Queen Elizabeth*'s manifest: Vera Frankel and Edith Ban, New York to Caracas, January 1947."

"But why talk to us now?" Vera asked.

"I can't believe *Time* magazine paid for you to come all the way to Caracas to interview two Hungarian refugees," Ricardo said with a look of disdain.

"I combined it with a story on Jewish immigration to Venezuela after the war," Doug replied easily. "Venezuela is one of the least anti-Semitic countries in the world. Last November, Venezuela supported the United Nations edict to establish a Jewish state in Israel. And it's given shelter to hundreds of Jews who had nowhere else to go."

"But how did you find us?" Vera wondered.

"I am a reporter. Caracas isn't a big place, and when you throw around a little of *Time*'s money, it's not hard to discover what you're looking for." He grinned. "I already spotted Edith tonight. She's as stunning as I remember." His eyes took in Vera's velvet evening gown. "I must say, Caracas society suits you. You've grown into a confident young woman."

"I'm afraid you wasted a trip." Ricardo's eyes were black. "Vera doesn't have time to speak to you. She's very busy."

"Not too busy to attend social functions," Douglas noted, and addressed Vera. "Perhaps we can squeeze in an interview on the terrace after the fashion show? Snap some photos of you and Edith together."

"I don't think so." Ricardo took Vera's arm and nodded. "Goodbye, Mr. Bauer. I hope you enjoy your stay in Venezuela."

Douglas reached into his pocket and handed Vera his card. "We are old friends and I came all the way here. I'm staying at the Majestic if you change your mind."

Ricardo pulled Vera away and the card fluttered to the floor. Ricardo's hand pressed harder against Vera's arm. He led her across the ballroom and she followed him, trying to ignore the anxious feeling rising in her throat.

Vera sat at her dressing table and removed her earrings. Ricardo had insisted they leave right after the fashion show, and he hadn't said a word on the drive home.

"Is it true?" Ricardo appeared behind her. His eyes were bright and he clutched a shot glass. "Did you kiss the journalist who was at the party?"

"It was nothing." Vera placed the earring in her jewelry box. Her hands shook slightly and she noticed her palms were sweaty. "I met Douglas on the *Queen Elizabeth* and he offered to read my writing. I went to his cabin and he tried to kiss me, but I slapped him and pushed him away. I never saw or heard from him again."

"He obviously harbored feelings for you. Why else would he come all the way to Venezuela?" Ricardo continued in a clipped tone.

"He's a journalist. When we met, he'd been traveling around Europe working on war stories for months," Vera replied nervously. "And we hardly exchanged two words tonight. You were with me the whole time."

"You don't understand Venezuelan society," Ricardo fumed. "A man doesn't speak directly to another man's wife. And do you really expect me to believe you didn't know he was here?" he said. "Perhaps he telephoned, or you exchanged letters."

"I've never written him a letter! Douglas was interested in our story. It got quite a bit of attention; it was in *LIFE* magazine," Vera's voice rose. She wanted to say that Ricardo had been rude, but she was afraid to upset him even more.

"And what kind of a woman goes to a man's cabin?" Ricardo persisted. "You wanted him to kiss you."

"I was young and inexperienced." Vera flushed. "Please, let's forget it. My head hurts and I'd like to go to bed."

The muscles in Ricardo's shoulders tightened and there was a trickle of sweat on his forehead. He opened his mouth to say something and then changed his mind.

"I'm going out. I need cigarettes."

"Ricardo, wait." Vera stopped him.

"I'll be home soon." He put his hand on her arm and gripped it tightly. "If Mr. Bauer calls, tell him if he comes near you he'll be sorry."

Vera heard the front door slam and sunk lower onto the stool. She hadn't seen Ricardo so angry since the night of her dinner with Edith and Marcus. Her mind went to the pistol in the bottom drawer and she shivered. But she was being silly. He would go for a drive and come home and apologize.

What if he was still angry when he returned? She couldn't go to Alessandra's again, and she didn't want to appear at her parents' bungalow in the middle of the night.

She climbed into bed and remembered the nights she and Edith slept in the Dunkels' barn and they were terrified a German soldier might appear outside. At least she felt safe inside the barn.

The minute Vera woke the next morning, she sensed something was wrong. Ricardo's side of the bed was undisturbed and when she ran to the window, his car wasn't there.

She walked downstairs, but the house was quiet. Her evening bag was where she left it and Ricardo's coat hung in the closet. He hadn't returned from wherever he'd gone last night.

Her heart pounded and she wondered what to do. Perhaps he slept at his office or took a drive to the beach? What if he went to the Majestic and talked to Douglas Bauer? Douglas might have said something to make Ricardo even more upset.

The windows were closed and the air felt hot and stale. Suddenly she couldn't sit there any longer. She would stay with her parents until Ricardo cooled off. She hurried upstairs to grab a suitcase, and prayed his car wouldn't appear before she was gone.

Vera set the table in her parents' kitchen. Her father would be home from the university soon and they were going to eat stuffed cabbage for lunch.

Ricardo hadn't called, and she was beginning to relax. She would tell him her mother was ill and she was going to spend the night. Tomorrow she would go home and Ricardo would apologize for his behavior and all would be forgiven.

The front door opened and she thought it was her father. Instead Ricardo stood in the doorway. His shirt was creased and his cheeks were dark with stubble.

"What are you doing here?" he demanded.

"I'm helping my mother make lunch," she greeted him. "She wasn't feeling well; I've been here all morning."

"I called your office and the secretary said you were home sick," Ricardo responded.

"It was easier to say that." Vera flushed at being caught in a lie. "I wanted to tell you, but you didn't come home."

"You're hiding something from me," Ricardo accused. His hands were shaking.

"You can ask my mother; she went to the neighbor's to borrow sugar," Vera said and tried to smile. "I'm glad you're here. I'll set another plate and we'll eat together."

"Don't take me for a fool!" Ricardo's eyes flashed. "You were waiting for me to go to work and then you were going to visit Douglas's hotel room. When I didn't come home, you decided to meet him here. Where is he? Is he in the bedroom or has he already left?"

"I wouldn't dream of going to a man's hotel room, and he hasn't been here," Vera responded. "I told you, I didn't know Douglas Bauer was in Caracas. I have no interest in talking to him."

Ricardo ignored her. "I went to the Majestic but he wasn't there. I even asked the concierge, but Bauer didn't leave word where he went. Where else would he be if he wasn't with you or Edith?"

"He could be anywhere; he's writing a piece," Vera reminded him.

"I know men like him; he wasn't about to give up," Ricardo insisted. "Maybe he's arranged a rendezvous in a few days' time when I have to deliver a car to a client in Maracaibo."

He was paranoid.

"You can ask your mother to stay at the house while you're gone," Vera implored. "You're tired and overwrought. Let me make you a cup of coffee and we'll go home."

"You weren't coming home." Ricardo glowered at her. "That's why you packed a suitcase."

Vera froze and her chest tightened. "How do you know I took a suitcase?"

"I searched your closet," Ricardo said and laughed. "My wife is missing when I come home. Do you really think I wouldn't try to find her?"

Vera took a deep breath. She couldn't show Ricardo that she was frightened.

"I told you my mother wasn't feeling well. I thought I'd spend the night if she needed help." She smiled at Ricardo. "I agree it was strange that Douglas appeared at Kitty's," she said, trying to appease him, "but I swear I had no idea that he was in Caracas. He's rude and I want nothing to do with him." She reached up and kissed him. "Please, Ricardo, you must believe me. I love you and I would never look at another man. Let's have lunch and then we'll go home."

Ricardo's lips were cold, and Vera recoiled. But the important thing was for Ricardo to calm down. She stepped forward and kissed him again.

"You say that now, but when it's time to leave, you'll stay here." Ricardo sank into the sofa and his voice faltered. "I love you more than I thought it was possible. When I found out you were pregnant, I was the happiest man in the world. But love can be an illness. It courses through my blood and takes over my brain."

"There's nothing wrong with being in love," Vera soothed him. "I'm in love with you and I'm terribly happy." As she said the words out loud she realized she was lying to herself. What was love without trust? But it didn't matter now; she and Ricardo were married and she was pregnant with his child.

Ricardo took Vera's hand and kissed it. "*Mi amada* Vera, if you could only understand jealousy. It's like the demon at the Christmas festival that darts around stealing children's presents. I see another man near you and I'm possessed. But it's only because I love you and can't imagine life without you."

"You don't have to," she whispered. "I'll always be by your side."

Ricardo put his head in his hands and sobbed. Then he looked up at Vera and his eyes were bright as the moon. "It's too late. I've made you afraid, and it will never be the same again."

"I could never be afraid of you; you're the father of my child," Vera assured him. "Why don't I fix you a brandy? My parents will come and we'll eat."

Ricardo's jaw relaxed and she turned to search for a glass. There was a rustling sound and then everything happened at once. Her parents arrived at the front door and Ricardo slipped something silver out of his pocket. There was a loud pop before she felt the bullet pierce her neck. She heard two more gunshots and then nothing.

CHAPTER TWENTY-FOUR

Vera gazed at the mirror in her dressing room and couldn't believe it had been two months since the terrible night when Ricardo shot her. The scar that the bullet had left was a dark kiss on her skin. She felt ill every time she saw her reflection. When she first woke up after that night and saw her mother at her bedside, she believed she was eight years old and had diphtheria. But she wasn't lying in her childhood bed in Budapest; she was in a hospital in Caracas.

The doctors said it was a miracle. The bullet grazed her neck, and she would make a full recovery. The baby survived as well. The two shots she heard weren't Ricardo shooting her parents, as she had feared; they were Ricardo turning the gun on himself.

Her hospital room was always full of visitors. For the first three weeks her mother slept in a cot beside her. Her father came every evening, and Edith often stayed late into the night. Julius hung a watercolor to brighten the room, Lola delivered food, and Marcus sent flowers. There were letters from Captain Bingham and Gina and Rosa, and cards and chocolates from everyone at the office. Sometimes she wondered if there would be a letter from Anton, but there never was.

Vera dreaded seeing Alessandra, who stayed away. But when she finally arrived, gaunt and haggard in a long black dress, they hugged each other and cried.

So many thoughts whirled through Vera's head. How could Ricardo have been desperate enough to try to kill her and take his own life? She pictured Ricardo with his hands around the pistol and longed to sleep forever. But then she remembered the baby and knew she had so much to be grateful for.

After six weeks she was allowed to return home, and that was almost worse than being in the hospital. How could she sleep in their bed and pass Ricardo's closet, which still held his dinner jackets and polished leather shoes? She didn't have anywhere else to go, and the Albees assured her that the house was hers. Her parents' bungalow was too small and she couldn't move back to Lola's five months pregnant.

Vera descended the staircase to the living room just before her lunch date with Edith. Last week her mother brought over her *lecsó* to fatten Vera up, and announced that her brother Tibby and his family had immigrated to Australia. Tibby invited Alice and Lawrence and Vera to join them. They could share their house on Bronte Beach. Tibby would get Lawrence a job at his accounting firm while he finished his law degree. Alice would help with the baby after it was born, and Vera could go back to work as a copywriter.

Vera listened to the offer and a weight lifted from her shoulders. It would be wonderful to go somewhere no one knew about Ricardo. But she couldn't desert Edith. She spent the last week fretting on how to broach the subject.

There was a knock at the door and Edith swept inside, wearing a belted dress and carrying a stack of magazines.

"Kitty sent some magazines." Edith placed them on the coffee table. "You can catch up on Hollywood gossip. Rita Hayworth met an Arabian prince named Aly Khan at the Cannes Film Festival and she's going to leave her husband."

Vera kissed Edith on the cheek. "Tell Kitty thank you. But I can't sit here all day, eating bonbons and reading magazines."

"You are doing something," Edith reminded her. "You're going to have a baby."

"Something else." Vera arranged a bouquet of flowers. "There's something I want to talk about. My mother's brother, Tibby, invited us to come live with them in Sydney."

"Sydney!" Edith repeated "In Australia?"

"I know it's very far, and I don't want to leave you"—Vera twisted her hands—"it's just I . . ."

Edith took her hand to calm her.

"You must go; Sydney looks beautiful," Edith interrupted. "I've had an offer too. I didn't want to mention it until you felt better. One of Kitty's friends loves my designs and wants to be my silent partner in a boutique."

"That's wonderful," Vera beamed.

"But the boutique wouldn't be in Caracas, it would be in Beverly Hills. The partner would sponsor me. I won't have any trouble getting into America."

"Beverly Hills? But we always dreamed of New York."

"New York is too cold, and Marcus says he can never relax because there's always someone younger and more talented eager to take his place. California sounds much nicer. Kitty's friend Betty Rosen is married to a big movie producer. Cary Grant and Gary Cooper come to their parties at Ciro's." Edith's eyes sparkled. "Can you imagine if I dressed Lauren Bacall?"

Vera pictured Edith sitting next to a kidney-shaped swimming pool sipping pink cocktails with Vivien Leigh and Katharine Hepburn, and for the first time since the bullet entered her neck she felt hopeful.

"They would be lucky to wear an Edith Ban design. One day I'll see your name on the credits at the movies and I'll pinch myself that you're my best friend." Vera's voice faltered. "You see, there is a reason for everything after all."

"A reason?" Edith asked curiously.

"It's nothing. I was thinking out loud." Vera waved her hand. "Do you remember the month in the ghetto when we were afraid something terrible would happen? And then on the train to Auschwitz we were sure we were being transported to our deaths. Then we spent a year on the Dunkels' farm, worrying that we'd get shot by Germans or freeze to death. Even when we arrived in Naples and there was music and laughter and all the pasta we could eat, you were certain that Stefan was dead and we thought our parents hadn't survived.

"And do you remember on the *Queen Elizabeth* when we sat at the captain's table and learned how to use a grapefruit spoon? We were certain our future would include college boys and country clubs. Then Sam Rothschild died and we had to go somewhere new." She looked at Edith. "I thought in Caracas we were finally safe and life would begin."

"We have had a good time," Edith said gently. "We made friends and I started a business and you're going to have a baby."

"It's hard to remember that when Ricardo is lying cold in the ground." Vera's eyes prickled. "The killing was supposed to stop with the war, but it goes on forever."

"Death is everywhere, but so is life," Edith said. "How many mornings did you make me get out of bed when I wanted to lie there missing Stefan? You taught me we have to give it our best try. We're young; we're going to lead happy lives."

Vera hugged Edith tightly.

"I can see it now. You're going to own a string of boutiques and an office in Paramount Studios," Vera laughed. "You'll marry some handsome movie producer and have a mansion in Beverly Hills and two children. But you have to promise me something."

"What is it?" Edith asked.

"Even when Elizabeth Taylor is in the dressing room insisting that the waist on her gown be tighter, you'll take the pins out of your mouth and ask your assistant to mail a letter," Vera said. "Because I won't last a week without hearing from you."

"I promise." Edith hugged her back. "I have to go. I'm going to tell Betty I accept her offer. What does Alessandra say about you moving to Australia with the baby?"

"I haven't told her," Vera admitted. "She's coming over this afternoon."

"Pedro and I have been talking," Alessandra said, sipping a cup of tea.

They were sitting in Vera's dining room and Vera had brought out tea and a plate of biscuits.

"We'll put this house in your name and create a trust fund for the baby," Alessandra continued. "You shouldn't live alone. Perhaps your parents could live with you or you can hire a nurse? We'd pay for it, of course."

"That's very kind," Vera replied. "But I had another idea. My mother's brother, Tibby, and his wife have immigrated to Australia.

They want us to join them. My father speaks good English and it would be easy for him to get a job. I'd live with my parents, and if I went back to work, my mother could care for the baby," she spoke quickly, afraid that Alessandra was going to stop her. "My aunt and uncle lost their son in the war and my aunt is pregnant. The baby would have a cousin to play with."

"Australia!" Alessandra gasped.

"Sydney is supposed to be beautiful," Vera continued. "There's a large Jewish community and friendly people. And I . . ." Her voice trailed off.

Alessandra looked at Vera. "You want a fresh start so you can forget everything that happened."

"It's terrible to take away your grandchild, but I don't know what else to do," Vera said worriedly. "Every day I think of Ricardo and wonder if I could have stopped him. Sometimes I can hardly breathe."

"You did nothing wrong," Alessandra assured her. "Do you remember when we met and talked about the university? I said the most important thing young people need to learn isn't piety or honesty, it's empathy. If we don't have empathy, we are finished. Losing a child for the second time is the most painful thing I could have imagined. But I have Pedro and two daughters and grandchildren." She paused. "If I were you, I'd leap at the chance to move to a new country without any memories."

"What are you saying?" Vera asked.

"Ricardo was my son and I loved him very much. But you have your whole life ahead of you and you deserve to be happy," Alessandra said. "If I stopped you from leaving, I would be acting against my own beliefs. I understand your misery. If you want to go to Australia, you have my blessing."

"I'll write and send photos every week after the baby is born," Vera said fervently.

"He's going to be a beautiful boy." Alessandra nodded.

"How do you know it will be a boy?" Vera wondered.

Alessandra picked up her teacup and smiled. "Even in times like this, one has to have faith in something."

After Alessandra left, Vera spent a long time going through items in Ricardo's study. She wanted to take to Australia some of Ricardo's things so their child would know him. There was a brochure of the New York Motor Show and a photo of Ricardo in front of his dealership in Caracas. Ricardo looked so handsome and proud, his dark hair gleaming in the South American sun. She had just started going through his books when there was a knock at the door. Vera answered it and Rabbi Gorem stood outside. His forehead was shiny from the heat and his coat hung on his thin frame.

"Rabbi Gorem," Vera said. "Please come in."

"I just played chess with your father," Rabbi Gorem said when they were seated in the living room. "He's not a very good actor; I always know when he lets me win."

"Why would he let you win?" Vera wondered.

"Lawrence is a smart man. If he won all the time, he'd lose his chess partner."

"My mother said you've played chess with him almost every day," Vera said. "I'm very grateful."

"Even tragedy comes with blessings. Let me tell you something," Rabbi Gorem said gravely. "I have a neighbor, Esther Blum, who survived Dachau and immigrated to Caracas with her daughter and grandson. Esther lay in a dark room every day and wouldn't talk to anyone. One morning, her daughter went to the market and left her son, Daniel, with his grandmother. Usually Daniel drove Esther crazy playing with his toys while she was resting. But that day the house was too quiet and Esther sensed something was wrong. She jumped out of bed and ran to the bathroom. Daniel's head was submerged in the bath and she thought he had drowned.

"Esther breathed into the boy's mouth until he started breathing. When her daughter came home, Esther and Daniel were sitting in the kitchen eating jelly cakes. Esther thought the Nazis had taken away her strength, but she found it again when she needed it." He paused. "For the first week, your mother was afraid you were going to die. Lawrence comforted her and promised everything would be all right," he finished. "Lawrence found his own strength, and he's not arguing with God so much as to why he lived through and survived the concentration camps."

Vera shivered. "I'm glad. I can't imagine what it's been like for them."

"And how are you?" Rabbi Gorem inquired.

"The doctors say I'm healed"—she touched her neck—"and the baby is fine."

"How are you here?" He tapped his heart.

Vera twisted her hands. The nurses had taken off her wedding ring, and she hadn't put it back on.

"I can't stop thinking about Ricardo," she admitted. "I don't understand how he could care so little about dying. My mother trudged for miles in the snow when they were taken from Flossenbürg, when it would have been easier to lie down and sleep forever. Even Stefan, when he was dying of scarlet fever, was planning how to get the diamond ring to Edith," She looked at Rabbi Gorem plaintively. "How could Ricardo try to kill me and take his own life when millions of Jews would have given anything to live another day?"

Rabbi Gorem was quiet for a minute. "In Judaism we take the study of the soul very seriously. God could not create the soul in everyone equally. Some people are born with souls that reach for the light like buds in the spring. For others it's more difficult to seek true meaning; their thoughts get in the way. Ricardo was a good man, but his soul carried a darkness he couldn't shake." He touched Vera's hand. "But God makes sure no one's life is for nothing. Every Jew who died in the camps left behind something: a piece of music or a poem or a new idea. Your son or daughter will continue what Ricardo started." He smiled gently. "Who knows what future generations of Albees will accomplish?"

Rabbi Gorem left, and Vera carried the tray into the kitchen. She felt a movement and turned around. There was no one there, and so she put her hand to her stomach. She felt the baby stir and she leaned against the counter and smiled.

CHAPTER TWENTY-FIVE

September 1950

Vera and her parents had been in Sydney for two years. Vera had sold Ricardo's house in Caracas and bought a redbrick cottage near Bondi Beach. She and her parents lived there with a small garden filled with fruit trees that Louis in Naples would have loved. Sydney had an excellent trolleybus system and Vera explored the entire city—from Vaucluse, with its leafy streets and grand houses, to Watsons Bay, with its beach and an amazing ice cream shop.

But she and her mother had felt most at home when they discovered Double Bay. Europeans who had owned jewelry stores and fashion boutiques in Hungary and Austria opened the same shops on the tree-lined streets. Every afternoon the cafés were filled with men and women speaking Hungarian and German and eating the kuglof and Dobos tortes displayed in glass cases.

The Australians were the friendliest people Vera had ever met. They loved to sit in a pub with a cold beer and listen to horseraces on the radio. The schoolchildren had sandy-blond hair and freckles and wore straw hats to protect their faces from the sun.

Andrew Lawrence Albee was born at Sydney Royal Hospital on

August 8, 1948. He had dark hair and Ricardo's brown eyes, and from the moment the nurse placed him in Vera's arms, she was in love.

Lawrence got an accounting job at Tibby's firm and was finishing his law degree at Sydney University. Alice took up sewing and spent most of her time pushing Andrew in his stroller around Centennial Park.

For months Vera debated going back to work. She loved every minute with Andrew, and the more he grew, with his sturdy arms and legs and bright smile, the more she hated the thought of being apart.

But Mr. Matthews had written her a glowing recommendation and she couldn't refuse the copywriter position at the Sydney branch of J. Walter Thompson. Her offices were downtown, and she could walk to the ferry at Circular Quay. She bought a wardrobe of suits to wear to work and had her own office and secretary.

Ten months into her position at J. Walter Thompson, Vera received a letter in the middle of the morning. She took out Edith's letter and unfolded it.

Dearest Vera,

So much has happened since I last wrote. The boutique is so successful that Betty hired two assistants. And you'll never believe it—Judy Holliday saw one of my dresses and asked me to design her gown for the Academy Awards. The moment she won the best actress award for Born Yesterday *wearing my gown was the most thrilling of my career.*

Marcus spends half his time taking pictures of movie stars. He bought a convertible, but I refuse to drive with him. He's as reckless as the teenagers driving Vespas in Naples and I don't want to die in a car accident on Pacific Coast Highway.

The big news is that I met the most wonderful man and I'm getting married! I can see you raising your eyebrows and demanding to know how I can get married without you. But Herman's mother is very ill and he wants to have the wedding while she is able to attend.

The wedding will be next Saturday at Betty's house. There will be an orchestra, and after the reception we'll stay in the bridal suite of the Beverly Hills Hotel. I'll send you photos of the dress. It's exactly like the dress Elizabeth Taylor wore in May, when she married Nicky Hilton.

I can't wait for you to meet Herman. He has a successful business and he's the most handsome man I have ever met. His grandparents escaped the pogroms in Russia, and he grew up in the Bronx. He's good and kind, and most important, he loves me. I forgot how wonderful it is to be in love! Yes! I am in love again and I'm so happy. We never run out of things to talk about and he always makes me laugh.

Next month we leave on our honeymoon and we're going to stay in Montreux with Dr. Abrahamson and his wife. I think Stefan would have liked Herman; they have so much in common.

I keep expecting to get a letter from you with similar news. There must be some Australian man who will sweep you off your feet! Give Andrew kisses, and I promise Herman and I will visit soon. I've enclosed his photo and business card; I'm the luckiest girl in the world!

Vera picked up the business card and read: *Herman Levin, certified accountant.* She studied the photo of a short man with a barrel chest and burst out laughing. Edith, who had adored Stefan's good looks and swooned over dark-haired boys in Naples, was in love with a Jewish accountant from the Bronx.

"Miss Frankel"—her secretary interrupted her thoughts—"your eleven a.m. client is waiting in the conference room."

"Thank you, Gwen." Vera checked her makeup in her compact. She wanted to make a good first impression on her new client, Trent Gotham, who represented an international company that was building a shopping arcade and hotel in Sydney.

When she arrived at the conference room, his back was turned to her and he appeared engrossed in a book. She coughed and he turned.

Her heart pounded and she reached for the table to steady herself.

"Anton," she whispered.

His hair was a little longer, but he looked exactly the same.

"Vera." Anton stood up. She had forgotten how tall he was and how handsome he looked in a sports coat and slacks.

"What are you doing in Sydney?" Her thoughts jumbled together and she could hardly breathe. She glanced up at the clock. "I have a meeting with a client; he'll be here any minute."

"I am the client," Anton said, and his eyes never left her face. "Anton Wight of Wight Hotels."

Her cheeks flushed and her hands rose to her throat. There was a small scar from the bullet, and she instinctively covered it. "That's impossible. My meeting is with Trent Gotham of the Gotham Group."

"I made up a different name. I didn't want to spoil the surprise," he said, and smiled. "You promise not to hate me for deceiving you?"

"I don't promise anything until I know why you're here," Vera remarked, trying to compose herself. Maybe Anton wasn't here to see her at all. Maybe he had simply heard J. Walter Thompson provided the best copywriting services.

"I'll tell you why I'm here," he said softly. He crossed the room and stood so close she could smell his aftershave. "I'm here because I couldn't forget you. It was the longest four years of my life and I couldn't live another day without you."

He touched her cheek and it took all her willpower not to kiss him. But she didn't know anything about his current circumstances, and they were in the middle of a conference room.

"Can we go somewhere and talk?" she asked.

"There are cabs downstairs. I'll buy you lunch and tell you everything."

Vera straightened her skirt and there was laughter in her eyes. "You're the client. I'll pay for lunch."

They sat in a restaurant in the Strand Arcade and ordered lunch.

"I wandered around Europe for months and became even more depressed," Anton began. "I thought that Naples had been destroyed, but Warsaw and Berlin were nothing but piles of rubble. In the Netherlands there had been a famine, and people ate tulip bulbs to survive. There were over three hundred thousand orphans. People who had lost their homes carried their belongings on their backs." His eyes were pools of misery. "I felt powerless and useless, so I decided to go home. My parents were thrilled to have me back and my father begged me to join Wight Hotels. I didn't put up much of a fight. My mother even tried to get me to attend dances, but that's where I put my foot down. How could I make cocktail conversation with debutantes who would never understand what I had witnessed? Several months ago there was a dinner party at the Astor residence that my father insisted I attend. When I arrived, I poured a large scotch and wandered around the house by myself." He smiled. "The interior was designed by Sister Parish and you know how I appreciate great design. I found myself in the study and noticed a framed photograph of two girls in a piazza in Naples. I immediately recognized you and Edith." He paused. "I must have stood there for an hour; the maid had to drag me into dinner. I asked our host where he got the photograph and he gave me Marcus's card with his contact information. I called Marcus and he gave me Edith's phone number." He looked at Vera. "Then I flew to see Edith in California—"

"You went to California?" Vera interjected.

"I called Edith but she wouldn't tell me anything about you." He grinned. "She didn't want me contacting you until she knew my intentions. So I took the first flight I could get on to see her. Then we sat for two hours and she told me everything about your life."

"Everything?" Vera gulped, thinking about her parents and Ricardo and Andrew.

"When Edith said your parents survived the war I wanted to cheer, and when she told me about Ricardo I wanted to board the next ship and hold you forever. But I couldn't show up in Sydney and ask you to move to New York. You had your parents and your son and a career. So I started researching Australia. The postwar economy is booming. Australia has let in almost two hundred thousand immigrants since 1945." He sipped his Coca-Cola. "The answer was simple: we could build a Wight Hotel in Sydney. It didn't take much to convince my father; he was looking for ways to expand." Anton drummed his fingers on the conference table and Vera was reminded of how impassioned he became when he was composing letters at the embassy in Naples. "Over the last six months we found investors and purchased the land and hired architects to design plans. Then I flew back to California and took the SS *Lurline* from San Francisco to Sydney and arrived three days ago."

Vera looked into Anton's blue eyes and the reserves she had built up over the last four years threatened to collapse.

"I've dreamed about this moment for months, but I understand if you don't want to see me." His voice was urgent. "I was a coward in Naples, and I let you down. But I knew if I told you in person, I wouldn't have the courage to let you go. I got it all wrong," he gulped. "Instead of running away, I should have done everything in my power to convince you that we had to be together and that I'd spend the rest of my life showing you how much I loved you."

Vera remembered when Anton proposed in Capri and she had never been so happy. She thought of arriving in Caracas and trying so hard to forget him. How many nights had she dreamed of Anton returning? But she wasn't a young girl who could be swept up by love anymore. Andrew was now the most important person in her life. She had responsibilities and commitments.

"Please, tell me what you're thinking," he beseeched.

"I don't know." She lifted her eyes to his. "So much is different. I've changed. I'm a mother and I have a career. What if it doesn't work?"

Anton leaned forward and traced the scar on Vera's neck. His fingers were soft, and a warmth ran down her spine.

"Please give me a chance," he begged. "Let me take you out and we'll get to know each other again. I never stopped loving you."

"All right," she agreed. "There's an Italian restaurant near the office. We could meet there after work."

"I was actually thinking of something different."

"Something different?" she repeated.

He took a piece of paper out of his pocket and smoothed it on the table.

"Tomorrow is Saturday. I could pick you up in the morning. First we'd ride the ferry to Taronga Zoo and see the kangaroos. Then we'd take the tram to Balmoral Beach. There's a cricket field and a restaurant that serves pink lamington cakes. After that we'd go to Hyde Park and see a puppet show."

"You want to visit the zoo and see a puppet show?" she asked incredulously.

Anton's face broke into a smile and he looked young and carefree.

"I was hoping Andrew could join us," he explained. "I don't know much about children, but I thought those are the things a two-year-old might enjoy."

"Then we'll do all those things," Vera laughed. "But Andrew is afraid of lions at the zoo and I don't let him eat cake at lunch."

Anton scribbled notes on the paper and slipped it in his pocket. His hand found hers across the table, and she didn't take it away.

CHAPTER TWENTY-SIX

September 1950

Anton was picking Vera up in half an hour and she had already changed her dress three times.

She had stayed awake most of the night thinking about everything he said. How had Edith not mentioned Anton in her letters? Edith was her best friend; she only wanted Vera to be happy. And had Anton decided to build a hotel in Sydney just so they could be in the same country? Then she remembered sailing on the *Queen Elizabeth* to New York to find Anton, and knew she could have easily done the same thing.

Halfway through the night she had gotten out of bed and stood in front of Andrew's cot. He was beautiful when he was asleep, with his long dark lashes and round fists clutching a teddy bear. Could she really introduce a man into Andrew's life?

There was a knock, and her mother appeared behind her.

"You look lovely." Alice nodded approvingly.

"Do you think so?" Vera turned around. "I was wondering if I should wear the yellow dress."

"It doesn't matter what you wear. Anton is coming to see you, not a piece of fabric," Alice said. "I got Andrew dressed and put on his shoes. He asked if he could bring his toy car."

Vera gave her hair a final brush and looked at her mother doubtfully.

"Do you think it's all right?" she wondered.

"What do you mean?" Alice asked.

"Taking Andrew to the zoo with Anton," she began. "I think about Ricardo never knowing his son and can't help feeling guilty."

"When Lawrence and I were on the ship to Caracas, I met an Austrian woman named Ida Rothstein. Every night she appeared at dinner in a mink stole and diamond earrings. She ate all the steak on her plate and asked for more. And she wasn't afraid to invite single men to dance.

"One day I ran into her on deck and noticed the tattoo on her wrist. She had been at Auschwitz, too. Her two sisters were sent to the gas chamber and her son died of tuberculosis. When she returned to Vienna after the war, she learned her husband had been killed at the Battle of Britain. Her husband, Wolf, despised Hitler so much he left for England in 1939 and volunteered in the British Army. All their family was in Austria and Ida begged him to stay, but he said the Allied forces would defeat Hitler in no time and he would return." Alice paused. "Ida never saw Wolf again."

"After Ida told me her story, she said: 'I know what you're thinking. How can I wear diamonds and eat steak when everyone I love is dead?' I nodded and she took off her eyeglasses and continued: 'Would they be any less dead if I stayed in my cabin and cried?'

"Ida put on her mink stole and diamond earrings every night because she recognized that life has to go on. Nothing will change what Ricardo did, and you've worked so hard to give Andrew a good life." She kissed the scar on Vera's neck. "It's only the zoo. Go have fun."

There was a knock at the front door and Vera jumped. She checked her hair in the mirror and ran to open it.

Anton stood outside. His arms were laden with wrapped gifts.

"I picked up a few things," he said sheepishly when they entered the living room. Vera scanned the plain sofa and drab paint and wondered what Anton would think of the cottage.

"These are for you." He handed Alice a bunch of lilies.

"Thank you, they're lovely." Alice nodded. "Please sit down."

Anton sat and twisted his hands. There was an awkward silence and Vera wondered if she made a mistake. Perhaps they should have met somewhere else and she could have introduced Anton to her parents later.

"When I met Vera at the embassy in Naples and read Captain Bingham's letter, I thought she was the bravest girl in the world," Anton said to Alice. "But then Vera told me what you suffered during the war and I understood where she gets her courage. She has a remarkable mother."

Alice beamed, and the air in the room seemed to expand. Andrew bounded into the room and Anton gave him the stuffed dog that was tucked under his arm.

"This is my father, Lawrence," Vera said when her father emerged from the bedroom. He had gained weight in the last year, and the lines in his forehead were smoother.

"Mr. Frankel, it's a pleasure to meet you." Anton jumped up and shook hands. "I brought you a bottle of brandy; I hope you like it."

"Please, call me Lawrence," he said, accepting the gift.

"Vera told me you are a chess champion." Anton slipped his hands in his pockets. "I was on the Yale chess team. Perhaps you would give me the honor of playing you."

"Anytime." Lawrence nodded. "But I have to warn you, I haven't lost a match in a year."

"I didn't know that," Vera said in surprise. "Rabbi Gorem said you let him win all the time."

"I had to let him win," Lawrence answered, and Vera noticed the old sparkle in his eyes. "In Caracas, God and I were still working things out. I needed Rabbi Gorem on my side."

Vera said good-bye to her parents and she and Anton and Andrew rode the ferry to Taronga Zoo. The zoo was built facing the harbor, and from the giraffe house you could see the Sydney Harbour Bridge and the boats crisscrossing the water. Anton carried Andrew on his shoulders, and they toured the elephant temple and the monkey pits. When Vera said it was time to leave, Andrew asked if they could come back to see the tigers.

"That was a wonderful morning," Vera said, sitting opposite Anton in the Balmoral Rotunda.

Vera had never been to Balmoral Beach. There was a swimming cove and an area for cricket and a restaurant with outdoor tables. Andrew played with a bucket and spade on the lawn, and she and Anton drank tea and ate scones and jam.

"I haven't been to a zoo in years," Anton said. "There's nothing more thrilling than lions and giraffes. When I was a kid, I dreamed of going on safari."

"Andrew is going to be talking about the elephants for weeks." She smiled. "Thank you for taking us."

"You don't know what it's like sitting across from you. I have to keep pinching myself," Anton said as he spread jam on a scone. "I thought about you the whole time I was in Europe. I bought a scarf in Barcelona because it brought out the green in your eyes, and I spent hours in the drama section of Shakespeare and Company in Paris. In Budapest, I rode a bicycle on Margaret Island because it was one of your favorite things to do."

"You went to Budapest?" Vera asked in surprise.

"Three years ago in 1947, before it became communist," Anton said. "The streets were empty and the people were grim; I didn't stay long."

Vera pictured her beloved Budapest with its opera house and green parks, and there was a lump in her throat. "We're very happy in Sydney; I don't think we'll ever go back."

"I took home a suitcase of souvenirs even though I knew I'd never have the chance to give them to you," Anton continued. "I saved one thing I hoped you might like."

He reached into his pocket and took out a velvet box. Inside was the diamond-and-sapphire engagement ring he gave Vera in Capri.

Vera gasped and her hand flew to her mouth.

"Gina sent it to me in New York," Anton explained. "Do you remember, I told you to sell it and get yourself a nest egg? You left it with Gina instead."

"It wasn't mine to sell," Vera responded.

Anton took her hand. "You are the only thing that matters. I loved you from the minute we met, and every day it's grown stronger. I was a fool to let you go and I would never make the mistake again. Vera, my darling. Would you marry me?"

Vera gazed at Anton's face that she loved so much. She was only twenty-three and there was no hurry. Why shouldn't they first have a proper courtship with Saturday movie dates and dancing? She didn't have to worry about a war taking Anton away, or not having enough money to support herself.

"I love you more than anything," Vera answered. "But ever since Edith and I were sixteen we've been waiting for something terrible to happen: first it was moving to the ghetto, and then it was Stefan being sent to the camps, and after that it was being put on the train to Auschwitz. Even in Naples and Caracas we couldn't enjoy being young girls because we were waiting to hear terrible news of Stefan and our parents. For the first time, there are only good things to look forward to: Andrew turning three and a promotion at work and my father earning his law degree. Getting engaged and marrying you would be the best thing of all, but I don't want to rush. Is it all right if I wait a little while to accept the ring?"

Anton looked at Vera and there was so much love in his eyes, her heart turned over. He leaned forward and kissed her. "I'll wait forever."

After they finished afternoon tea they took the ferry back to Circular Quay. They sat on the outside deck and Vera gazed at the sailboats and green inlets and brick buildings of downtown Sydney

"What are you thinking about?" Anton asked.

"How bright everything is here. The houses are beautiful and the harbor is full of boats, and there are flowers and sunshine. Everyone seems happy; Europe and the concentration camps are in the past." She looked at Anton. "What if people forget and all the unimaginable atrocities happen again?"

"One of the great things about human beings is their capacity to learn," Anton commented. "We'll tell the story to our children, and they'll tell their children, and no one will ever forget."

Vera remembered when Alessandra said to her that the young must study history, literature, and geography to learn empathy. She thought about Rabbi Gorem saying every Jew who died in a concentration camp left behind something. Perhaps she would write a play about the war. As Andrew's sleeping head pressed against her, she vowed to do everything she could to make others remember.

Anton took her hand and she rested her head on his shoulder. The sun made patterns on the deck and spread golden rays onto the blue water. She shielded her eyes and had never seen a more beautiful light.

AUTHOR'S NOTE

My mother, Vera Frankel, was born in April 1927 in Budapest, Hungary. Her mother, Alice, was one of eight children, and her father, Lawrence, was an attorney with a practice in Budapest. Three of my grandmother's siblings died in concentration camps, and my grandfather Lawrence spent four years in a forced-labor camp.

Miraculously, my mother and her parents survived the Holocaust. Because of their experiences, I heard many stories about the war as I grew up. My mother told me that in Budapest from 1944 until the end of the war, Jewish children wore the standard yellow star and weren't allowed to attend school. Half a dozen families lived in one apartment and the most basic necessities like toilet paper were almost impossible to find.

The brunt of the war came late to Hungary. In 1940, Germany pressured Hungary to join the Axis powers, and for the next four years, Jews in Hungary led restricted lives. They lost their businesses, and Jewish men were sent to labor camps, but they were not yet part of Hitler's Final Solution. In late 1943 and dragging on into the early months of 1944, Hungarian Prime Minister Miklós

Kállay secretly engaged in negotiations with the United States and Great Britain. Hitler discovered the betrayal, and in March 1944, German troops invaded Hungary. Budapest was occupied and all Jews were moved into ghettos. In the subsequent twelve months, a staggering 550,000 Hungarian Jews died at Auschwitz and other concentration camps.

My mother and her best friend, Edith, escaped from the train that carried them and their mothers to Auschwitz. From there, their desperate journey took them six years and across four continents. At times their situation was so full of anguish and heartache, I couldn't imagine how they found the strength and willpower to survive.

Armed with the knowledge of inconceivable atrocities, I began to ask questions. How were the Jews in Hungary and all over Europe able to live through a time when human decency, respect for individuals, and hope for a future had been shattered? What kinds of deprivations did they suffer, and even more than that, how were those who survived able to put the past behind them?

When I started doing research for this book, I obtained the ship manifest with the details of my mother and Edith's arrival at Ellis Island. I found pictures of my mother from when she was young and I learned all I could about the places she ended up. During my research, I discovered much more than facts. I learned the historical significance of empathy, and that we all leave something of value behind. I learned to cherish family and to believe true love perseveres. And mostly, I learned how during a time of unfathomable evil, the strength of the human spirit prevailed.

In today's challenging world, I hope my mother's story will help readers to believe in themselves, in love, and in the goodness of life and humanity. When people talk about the Holocaust, the phrase that recurs is to "never forget." That sentiment is more important than ever. In writing my mother's story, I hope to honor a whole generation of courageous people. They didn't have the luxury of simply turning away. I hope that present and future generations show the same kind of courage by never letting it happen again.

ACKNOWLEDGMENTS

Huge thanks to my agent, Johanna Castillo, whose direction to "write from the heart" I take every day. You have been an inspiration since our first conversation, and I'm so grateful. Thank you to my editor, Kaitlin Olson, for your meticulous and thoughtful editing. You made me a better writer and this a better book. It is such a pleasure to work together.

The Light after the War could not have a found better home than at Atria/Simon & Schuster. Thank you to the publisher, Libby McGuire, and editorial director, Lindsay Sagnette, and Isabel DaSilva and Mirtha Pena in marketing and publicity. And thank you to Olga Grlic for the luminous cover.

This book is so much about friendship and I couldn't have written it without my friends. Traci Whitney and I have been friends since we were sixteen and still share things every day. Andrea Katz always knows the right way forward and Sara Sullivan is the truest friend I could ask for. Thank you also to David Perry for your wisdom, and Jill and Sally Fales for your graciousness. And many thanks to Kelly Berke, Pat Hull, and Laura Narbutas for always listening.

I'm so fortunate to have my children who make me incredibly happy: Alex, Andrew, Heather, Madeleine, and Thomas. This book is for you. My mother would have been so proud of you and so am I.

ABOUT THE AUTHOR

Anita Abriel was born in Sydney, Australia. She received a BA in English literature with a minor in creative writing from Bard College. She lives in California with her family. *The Light After the War* was inspired by her mother's story of survival during World War II.